PRAISE FOR

the promise of forgiveness

"There's a big promise in this book: love, redemption, and a story so gripping I couldn't put it down."

—Debbie Macomber, #1 *New York Times* bestselling author of *Silver Linings*

"A heartfelt novel of mysteries hidden in lonely hearts. Marin Thomas gives us characters that jump off the page, people we root for and who dare to reach for love. A keeper!"

—Curtiss Ann Matlock, *USA Today* bestselling author of *Love in a Small Town*

"Resonates with the power of redemption and absolution while exploring the idea of choosing your own family. A complex novel that examines the mother-daughter bond and the lengths a person will go to to be forgiven."

—Kate Moretti, *New York Times* bestselling author of *Thought I Knew You*

"I loved the book! Marin Thomas has a wonderfully fresh writing voice that makes *The Promise of Forgiveness* an unputdownable novel. It is a compelling story of forgiveness with a warm heart at its center. You won't want to put it down!"

—Joan Johnston, *New York Times* bestselling author of *Shameless*

continued . . .

"*The Promise of Forgiveness* takes a heartfelt look at the complexities inherent in familial relationships. It's authentic and poignant, and will have you turning pages well past bedtime."

—Emily Liebert, author of *Those Secrets We Keep*

"The flawed, frail but deeply human characters in *The Promise of Forgiveness* will have you rooting for them from the first page and cheering by the last. This is a story to savor—and remember."

—Yona Zeldis McDonough, author of *The House on Primrose Pond*

"Marin Thomas writes with warmth and empathy about raising a daughter when the path isn't clear and history provides little guidance. The beauty of the Western landscape, the difficulty of navigating parenting on all levels, and a beautiful romance round out this hopeful book, filled with complexity and love."

—Ann Garvin, author of *The Dog Year*

"I loved the ranch in Unforgiven, Oklahoma, the mysteries no one wants to talk about, and Ruby Baxter, who flew right off the page, fists swinging, boots tapping. She was one of those true-as-life characters you don't forget."

—Cathy Lamb, author of *My Very Best Friend*

"With its colorful characters and raw emotions, *The Promise of Forgiveness* delivers a tender story about family and love. Readers will root for the feisty Ruby as she uncovers painful secrets about her past and seeks to find redemption in the most unlikely of places: Unforgiven, Oklahoma."

—Amy Impellizzeri, author of *Lemongrass Hope*

"Marin Thomas writes with charm and a wise understanding of how relationships work. *The Promise of Forgiveness* is a heartfelt novel set in rural Oklahoma that explores what happens when one woman takes a risk to find where her heart truly belongs. Lovely novel."

—Tina Ann Forkner, author of *Waking Up Joy*

"Full of warmth and wisdom, Marin Thomas's beautifully written *The Promise of Forgiveness* proves that the past doesn't define the future, family is what we make it, and, most important, it's never too late to become the person you want to be. This is a truly special read that will stay with you long after the last page."

—Kristy Woodson Harvey, author of *Dear Carolina*

"In this heart-wrenching but ultimately hopeful novel, Marin Thomas delivers a story with more twists than a hand-braided lariat as she spins out her story of a resilient single mother determined to make a better life for herself and her stubborn teenage daughter. What makes this novel rise above the rest are the quirky but believable characters, the surprisingly sensual details of a dusty Oklahoma town, and the way Thomas writes about even the most flawed characters with grace, affection, and humor."

—Holly Robinson, author of *Chance Harbor*

the promise of forgiveness

MARIN THOMAS

NAL ACCENT
Published by New American Library,
an imprint of Penguin Random House LLC
375 Hudson Street, New York, New York 10014

This book is an original publication of New American Library.

First Printing, March 2016

For more information about Penguin Random House, visit penguin.com.

LIBRARY OF CONGRESS CATALOGING-IN-PUBLICATION DATA:
Names: Thomas, Marin, author.
Title: The promise of forgiveness/Marin Thomas.
Description: New York City: New American Library, [2016]
Identifiers: LCCN 2015038161 | ISBN 9780451476296 (softcover)
Subjects: LCSH: Mothers and daughters—Fiction. | Man-woman relationships—Fiction. | Domestic fiction. | BISAC: FICTION/Contemporary Women. | FICTION/Family Life. | FICTION/Psychological. | GSAFD: Love stories.
Classification: LCC PS3620.H6348 P76 2016 | DDC 813/.6—dc23
LC record available at http://lccn.loc.gov/2015038161

Printed in the United States of America
10 9 8 7 6 5 4 3 2 1

Designed by Laura K. Corless

PUBLISHER'S NOTE
This is a work of fiction. Names, characters, places, and incidents either are the product of the author's imagination or are used fictitiously, and any resemblance to actual persons, living or dead, business establishments, events, or locales is entirely coincidental.

Penguin Random House

To my mother,
Phyllis June Smith

the promise of forgiveness

Chapter 1

Unforgiven, Oklahoma, was as ugly as it was hot.

There wasn't a soul in sight, but Ruby Baxter's skin prickled. Someone was watching.

A gust of blistering July heat plastered her overprocessed blond hair to her face. Accustomed to Missouri's lush green foliage and high humidity, she wouldn't be surprised if the Panhandle's harsh sun, blowing soil, and never-ending wind sucked the life right out of its Okies.

She fondled the gemstone dangling from the gold chain around her neck and studied the only paved street in Unforgiven. The side alleys consisted of sparse gravel and packed dirt. The buildings to her left listed slightly—kind of like her single-wide after a fierce storm had blown through Pineville, Missouri, and almost shoved the tornado magnet off its cinder blocks.

"Not much of a town, is it?" Ruby reached out to brush a strand of hair from Mia's face, but her daughter jerked away. Lately everything she did or said made Mia angry, leaving a sick feeling in Ruby's gut that never went away.

"Enjoy your stay, ladies." The bus driver set their bags in the dirt, and then the Greyhound drove off, farting black exhaust in their faces.

Mia kicked a stone, sending it sailing through the air, where it pinged off the No Parking sign ten yards away.

This pit stop had been a bad idea. Her relationship with Mia was in shambles, and the last thing Ruby needed was to lose focus on what mattered most—her daughter. There was no guarantee anything positive would result from Ruby meeting her biological father, but the instant she'd opened the certified letter from a lawyer representing Hank McArthur—a man she hadn't known existed until a few weeks ago—the fresh start in Elkhart, Kansas, that she'd promised Mia had taken a detour.

Hank McArthur had summoned Ruby home to her birthplace to claim her inheritance—whatever that was—and a five-hundred-dollar cashier's check had been included with the note. Ruby glanced at her daughter. "Maybe I should have bought a used car with the cashier's check instead of bus tickets." If Ruby had a set of wheels, they could leave this hole in the wall whenever they wanted. But she'd doubted a clunker would have made the four-hundred-fifty-mile trip, so she'd opted for reliable transportation—bus tickets to the Sunflower State with a layover in Unforgiven.

Ruby wished she and Mia were on better terms, because she had no one to confide in about her reasons for meeting Hank McArthur. Aside from wanting information about her medical history, which was also important for Mia, Ruby wished to know if she shared any traits with her biological parents. After she discovered she'd been adopted, she'd fantasized that the McArthurs were important people and that she hadn't yet lived up to her potential.

That life had more in store for her than barely scraping by.

"Are we just gonna stand here and look stupid?"

"Give me a minute to think." The sweltering mid-July temperature might as well have melted the heels of Ruby's cowboy boots to the blacktop, because she couldn't have moved her feet if she'd tried. All these years she'd believed she was the biological daughter of a trucker and a self-taught hairstylist. Her parents had gone to their graves in a head-on car crash without ever having told her she'd been adopted.

The answers to her questions were here, but what if she ended up not liking the real Ruby Baxter? Then again, Mia would argue that the adopted Ruby Baxter was nothing to brag about, either.

"We won't stay long," Ruby said, whether to reassure herself or Mia, she had no clue. Only two buses a week stopped in Unforgiven—Tuesdays and Thursdays. Today was Thursday. Unless they wanted to hitchhike to Kansas, they were stuck for a while.

"This place is lame," Mia said.

Annoyance mixed with fear crawled up Ruby's throat, but she flattened her lips, trapping the F bomb inside her mouth. It wasn't as if Mia hadn't heard her mother swear before. F-u-c-k had been one of her daughter's first words. Ruby had taken her then-eighteen-month-old to Dollar Island, and when she'd refused to buy her a stuffed animal, Mia had blurted, "Fuck you, Mommy."

Ruby had put the blame for that one squarely on her own shoulders. She'd been seventeen when Dylan Snyder had knocked her up. She'd expected him to do right by her. He hadn't. Rather than say *I do*, he'd come and gone as he pleased—his visits ending in slamming doors and *fuck you*s. She should have ended things between them after Mia was born, but she'd let Dylan stay in her life because she'd been afraid to be alone. He'd been her first bad boyfriend decision and he wouldn't be her last.

One afternoon when she'd returned home from her hostess job at Carmen's Chicken Fry, she'd found Dylan passed out naked on the bed with a condom hanging off his ding-dong. That he'd used her trailer to have sex in with some other girl had made her realize he'd never be the kind of father Mia deserved, or the boyfriend she deserved. Ruby decided Dylan had used up his last second chance, and with great pleasure and a whole lot of satisfaction, she'd planted her pointy-toed Dingo right up his lily-white ass. From then on Dylan had steered clear of the Shady Acres Mobile Home Park.

"Give it a chance. The town might grow on us."

Mia snorted.

At the end of the month Ruby would begin a new job as the night manager for the Red Roof Inn in Elkhart. The late hours wouldn't be easy, but she'd be home when Mia returned from school, and spending more time with her daughter was part of Ruby's plan for a fresh start.

She shielded her eyes from the sun's glare and stared down the block. The ramshackle buildings looked as if they'd been abandoned during the Dust Bowl Era and then reclaimed years later. The wooden sidewalks and false storefronts were straight out of an Old West film set. A life-size cigar-store Indian wearing a black-and-blue war bonnet stood outside the Trading Post Mercantile. The faded outline of a Castrol Motor Oil emblem decorated the brick exterior of Dwayne's Billiard Hall, where a giant cue stick served as the handle on the front door. Hidden in the shadows of the pool hall sat the Possum Belly Saloon, its windows spray-painted black—either to represent the color of oil or to conceal the shady dealings of its patrons.

A pair of rusted antique Chevron gas pumps with their hoses ripped off baked in the sun across the street in an empty lot littered with trash and weeds. A newer station with a repair bay sat adjacent to the abandoned one. The sheriff's office was located at the end of the block, sandwiched between Panhandle Realty and Petro Oil. No bank—hopefully there was an ATM inside one of the businesses.

"I don't see any place to eat unless the pool hall has a grill," Ruby said. They'd boarded the bus at six fifteen in the morning and it was now after one o'clock.

Mia motioned to a silver 1960s Airstream with *Jailhouse Diner* written in black cursive along the side. A handful of dusty pickups and a patrol car sat parked out front. Yellow plastic ribbons tied to the AC unit in the window flapped in the air, reminding Ruby they stood baking in the sun. She picked up her luggage. "Let's give the diner a try."

As they approached the Airstream, a Chevy truck cruised past and the driver stuck his head out the window to get a look-see at Ruby. *Yeah, you think you're gonna get lucky, fella.* She'd hitched enough rides with handsome rednecks to leave her with a lifetime of brief relationships.

Mia waved at the drive-by cowboy.

"Knock it off. He's too old for you." At fourteen Mia showed signs of inheriting Ruby's generous bust size. Her blossoming bosom, coupled with honey-blond curls, drew attention from men who had no business looking at girls her age.

A little more than two months ago Ruby had walked in on her daughter and a high school freshman naked in bed. After all of their chats about boys and sex, she'd never expected Mia to lose her virginity at such a young age. Ruby had been no saint in high school, but she'd waited until she'd turned seventeen to get naked with a boy.

Not that it had mattered how long Ruby had waited to pop her cherry. Everyone in Pineville knew she test-drove men faster than an Indy 500 car circled a racetrack. It shouldn't have surprised her that people would assume *like mother like daughter*, making Mia an easy target for boys like Kevin Walters. The only way to give Mia a fighting chance to save her reputation was to move out of town and enroll her in a new school, where her classmates wouldn't know she'd slept with a boy in eighth grade or that her mother had a history of failed relationships.

"Maybe someone in here will tell us how to get to your grandfather's ranch."

"He's not my grandfather. He's *your* father."

Not as far as Ruby was concerned. Hank McArthur had forfeited his fatherhood rights when he'd given her away. She could have done the same with Mia after she'd been born, but she hadn't. Ruby wasn't a perfect parent, but she loved her daughter.

When they entered the Airstream, the men seated at the lunch counter—four cowboys and a lawman—spun their red leather stools and sized them up.

Ruby smoothed a hand down the front of her peach sundress and straightened the belt at her waist. The outfit hadn't been comfortable to travel in, but she'd wanted to look nice when she met Hank McArthur for the first time. Not to impress him but to show him what he'd tossed away.

Before the stare-down between her and the group at the counter grew uncomfortable, the kitchen door swung open and out strolled Elvis—the Native American version. Tall and thin with a wide forehead, flat nose, and tanned skin, he wore jeans cuffed to the ankles, and his black T-shirt sported an image of the infamous icon. One rolled sleeve held a pack of cigarettes, and he'd combed his jet-black hair into the famous pompadour style, complete with wet locks falling onto his forehead and muttonchops.

"You ladies lost 'n' looking for directions, or are you here to eat?" he asked.

Aware the men at the counter continued to eyeball them, Ruby said, "We're eating."

"Seat yourselves."

Mia picked the booth near the air conditioner, and they shoved their bags beneath the table.

"What's up with that guy's hair?" Mia whispered.

"He's impersonating a singer from the fifties."

"Weird." Mia popped her chewing gum while she perused the menu.

The diner walls were plastered with Elvis memorabilia—a framed *TV Guide*, an artist's rendition of Graceland, album covers, signed posters, movie photographs, and a display case filled with Elvis bobblehead dolls. The black-and-white-checkered linoleum floor was covered in scuff marks, and the old-fashioned jukebox gave the motor home a teenage malt-shop feel. The place stuck out like a sore thumb in the spaghetti-western town.

"I'm ordering dessert and a soda pop." Mia glared defiantly and tapped a neon-green fingernail against the sparkly tabletop.

"Go ahead."

"Fine. I will." Mia dug out her iPod and stuck in the earbuds.

Ruby had to pick her battles with Mia, and keeping her from turning into a slut trumped concern over a poor diet. Ruby wished her daughter understood that the choices she made now would impact her for the rest of her life.

After Mia had had sex with Kevin, Ruby had forbidden her from seeing the boy. She'd considered speaking with Kevin's father, but Biggs Walters was an unemployed alcoholic who had nothing good to say to anyone—especially women—after his wife had left him a year earlier.

Ruby had resorted to one of her lectures on the dangers and consequences of having sex at such a young age, but Mia had shut her out and would never say why she'd slept with Kevin.

If there was one upside to Mia's rebellion, the timing couldn't have worked out better for a move. Ruby had split with her boyfriend a week before catching Mia and Kevin in the act. She and Sean had been together nine months—the longest she'd lived with a guy before handing him his eviction notice.

A month earlier Ruby had begun growing uneasy when Sean had ignored several of her text messages. She'd feared that he was losing interest in her, and with each passing day she'd become more anxious. Then one night he hadn't come home—his reason: he'd stayed at a buddy's house after drinking too many beers. Ruby hadn't bought it and had asked him to move out. Sean had begged and pleaded with her not to break up with him, insisting he hadn't done anything wrong. That the reason he hadn't returned her texts was because the guys at work had made fun of him for having to answer to her for everything he did. Ruby wanted to believe Sean, but if she let him stay, his buddies at work would keep badgering him until they convinced Sean he could do better than Ruby. So she'd stood her ground, insisting he pack his bags and vamoose. She'd barely caught her breath after he left before Mia had blindsided her.

Elvis delivered glasses of water to their table and Mia removed her earbuds. "Everyone 'round here calls me Jimmy," he said. "Or you can use my Osage name, Ha-Pah-Shu-Tse. Means 'red corn.'" He flashed a gilded-toothed smile.

"Is that real?" Mia asked.

"Solid gold." He dipped his head toward Ruby. "We don't get many women passing through Unforgiven. Where're you ladies headed?"

"Kansas. I'm Ruby Baxter and this is my daughter, Mia. We stopped in town to visit Hank McArthur."

"He's my mom's *real* dad."

Ruby shot Mia a stern look. She knew not to tell strangers their personal business. "Is the Devil's Wind Ranch nearby?"

"West of here. 'Bout a half hour by car."

Ruby should phone Hank and warn him that she'd arrived, but the call could wait until after lunch.

Coward. Okay, she was delaying the inevitable. So what? It wasn't like she had places to go and things to do the rest of the day. "I didn't notice any motels in the area."

"If you want a room, you'll have to go to Guymon." Jimmy pointed his thumb over his shoulder. "I got a pop-up trailer out back you can sleep in for twenty bucks a night. I'll let you use the bathroom in here before I open in the mornings."

Ruby ignored Mia's groan. "We might take you up on the offer." If Hank turned out to be a schmuck, they'd bunk down in the King's trailer while they waited for the next bus out of town.

The diner door opened and in walked a pair of dusty jeans, a faded red Oklahoma Sooners T-shirt and a matching baseball cap. The newcomer glanced Ruby's way, startling her with his empty brown-eyed stare. He nodded, although it sure didn't seem like he saw her, and then walked up to the counter, choosing the stool farthest from the others.

"This is your lucky day," Jimmy said. "You might be able to hitch a ride to the Devil's Wind with Joe."

"Joe?" Ruby asked.

Jimmy nodded to the man with the vacant gaze. "Joe Dawson. He's the foreman of the ranch."

Chapter 2

Joe Dawson looked more like a cotton farmer than a cowboy.

"Can you vouch for him?" Ruby asked the diner owner.

"He's been working for Hank 'bout a year and never caused any trouble that I heard of. You gals know what you want?"

"Apple cobbler and a root beer." Mia stuck her earbuds in and lip-synched to a song.

"I'll have a cheeseburger—no onions—and a Diet Coke," Ruby said.

Before Jimmy went into the kitchen, he set a glass of water in front of the Devil's Wind foreman. Ruby ogled Joe. If he felt her eyes on him, he didn't care, because he never glanced her way. After a minute she lost interest in the granite statue and gazed out the window while Mia pretended she didn't exist.

Ten minutes later Jimmy delivered their food. Ruby chewed her burger and recalled the dream she'd had the night after opening the lawyer's letter. The scene had unfolded in front of a white clapboard house with a lush green manicured lawn and a pot of yellow daisies by the front door. There hadn't been a single cloud in the periwinkle sky as butterflies fluttered in the air. Hank McArthur stood on the porch, his arms open in welcome as he shared a sad tale of how he'd been forced against his will to give Ruby up for adoption. She'd woken before she'd learned whether she'd forgiven him or not. She shoved a fry into her mouth, then froze when a shadow fell across the table.

"I hear you're looking for a ride."

"I'm Ruby Baxter." She wiped her fingers on her napkin before offering her hand.

"Joe Dawson." His grip was firm, and she appreciated that he didn't break eye contact to check out her boobs the way most men did.

"My daughter, Mia." She nodded across the table. "We don't want to get in the way of your business in town, but we could use a lift to the Devil's Wind."

"I need an hour."

"That's fine. As soon as we finish our lunch, we'll go over to the mercantile and look around until you're ready to leave."

After the door closed behind him, Mia spoke. "He's got sad eyes."

Not sad—haunting.

Someone at the counter told a joke and the others guffawed. It was time to leave. "Finish your cobbler." Ruby rummaged through her purse for money.

"He keeps staring at you."

"Who?"

Mia tilted her head. "The cop."

There was nothing memorable about the lawman's face or neatly trimmed brown hair, but when their gazes connected, his mouth curved into a nice smile. Even if she hadn't put dating on the back burner, the boy next door wasn't her type. She'd celebrated her thirty-first birthday last month, but the crow's-feet fanning from the corners of her eyes had cropped up years ago—each line representing a bad choice, mistake, or regret. She was way more than the fresh-faced officer could handle.

"Let's head over to the mercantile and wait there for our ride." Ruby signaled Jimmy for the bill.

"I don't take credit cards or personal checks." He set the ticket on the table. "Cash only."

"Who are the cowboys?" Ruby asked.

"They ride for the Bar T. Roy Sandoval's ranch borders the Devil's Wind."

"Is Mr. Sandoval a friend of Hank McArthur's?"

"Just neighbors." Jimmy took the twenty-dollar bill Ruby held out. "You want change?"

"We're good."

She and Mia removed their belongings from beneath the table.

"Excuse me, ma'am."

She turned and came face-to-face with the boy next door.

He tapped a finger against the brim of his Stetson. "Deputy Paul Randall."

"Ruby Baxter."

"What brings you to Unforgiven?" he asked.

"Hank McArthur."

"You related to Hank?"

"He's my father," Ruby said.

The deputy's lips stretched until his smile vanished into his cheeks. "Didn't know Hank had a daughter."

"Nice to meet you." She urged Mia toward the door, but the lawman followed them outside.

"Must have been something important to keep you away from home all these years."

"Unforgiven isn't home." Ruby watched Mia's retreating back. "I'm in a hurry."

"If you need anything during your stay, feel free to call on me."

"Thank you, Deputy—"

"Paul." The nice-guy smile returned. "We're a close-knit community." He got into his patrol car and sped off.

"The deputy's nosy," Ruby said when she caught up with Mia outside the mercantile.

"Is he joining your boyfriend-of-the-month club while we're here?"

Ruby squeezed the suitcase handle until her fingers grew numb. Before Ruby's breakup with Sean, Mia had never voiced an opinion about her mother's numerous relationships.

"We're not buying anything." Ruby opened the door and ushered Mia inside the musty-smelling store.

The sun streaming through the front window illuminated the dancing dust fairies around their heads. Wall-to-wall shelving displayed a variety of goods—canned food, cleaning products, fishing tackle, camping supplies, and boots. Three circular clothing racks held an assortment of men's shirts, lightweight jackets, and hoodies. Jeans stacked two feet high sat on a table next to a shelf of white undershirts and BVDs. There wasn't a stitch of female clothing in the entire store.

Mia wrinkled her nose at the stuffed critters mounted on the wall above the checkout counter. Ruby identified the deer head, raccoon, possum, and fox, but the animal with a tubelike head and a bushy tail perplexed her.

"That there's a South American anteater." A little person stepped out from behind a display of fishing tackle. The miniature, short-limbed senior couldn't have been more than four and a half feet tall. Grizzled beard stubble covered his face, and a large bald spot on the top of his head gleamed beneath the fluorescent lights. The remaining ring of snowy hair stuck up at angles, and tufts of fuzz sprouted from his ears. His Roman nose, wide mouth, fleshy lips, and dark eyes hinted at a Greek heritage. Taken separately, his features were much too large for his small stature, but together they created a compelling face.

"You two got off the bus."

Had it been this man's eyes that she'd felt on her earlier? "I'm Ruby Baxter, and this is my daughter, Mia."

"Folks call me Big Dan. Name's a keepsake from my days as a carnie."

"What's a carnie?" Mia asked.

"Someone who works for a traveling carnival," Ruby said.

Mia wandered over to a display of tourist trinkets and examined the key chains, snow globes, and magnets.

Big Dan climbed onto a stool behind the register. "If you need something, say so. I'll tell you if I have it. If you're killing time until your ride comes, I got week-old newspapers you can read."

"How did you guess we were waiting for a ride?" Ruby asked.

He opened a can of Kodiak chewing tobacco and placed a pinch between his cheek and gum. "I know everything that goes on in this town." The statement was so matter-of-fact that she took him at his word.

"Bought the store in eighty-three. Seen thousands of roughnecks pass through Unforgiven."

"Are there any women here?"

"The ranchers' wives shop in Guymon."

"What about the wives and girlfriends of the oil workers?"

"Most of the men live near the drilling sites. And the married ones leave their families back home."

"I want this." Mia held up a magnet of the state of Oklahoma.

"That'll be two sixty-eight," Big Dan said.

Mia shoved the trinket into her pocket, then sat on the bench by the front window and listened to her iPod.

Ruby's daughter had been testing her ever since Sean packed his bags. As much as she wanted to refuse to pay for the souvenir, she forked over a five-dollar bill in order to avoid a public spat.

Ignoring her open hand, he placed the change on the counter. "Enjoy your stay at the Devil's Wind."

How did he know where she was headed? She hadn't mentioned the ranch. Big Dan's gaze fixated on something over her shoulder, and Ruby spun to see what had caught his attention.

Joe.

His bootheels *thunk*ed against the plank floor, the warped boards popping beneath his weight. He stopped a good distance from the checkout.

"Our ride's here," Ruby said. "It was nice meeting you, Big Dan."

"See you next time."

Ruby and Mia followed Joe to the black Dodge pickup parked in front of the mercantile. He opened the passenger-side door for Ruby, then slid behind the wheel and waited for Mia to buckle up before backing out of the space. He cruised through the four-way stop at the end of the street and then pressed on the gas when he hit the open road.

She waited for him to make conversation or flip on the radio. He did neither. After a mile of silence, Mia fell asleep. Ruby's eyes drifted to Joe. He drove with one hand on the wheel, the other arm resting on the door.

"What kind of ranch is the Devil's Wind?" she asked.

"Cattle and oil." He shifted toward her. "I manage the cattle."

"Who handles the oil?"

"Petro Oil leases the pumps, and Hank spends most of his time caring for a few abused horses."

The sympathetic rancher seemed at odds with a man who'd give his daughter up for adoption. But if neglected horses were willing to trust Hank McArthur, then maybe Ruby shouldn't write him off too soon.

"Does anyone else live on the property with you and Hank?"

"It's been just the two of us since he hired me a year ago in May."

She turned her attention to the giant grasshoppers bobbing across the land and wondered what kind of reception she'd receive from her estranged father.

As a young child Ruby had been the apple of her adoptive father's eye. Every Friday afternoon when Glen Baxter returned from his weekly truck route, he'd take Ruby fishing, to the movies, or bowling. On occasion they'd stop at Charlie's Place and she'd eat cheese popcorn while he drank draft beers with his buddies. When she reached the age of sixteen, their relationship changed overnight. Her father began working extra hours and stayed away from home. Even though he'd been dead for years, his behavior still haunted Ruby. To this day she'd never been able to figure out what she'd said or done that had caused her dad to pull away from her.

That Hank McArthur had turned his back on Ruby, too, left her with little hope he'd be a better man than Glen Baxter. His summons had ripped open an old wound, and the only way to stop the bleeding was for Ruby to find out why she'd been left behind.

"You've probably figured it out by now, but in case you haven't, I'm Hank's biological daughter."

"I heard."

"I'm surprised. Usually men don't wag their tongues like women."

He chuckled.

"I'm nervous about meeting Hank. Care to share any insight into the man?"

"He keeps to himself mostly. Doesn't have a whole lot to say."

"Neither of you have to worry about us girls invading your territory. This will be a short visit." If she could coax the man who didn't have much to say to talk to her.

Chapter 3

Joe steered the Dodge over to the shoulder of the road, then turned onto a dirt path and drove across a cattle guard. The vibration jarred Mia awake.

The entrance to the ranch was hardly special—two lodgepoles held up a third log spanning the top. The name *Devil's Wind* had been etched into the wood. Ruby pointed to an outcropping of jagged rock that resembled the bony plates of a petrified stegosaurus. "What's that over there?"

"Fury's Ridge," he said.

Appropriately named—the rocky mass looked angry.

Cumulus clouds dotted the heavens, the puffy cotton balls casting giant shadows over the land. Off to the west the skies grew ominous. Gusts of wind moved the buffalo grass in giant waves across the ground, forcing the bleached utility poles and their sagging wires to bend against their will. The desolate scenery belonged in a sci-fi movie.

The truck whizzed by an antique wind pump, its rusted blades spinning fiercely. Not far from the pump sat a water tank and a lean-to for cattle, which were nowhere in sight. The road sloped upward, and at the top of the incline a two-story house, barn, corral, and shed came into view.

The ranch house looked nothing like the residence in Ruby's dream. Years of incessant wind and sandy grit had peeled away the white paint, leaving behind sun-bleached gray boards. The once emerald roof had faded to mint green, and hailstorms had left fist-size divots in the asphalt shingles. The structure had no gutters, and only a few blades of grass poked through the dirt. The yard would turn into a mud bog after a downpour. A pair of rusty shell-back chairs sat on the porch beneath the overhang, which provided shade from the sun and protection from an air-conditioning unit balanced precariously on a second-floor window ledge. The red flowering rosebushes in front of the porch were the only sign of life in the otherwise depressing scene.

If this was her inheritance . . . *No, thanks.*

"Hank's inside." Joe got out of the truck. "I'll be in the barn if anyone needs me." He walked off, and Ruby almost called him back to help break the ice between her and Hank.

Mia leaned over the seat. "The house is worse than our trailer."

That was saying a lot, considering they'd spent the past four years living in a 1990s mobile home with turquoise trim and plastic sheeting nailed over the windows.

"I bet there's cockroaches inside."

"If it's infested with bugs, we won't stay."

Ruby played with her necklace—a nervous habit that had grown worse since leaving Pineville. She hadn't thought to ask Joe if he'd warned Hank he was bringing her and Mia to the ranch. "Maybe you should stay in the truck."

"It's too hot," Mia said.

"Then keep the door open." Ruby crossed the yard, her calf muscles tightening as the dusty ground sucked at her feet. She climbed the porch steps—five of them—then stared at the polished horseshoe knocker behind the screen.

Fancy decoration for a house in need of a wrecking ball.

She pulled back the screen door, lifted the iron talisman, then let it bang into place. A shadow passed by the front window right before the door cracked open and the barrel of a shotgun slid out to greet her.

"Are you always this neighborly?"

"I wasn't expecting visitors. Who the hell are you?"

She wished she could see his face, or at least his eyes, to determine if he was mentally deranged or just ornery. "I'm Ruby Baxter." She held up an envelope. "According to this notarized letter, you're my biological father."

"Who else is out there?"

"My daughter, Mia."

"You got a husband?"

"No. Are we welcome?"

"You're welcome." He turned his back and walked away. Hank McArthur was as friendly as a rattlesnake.

Ruby stepped inside the house, then breathed a sigh of relief when she spotted the firearm leaning against the antique umbrella stand in the foyer.

"You gonna let all that dadgum dust blow in here?"

"Sorry." She moved aside and closed the door—but not all the way.

The sun spilling from a room off the foyer cloaked Hank McArthur in shimmering light—the kind reserved for angels, not fathers who rejected their daughters. He'd probably been taller in his youth, but now he stood only a few inches over Ruby's five feet six. She'd inherited her blue eyes from him, except a murky haze covered his—cataracts. His bushy eyebrows reminded her of a milkweed moth with its white-, gold-, and dark-colored spikes sticking up in all directions.

Decades of toiling in the sun had turned his skin to cracked leather. The wrinkles near his eyes bled into his cheeks, the lines deepening as they drew closer to his chin. A permanent fissure split his lower lip in half, and the left side of his mouth folded inward—a telltale sign of missing teeth. His stooped frame offered a view of the top of his head—splotches of pink scalp with brown spots peeked through thinning gray hair in need of a trim.

As far as first impressions went, Hank McArthur wasn't at all what Ruby wished for in a father.

"Where's that kid of yours?" His throaty rasp and the cigarette pack in his shirt pocket ID'd him as a lifelong smoker.

"She's waiting outside."

He left her standing in the foyer.

Jeez, the least he could do was act as if not seeing her for thirty-one years affected him. She followed him through the hallway, noting the half bath tucked beneath the staircase. When she entered the kitchen, a mongrel the size of a Great Dane *woof*ed at her. The ugly mutt sniffed the air but didn't budge from his bed pillow in the corner.

"Found him wandering in the road," Hank said.

"What's his name?"

"Didn't give him one."

He cared enough to rescue a homeless hound but not enough to name it?

Hank struggled to hold a can of dog food, while his gnarled fingers fumbled with the opener. A short-sleeved cotton shirt and worn jeans hung on his scrawny frame, and his saggy skin was mottled with moles and scabbed-over sores. His shoulders curved inward, forcing his torso toward the floor, gravity tugging him closer to the grave—half buried already by the fine layer of dust that coated his skin and clothes. He dumped the moist food into a bowl, mashed it with a fork, then bent, his knees crunching, and placed the meal before the dog.

While the mutt ate, Ruby scrutinized the kitchen. Burn marks marred the linoleum floor—ash from Hank's cancer sticks. The aging vinyl curled up along the baseboards, and the pattern had been worn off two of the squares in front of the cast-iron sink. The black refrigerator clashed with the white stove. No dishwasher. A table and four chairs sat in front of the window overlooking the backyard. A crock of cooking utensils and a tin canister set—their faded red letters spelling *Flour*, *Sugar* and *Tea*—sat on the gold-flecked Formica counter next to the toaster. Decades of frying food in the kitchen had coated the maple cabinets with a thick sheen of grease. Even though there was no trace of a woman's touch, the shabby room possessed a homey feel.

Ruby crossed her arms over her chest. The Devil's Wind wasn't home and never would be.

"Didn't expect you this soon," he said.

That Hank had expected her to show up at all pissed Ruby off. Had it never crossed his mind that maybe she wouldn't want to meet the man who'd given her away?

His eyes studied her. "Where'd you get the necklace?"

"From my parents. Why?"

He shrugged.

"How do you know for certain that I'm your daughter?"

"You look like your mother."

"Where is my mother?"

He wet a dishrag, then rubbed at an invisible spot on the counter. "Haven't seen Cora since right after you were born."

So her birth mother had left him, too? "Where did she go?"

"Sometimes a person doesn't want to be found." He pressed his bony hand against his chest and stared into space.

"What's the matter?"

"Had a pacemaker put in a while back."

Suddenly Ruby understood why he'd tracked her down. "You sent for me because you're going to die soon and you want to clear your conscience."

"My conscience is clear."

"You have no regrets about putting me up for adoption?"

"Didn't have a choice."

"Everybody has a choice." Ruby choked back a curse. So much for pretending she was tough enough to handle the truth. "I became pregnant with my daughter by accident, but I kept her."

"I got things to settle before I leave this earth."

She didn't want to care about Hank's health. But the fact that his heart needed help beating properly was cause for concern. She'd hate to see him keel over before she learned more about him and Cora, not to mention other health issues aside from a weak heart that she and Mia needed to be aware of.

He pointed to the door on the opposite side of the kitchen. "Made the back porch into a bedroom. Cooler out there at night." He picked up the empty dog bowl and rinsed it in the sink. "Joe'll clear his things out later. You 'n' . . . What's your daughter's name?"

"Mia."

"Can bunk down on the porch."

Ruby didn't know which was worse—sleeping on Hank's porch or in Elvis's pop-up trailer behind the diner.

A scuffling sound alerted her that she and Hank weren't alone. "I told you to wait in the truck." Not that she'd expected Mia to listen to her. The teen had a mind of her own—like her mother.

"You're my grandfather?"

Hank's expression softened as he peered at his granddaughter. "You have an unusual name, Mia."

"Mom named me after a stupid character in *The Princess Diaries*. They made a movie out of the books."

"You don't say."

"Did you name my mom Ruby?"

Of all the questions that had come to mind when Ruby had learned she'd been adopted, who had named her hadn't been one of them.

"I'm afraid I didn't."

Good. Hank hadn't earned the honor of naming her.

"Your grandmother called her Faith," he said.

"Why?" Mia asked.

Hank's gaze traveled around the room, skipping over Ruby. "When she held your mother in her arms, she said she knew the baby would remain loyal."

Loyal to whom? Hank, herself, or—Ruby glanced at Mia—her daughter? The old man was in for a big surprise if he believed he'd win her over with a sentimental story about her birth moniker.

He lifted a cowboy hat from a hook on the wall and clucked his tongue. The hound padded after him through the porch and out to the backyard, where he stopped to light a cigarette.

Mia watched the pair through the kitchen window. "What's the dog's name?"

"It doesn't have a name."

"Your dad's not very friendly."

"No, he's not."

Chapter 4

"Are we gonna stay?" Mia asked Ruby.

"Hank said we could sleep on the porch. Let's take a look at our accommodations and then decide."

Ruby surveyed the cramped quarters. A washer and dryer had been placed in the corner across from the door that opened to the backyard. A generic brand of laundry detergent and a jug of bleach sat on the shelf next to the machines. Old-fashioned roller shades, yellowed from age, hung above the window screens. An inch of dust coated the furniture, and when Ruby walked across the rug in front of the queen-size bed, puffs of dirt swirled next to her feet. The only sign that anyone occupied the room was the pair of men's athletic shoes resting beneath a chair in the corner and the quarter, two dimes, and penny left on the nightstand.

Ruby had slept in worse places, but she didn't feel right about evicting the foreman from his room. Why hadn't Hank suggested they use one of the second-floor bedrooms? Mia pointed the remote at the TV on the dresser, then stretched out on the bed.

"What do you think?" Ruby said. "Is it okay with you if we stay?"

Silence.

"If Hank makes you feel uncomfortable, we can leave."

No answer. Ruby was damn tired of being ignored, but she squelched her frustration. "It doesn't matter to me whether we stay or not. It's more important that you feel safe here."

Mia flipped over on the mattress. "Why wouldn't I feel safe?"

Well, for one thing, your grandfather answered the door with a shotgun in his hands. "I'm not saying it isn't safe. It's just that—"

"You want me to decide. Then if anything goes wrong, it's not your fault." The accusatory glower in Mia's eyes cut Ruby to the bone.

"Let's not make this into a big deal."

"Fine. We can stay."

Breathing a sigh of relief, Ruby went out to the pickup to retrieve their luggage. One bag slung over her shoulder and two more in hand, she returned to the porch just as the back door opened and Joe stepped inside. He froze when he saw Mia on the bed.

"Hank said we should sleep here tonight, but if you'd rather . . ." Ruby's words spurred Joe into action. He removed a duffel bag from beneath the bed, tossed his shoes inside, and then emptied out a clothing drawer before collecting his change from the nightstand.

"Clean sheets are in the upstairs linen closet." He stopped at the foot of the bed. "It gets windy out here at night. You'll want to use the latch hook on the screen door to keep it from blowing open." Then he was gone.

"Is he mad that we took his room?" Mia asked.

"I don't think so." If he was, he'd hidden it well. "I'll find the sheets. Then you can help me make the bed."

Ruby climbed the stairs to the second floor. She paused on the landing and counted the doors—three plus the linen closet at the far end of the hall. Faded yellow wallpaper with pink roses clinging to mint-green vines buckled in the corners where brown water splotches marred the ceiling. The floorboards needed a new coat of stain, and the only footprints in the hallway led to the two doors on Ruby's right. The dust in front of the door to her left remained undisturbed. No one had gone into that room in ages. *Why*?

She checked out the bathroom—toilet, tub, and pedestal sink. Next, Hank's room—bed, dresser, and a brown rug that covered the wood floor in front of the bed. There were no photographs, artwork, or anything personal that hinted at a woman having ever shared the space with Hank. The door across the hall beckoned her. Who cared if he noticed her footprints? She tested the knob, then poked her head inside—pink walls and white baby furniture.

What the . . . ? She tiptoed into the room and ran her hand across the crib rail. Then she fingered the satin ruffles on the bassinet before giving the rocking chair in the corner a gentle push. The top drawer of the dresser held a supply of pink hair bows and ruffled socks. The middle drawer was filled with disposable diapers—yellowed with age—and flannel baby blankets had been stowed in the bottom drawer.

The evidence in the room suggested Hank and Cora had never intended to give Ruby up for adoption. What had changed their minds about keeping her? And why after three decades hadn't Hank painted the nursery a different color and gotten rid of the furniture?

Maybe there were other children after you.

Ruby didn't have time to ponder the possibility because she heard the front door open. She ducked from the bedroom, then hurried to the closet at the end of the hall.

Hank appeared on the landing. "What are you doing?"

"Getting fresh sheets for the bed." She wiped her sweaty palms against her dress before removing a set of dingy linens from the shelf.

His gaze tracked her footprints to the nursery, and the parentheses lines bracketing his mouth deepened. "You can use the bathroom up here, but keep out of the other rooms."

"We need to talk." She hovered in his bedroom doorway.

"I have to exercise one of the horses." He sat on the bed and switched to a different pair of boots.

She exhaled a noisy breath through her nostrils. "I didn't come here to be ignored."

"You in a rush to leave?"

Yes. No. *Maybe.* "I have to be in Kansas two weeks from now."

"Then we have time to talk."

Ruby let him win this round and stepped aside. "Did you have plans for supper, or would you like me to throw a meal together?"

"Make what you want. Joe and I go our separate ways." He hitched his drooping pants, then descended the stairs and walked out the front door. Ruby went into the parlor to snoop.

The room smelled of musty wood and moldy fabric. Nose twitching, she walked past a love seat and matching chair to check out the piano against the wall. Had Cora played the instrument? She ran her fingers over the yellowed keys, picturing a blond-haired woman singing as she played.

Faith. Cora had named her Faith. The gentle-sounding moniker conjured up images of charity work and Sunday sermons—things Ruby had no experience with. It was a good thing her adoptive parents had changed her name. She'd never been one to hold much faith in anyone—certainly not herself.

Ruby returned to the back porch, finding it empty. She peered through the window and saw Mia and the ugly dog out by the corral, watching Hank put a harness on a horse. Feeling the need to supervise their interactions—at least until she was convinced Hank wouldn't say or do anything to offend Mia—Ruby dropped the sheets on the bed and went outside.

Hank held the rope and turned in a slow circle, forcing the horse to trot around him.

"I'm bored." Mia waved her arms in the air.

Hank ignored her.

"I said, I'm bored!"

"I heard you the first time." His focus remained on the horse. "You ever ridden before?"

"No, but I rode a motorcycle once."

Ruby stopped at Mia's side. "When?"

"Sabrina's brother gave me a ride to their house once after you went to work."

What else had Mia's friend talked her daughter into doing? Had she been so caught up in her troubles with Sean that she'd missed all the warnings signs that Mia was testing her boundaries?

Hank clicked his tongue and the horse slowed. "How old are you?" he asked.

"Fourteen. How old are you?"

"Seventy-one."

"You look older than that."

"Reckon I do."

"My mom makes me wear sunscreen, but she never does." Mia stared defiantly at Ruby. "And she said I couldn't get a tattoo, but she got one on her boob."

Why was Mia intentionally trying to make her look bad in front of Hank?

After a ten-second glare-down with her daughter, Mia looked away and spoke to Hank. "I can see his bones. Is the horse gonna die?"

"He'll be okay, once he fattens up."

"What happened to him?"

"He was abused."

"How?"

"His owner moved away and left him without food."

"What happened to my grandma?"

"You ask a lot of questions," he said.

"So?"

It was difficult to tell with the late-afternoon sun in her eyes, but Ruby swore Hank's mouth lifted in a smile.

"Where's my grandma?" Mia asked.

"Don't know."

"How come you don't know?"

"Your grandmother left after your mother was born."

"Were you mean to her?"

Hank scowled, and his eyes disappeared into his wrinkles. "You always speak your mind, young lady?"

"I'm afraid she does," Ruby said.

He clicked his tongue and the horse stopped. "I didn't beat your grandmother."

"Then why'd she run off?"

"If I knew, I'd tell you."

"Do you have the Internet in your house?"

"Don't have any use for a computer."

"Everyone needs a computer. I found out Pinky's boyfriend got her pregnant on the Entertainment News website."

"Never heard of Pinky," Hank said.

"She's a singer in a band from England."

Hank walked the horse closer to Mia.

"Can I pet him?" she asked.

"Be gentle. He's not used to strangers."

Ruby got the feeling no one on the ranch—the horses, Hank, or Joe—was used to being around people.

Mia stroked the animal's neck. "He's sweaty."

"Where's your father?" Hank glanced between Ruby and Mia.

"Dylan and I never married," Ruby said.

Hank must have been satisfied with her answer, because he changed the subject. "You want to feed the horses?"

"Sure," Mia said. "What's this one's name?"

"Didn't name him."

"How come?"

When Hank didn't answer, Mia rubbed the horse's nose and asked, "Can I name your animals?"

"Suit yourself."

"I'm gonna call your dog Friend."

"That's a stupid name."

"Is not." Mia pointed to the hound. "He follows you everywhere just like a friend."

"Guess you got a point there." Hank pulled a pack of Winstons from his pocket, then flicked his lighter.

"Cigarettes cause cancer."

"We all gotta die of something, kid."

"And they make you stink." Mia met Hank and the horse at the gate. "A grandfather shouldn't smell like an ashtray."

Hank dropped his smoke on the ground and stomped it with his bootheel, then looked at Ruby. "You coming?"

Mia's cold stare warned Ruby to stay behind. "I have to make the bed." She drew in a ragged breath as she watched the pair saunter off. She and Mia had been at the ranch less than an hour and already her daughter and Hank were bonding, which left Ruby feeling like a third wheel.

Hank was *her* father, not Mia's.

Oh, hell. What kind of mother was jealous of her own child? Ruby had been thinking only of herself when she'd made the decision to meet Hank McArthur. She hadn't considered how the visit might impact Mia.

Before arriving in Unforgiven, Ruby had made up her mind that she wasn't going to like her biological father. But Hank's unconditional acceptance of his granddaughter chipped away at her plan to keep him at arm's length.

First the animals, and now Mia saw something worthwhile in the old man. Maybe Ruby should give Hank a chance even if she had to wait in line behind her daughter for his attention.

Chapter 5

Joe sidled up to the bar at the Possum Belly Saloon—the only place in town whose name was connected to the oil and gas business. A possum belly is a receiving tank found at the end of a mud return line, and the roughnecks who frequented the bar looked like they'd spent the day in a sludgy cistern.

The owner, Stonewall Davis—called Stony by the regulars—ignored Joe. What the retired oil worker lacked in height he made up for in muscle and tattoos. His short-cropped hair, neatly trimmed goatee, and clean, well-manicured fingernails contradicted the mish-mash of multicolored skulls and fire-breathing dragons that wrapped his arms from wrist to shoulder.

Joe wasn't a regular at the bar—too much alcohol ripped the scabs off old wounds. But Ruby and her daughter showing up out of nowhere today had reminded him of the wife and child he'd lost, and he needed a drink to settle his nerves.

Davis made his way toward him, and Joe pulled his wallet from his pocket. "Whiskey. Make it a double."

Stony measured the liquor, then banged the shot glass on the bar, splattering Joe's T-shirt with drops of amber liquid. He'd run into Davis's kind before—bullies who enjoyed intimidating people if for no other reason than they could. Not in the mood for the man's games, Joe carried his drink to a table in the corner. His back to the wall, he fixated on his Johnnie Walker, fingers clenching the jigger as if he could choke off the memories that always followed the first sip.

It had been seven years since the night he'd drunk enough whiskey to quiet his spirit for eternity. Death would have been a blessing, but a sadistic voice in his head had coaxed him to put the bottle down before he'd smothered the pain for good. He hadn't understood why he'd survived the drinking binge until days later, when the alcohol fog had lifted and his conscience revealed his sentence—a lifetime of guilt. But unlike Jesus Christ, the cross Joe carried held his son's lifeless body. Hand trembling, he raised the glass to his lips. The alcohol seared his throat, but he savored the sting.

The saloon door burst open, smacking the wall. A handful of roustabouts shuffled inside, the sheriff's deputy bringing up the rear. When Randall spotted Joe, he changed direction. Joe tossed the remainder of the whiskey down his gullet.

"Invite me to sit, Dawson."

Using the heel of his boot, Joe pushed the chair out on the opposite side of the table.

Randall straddled the seat, then caught the bartender's eye and pointed to the empty shot glass. Stony came over with a whiskey bottle and refilled Joe's drink and left a glass of water in front of Randall.

"Thanks." The deputy waited for Stony to walk off before he spoke. "Heard you drove Ruby Baxter and her daughter out to the Devil's Wind earlier today."

The ride to the ranch with Ruby and Mia had been uncomfortable but in a good way. Their presence had brought back memories of a life Joe had been trying to forget for years. He hadn't realized how much he'd missed hearing a woman's voice. He liked Ruby's matter-of-fact tone and that she didn't mince her words.

"What does Ruby want from Hank?"

"She didn't say." Although their conversation had been only a handful of sentences, Joe hadn't stopped thinking about Ruby. She looked nothing like his ex-wife. Melanie had short dark hair and big brown eyes. They'd had a good marriage up to the end. But not even a good marriage had been enough to overcome their personal tragedy.

"Is Ruby planning to stay?"

"I don't know." The length of her visit wasn't any of his business.

"How's Hank feeling?"

Like Randall gave a crap. "He's got no complaints." A few weeks ago Hank had suffered chest pains after he'd learned that a section of fence bordering the Bar T had been opened up with bolt cutters and five steer had gone missing. Joe had asked Roy Sandoval to check his herd for the Devil's Wind brand—666—but the rancher had balked. When Hank reported the missing cattle to the law, the sheriff had put Randall on the case and the investigation had gone nowhere.

"Hank's daughter might be a gold digger, looking to cash in after his ticker stops"—Randall smirked—"ticking."

Hank's heart had better hold out. Joe needed his job. Needed to feel exhausted at the end of the day. Needed some kind of purpose in his life—a reason to get up in the morning. The Devil's Wind was the first place he'd felt a sense of peace. A glimmer of hope.

"Excuse me." A man stopped at their table and removed his ball cap, revealing a farmer's tan forehead. Joe had run into the guy and his two sons outside the mercantile after he'd hired on with Hank. He remembered the young boys had looked as if they hadn't had a decent bath in months.

"How are the twins?" Randall asked.

"Good." Pete nodded over his shoulder. "They're waiting outside for me right now." He rubbed his finger back and forth over the edge of the ball cap. "I wanted to thank you for picking up the tab for their Little League fee this summer."

"Glad to do it. Any luck finding a new job?"

Pete's gaze dropped to the floor. "Not yet."

"You tell Chris to keep his eye on the ball when he's in right field, and Craig needs to choke up on the bat before he swings."

"Will do."

"When's their next game?"

"Saturday morning."

"I'll drop by the field and watch," Randall said.

Pete put his cap on, then glanced at Joe. "Sorry for the interruption."

"Are the oil fields laying off?" Joe asked once the father left.

"No. Pete can't keep his hands off the bottle. He got fired for drinking on his shift."

"Does his wife have a job?"

"She works for one of those maid services in Guymon."

Randall didn't seem like the kind of guy who cared about other people's misfortunes. "Didn't know you were a Little League fan. Did you play when you were a kid?"

"No." The deputy shoved his chair back and stood. "Tell Hank I'll stop by the ranch tomorrow and update him on his missing cattle."

Joe suspected there was no update on the investigation—Randall needed an excuse to grill Ruby. An image of Hank's daughter flashed before his eyes, and he drained the half inch of whiskey left in the shot glass. Ruby was an attractive woman, if a little rough around the edges. The few times they'd glanced at each other, he'd recognized the guarded look in her blue eyes. Those same shadows greeted him in the mirror each morning. As if his thoughts had summoned her to the saloon, Ruby walked through the door and a hush fell over the crowd.

"What's wrong? Haven't you seen a woman in town before?" Ruby leered at the oil workers. When the men turned their backs to her and resumed drinking, she marched up to the bar. "I like your dragon tattoos." She nodded to the bartender's muscular arms.

"You must be Ruby."

She wasn't surprised that the news of her and Mia's arrival had spread from the diner to the mercantile and now the saloon.

"Stonewall." He held out his hand. "Everyone calls me Stony."

"Nice to meet you. I'll have an iced tea, please."

"A Long Island tea?"

"Regular, no alcohol." She'd borrowed Hank's rust-bucket pickup and had driven into town for a cold drink with Elvis, but a CLOSED sign hung on the Airstream's door. "Thanks," she said after Stony filled her drink order. She'd taken only two sips of tea when her neck began to itch. She glanced over her shoulder. *Joe.* She weaved through the male bodies and stopped by his table. "You couldn't sleep, either?"

He inclined his head toward the empty chair and she sat. "It's hotter than hell on that porch. I don't know how you survived out there with no air conditioning."

"You get used to it."

She studied him. Mia was right—he had sad eyes. "I went outside to catch a breeze and got a nose full of flying grit." She'd sat in the dark on the porch step, listening to the cry of a coyote. The lonely howl had reminded her of Hank, who'd asked Mia to help him groom the horses after supper rather than answer Ruby's questions about why she'd been given up for adoption. She brushed at the thin layer of silt covering the back of her hand. "How do you stay clean in this place?"

"I like to think of it as an all-year-round tan."

She laughed. "Next you'll tell me wearing dirt is better than sunscreen." A light flashed through his eyes and the brown orbs warmed to dark chocolate. Ruby hardly knew Joe, but his calm demeanor put her at ease. "I feel bad that you have to sleep in the barn."

"I've slept in a lot worse places." He shrugged. "There's a cot in the storage room. It's comfortable enough."

"What else do you do for Hank besides look after the cows?"

"Run errands and repair things."

"Mind if I add something to your to-do list?" she asked.

"What's that?"

"Tear the house down."

He chuckled. "I offered to paint it when Hank hired me, but he wasn't interested."

"Did you know there's a nursery on the second floor?"

He shook his head. "The only room I've been in up there is the bathroom."

"You and Hank don't say a whole lot to each other." She waved a hand in front of her face. "Not that Hank cares to converse with anyone. Is he always so blunt with people?"

"The boss man doesn't engage in meaningless chatter."

Is that what Hank thought—that the circumstance of her adoption was babble? "What about you?"

"What about me what?"

Joe had said more to her in the past few minutes than he had in the past ten hours. Her gaze dropped to the empty shot glass rolling between his fingers. Maybe his talkativeness was a result of alcohol consumption. "You don't seem to mind talking. Where are you from?"

"Born and raised in Tulsa."

"Mia and I are from Pineville, Missouri." She studied his face while she took another sip of her tea. Like her, the lines around his eyes remained visible when he wasn't smiling. The strands of gray hair at his temples, his prominent cheekbones, and his angular face hinted that he was in his mid- to late forties. "How old are you?"

"Thirty-eight."

More than toiling in the hot sun and wind had aged Joe Dawson.

"How old is your daughter?" he asked.

Ruby expected him to ask her age, not Mia's. "Fourteen. Why?" He'd better not be a pervert who preferred young girls to mature women.

"I thought she might be close to my son's age if he'd . . ." His voice trailed off, following his gaze into space.

He couldn't drop a bomb like that and expect her not to ask . . . "If your son what?"

His eyelids lowered and his chest shuddered. "Aaron passed away seven years ago."

A nauseating knot formed in Ruby's stomach. No wonder there

were shadows in the man's eyes. "I'm sorry." She chewed her lip, debating whether or not to prod him for details. As a mother, she couldn't imagine coping with the pain of losing a child. It certainly put her relationship troubles with Mia into perspective.

"It was an accident." Joe curled his fingers into his palm.

Ruby caught Stony's eye and motioned for drink refills. He brought her another iced tea, then set a half bottle of whiskey on the table before walking off.

Joe tossed back two shots—one right after the other.

"You don't have to talk about it," she said.

"I talk about it every day in my head."

"His name was Aaron?"

He nodded. "After his sixth birthday I was promoted to supervisor at Axis Exploration in Tulsa County."

So Joe Dawson hadn't always been a ranch hand.

He traced the label on the liquor bottle. "It happened on a Saturday. Melanie took off with her girlfriends and left Aaron at the house with me. There was a problem at one of the company sites, and I told Aaron that he had to go with me to check on a well. He wanted to stay home and play with a friend who'd gotten a new video game." Joe shook his head. "I knew the parents wouldn't mind watching Aaron that afternoon, but I'd been on the road all week and I wanted to spend time with my son." He rubbed his brow, his fingers leaving deep dents in the skin. "I went into the bedroom to change clothes, and a few minutes later someone rang the bell and shouted my name."

Ruby couldn't take her eyes off the front of Joe's T-shirt, where his heart was pounding so hard it moved the cotton material.

"Aaron had taken off on his bike." Joe swallowed twice before he spoke again. "The neighbor lady said he came out of the driveway so fast she had no time to stop."

Aaron had been hit by a car.

"Melanie and I were adamant about him wearing a helmet. He knew the rules." Joe's tortured gaze begged Ruby to explain why his son hadn't worn the protective headgear.

She wanted to assure him that he'd done nothing wrong, but she'd yet to win any mother-of-the-year awards. Ruby had thought she'd done all the right things with Mia. She'd been open with her daughter about sex and willing to answer questions. Then she'd discovered Mia in the act and had felt like the biggest failure ever. After she'd chased Kevin's buck-naked ass out of the trailer and Mia had locked herself in the bedroom, Ruby had cursed God, her dead parents, Mia's father, Sean, and lastly, herself.

Once she'd spread the blame around, she'd accepted that maybe she hadn't been a good role model for her daughter. That maybe her tendency to swap out boyfriends as often as she changed underwear had given Mia the impression that relationships were all about sex. But how could Ruby explain what a meaningful, lasting relationship was when she'd never experienced one?

So Ruby had done the only thing she was certain would prevent Kevin Walters from getting Mia pregnant—she'd moved them out of town.

"Melanie and I grew apart after Aaron died." Joe's voice startled Ruby out of her reverie. "I quit my job and hit the road, looking for work where I could find it."

"And you ended up in Unforgiven." A town with no children, women, or families. No reminders of what he'd lost.

Joe crossed his arms, his fingers pressing into his biceps. The raw emotion in his eyes tapped into Ruby's own uncertainty and fear about her relationship with Mia.

She tossed a ten-dollar bill on the table and stood. "I'll drive you back to the ranch. You can get your truck in the morning." She left the bar first, stopping on the sidewalk to draw in a lungful of humid air, then jumped inside her skin when a voice floated through the darkness.

"Nice evening for a stroll." Big Dan emerged from the shadows. The man had a nasty habit of popping up unexpectedly. "The threatening weather earlier today took a detour. It'll be back tomorrow." He tottered off into the darkness.

Joe came out of the bar and they crossed the street to Hank's pickup. Neither one of them was in the mood for more conversation. Not until Ruby pulled up to the house thirty minutes later did Joe speak.

"Deputy Randall plans to pay Hank a visit tomorrow."

"What does he want?"

"A month ago Hank reported some missing cattle."

"Were his cows ever located?"

"No."

"Then why's the deputy coming out?"

"He's looking for an excuse to talk to you."

The officer might have been pleasant to Ruby in town, but she doubted he was Unforgiven's Welcome Wagon.

Eyes stinging, Ruby watched Joe disappear into the barn. Although their chat tonight hadn't been uplifting, she was grateful he hadn't excluded her like Mia and Hank had.

Chapter 6

Ruby woke to the sound of birds chirping and bright sunlight flooding the screened-in porch. With only one tree on the property, she wouldn't expect any feathered creatures to take up residence. Then again, Hank McArthur appeared to have a soft spot for animals—maybe he'd hung feeders for his winged friends.

She checked the time on her cell phone. It was nine a.m. Normally she'd have gotten dressed by six thirty, but after her trip into town last night and learning about the death of Joe's son, sleep had eluded her. She'd lain in bed and listened to Mia's soft snoring, thanking the heavens above that her child was alive and well. Aaron's death had put things into perspective. Ruby wasn't happy that Mia had lost her virginity already, but she'd rather deal with that reality than Joe's—life without his child.

She'd contented herself with the knowledge that things hadn't always been strained between her and Mia. Before her daughter had entered her teens, they'd gone to the movies together, enjoyed shopping, and had given each other manicures. But when Mia had entered junior high, she'd begun pulling away from Ruby, choosing to spend time with friends rather than her mother, which was why Ruby had been stunned when she'd caught Mia with Kevin. She hadn't even been aware the two were hanging out.

Right now she and Mia were going through a rough patch, but Ruby was confident they'd weather this storm, and once they settled into their new home in Kansas, things between them would return to normal.

Ruby swung her legs off the bed and rubbed her eyes, then fumbled in the nightstand for her toiletry bag. When her fingers bumped the journal, she removed the notebook and studied the floral design on the leather cover. She'd never seen her mother write in the diary and hadn't discovered it until after her parents died.

Burying her parents, settling their estate, and being a single mother of a newborn was more than Ruby had been able to handle. The diary had gotten tossed into a box with other mementos, then stowed and forgotten. Not until she and Mia had cleaned out the trailer in preparation for their move had she come across the journal again.

She'd intended to read it, but then the letter from Hank's lawyer had arrived, knocking her legs out from under her. She'd been hurt and angry that her parents had kept her adoption a secret. The news had stirred up memories of her troubled relationship with her father, and now she didn't have the courage to read her mother's words, for fear she'd discover her parents hadn't loved her as much as she'd believed.

She returned the diary to the drawer, grabbed a pair of clean underwear, denim shorts, and a hot-pink tank top, then padded through the house, the smell of burned toast and coffee accompanying her to the second-floor bathroom. She showered and dressed, then pulled her damp hair into a ponytail before heading outside to inform Hank that the deputy might stop by.

The horses stood in the corral but grandfather and granddaughter were nowhere in sight. Hank's truck sat next to the shed—not where she'd parked it last night. He must have given Joe a lift into town to retrieve his vehicle. Squinting against the bright sun, she hiked across the dirt drive to the barn, pausing inside the doorway while her eyes adjusted to the dim light.

"I'm gonna call the black one Pretty Boy, because he was beautiful before he got all marked up." Mia's voice echoed from the rear of the structure. "How come he has so many scars?"

"Tried jumping a fence to get to water and got tangled in barbed wire," Hank answered.

Ruby stepped into the open but saw only a wheelbarrow filled with soiled hay. The pair must be cleaning stalls. She had trouble envisioning Mia shoveling horse crap when her daughter had never once taken the garbage to the Dumpster in the trailer park.

"The gray one is Sugar, 'cause she loves sugar cubes," Mia said. "I'm not sure about the brown horse. I might call him Lonesome. He always stands by himself in the corral."

"Don't expect 'em to come when you say their name. They're too old and set in their ways to learn new tricks."

Maybe that same logic applied to Hank, and Ruby should adjust her expectations.

"I want a dog, but my mom says it costs too much to take care of one."

"Animals need more than food and water. They need vaccinations and—"

"Did you take Friend to the vet after you found him?"

"Yep. He got all his shots."

Ruby felt a twinge of guilt for eavesdropping, then shoved it aside. This was the most talkative Mia had been in weeks, and she didn't want to miss hearing anything that might help her understand why her daughter was shutting her out.

"I bet if I lived with you, you'd let me have a dog."

Hank remained silent.

"Do you have a girlfriend?" Mia asked.

"What would I do with a girlfriend?"

"She'd keep you company."

"I've been on my own all these years. No sense changing that now." Hank coughed, the rattle in his chest bouncing off the barn walls. Then he hacked up phlegm.

"That's gross," Mia said.

"Got to clear out my chest in the morning."

"I could help you quit smoking if you let me stay with you."

Mia would rather live with a practical stranger than her own mother. Beads of sweat bubbled across Ruby's upper lip, and she wiped away the perspiration with the back of her hand. Since Mia had been caught in bed with Kevin, she'd given Ruby the cold shoulder. Ruby had backed off, deciding to wait until they arrived in Kansas before addressing the subject again. But if Mia continued to avoid Ruby, they might have to duke it out at the ranch.

"Why would you want to live with an old man like me?"

"You've got horses and Friend."

"You like animals?"

"Animals love you no matter if you've done bad stuff," Mia said.

Ruby's heart hurt for her daughter. Was she worried that her mother wouldn't love her after she'd slept with a boy?

"And animals never leave you."

Who was leaving Mia? Ruby had always been there for her daughter.

"I'd rather live here than in Kansas," Mia said. "My mom got a job at a motel in some stupid town called Elkhart."

"I'm guessing you don't want to live in Elkhart," he said.

"Not hardly."

"What does your father say about you and your mom moving?"

"He doesn't care."

If Hank wanted to know more about Dylan, why didn't he just ask her?

"My mom said my dad got her pregnant in high school. She thought he'd marry her, but he didn't."

Which was why Ruby had to make Mia understand that sex had serious consequences and she was way too young to handle them.

Ruby had run into Dylan—literally—at the roller rink. Some twit had cut her off during the girls-only skate and she'd careened into the half wall, where Dylan stood with his back to the rink. The jolt sent his Dr Pepper flying, and the drink had splashed his date—a girl named Penny.

Penny had flown into a rage, but it had been Dylan whom Ruby couldn't take her eyes off. Apparently he'd found her just as interesting. Later that night he'd dumped Penny and given Ruby a ride home. She'd known Dylan was nothing but trouble, but she hadn't cared, because he'd wanted to be with her. After only three dates she'd handed him her virginity, and then a few months later the stick had turned blue.

And Ruby had blamed her pregnancy on Glen Baxter.

Every summer after Ruby had turned eight, she'd spent two weeks on the road with her father. Hands down, it had been the best part of her school break. No set bedtime. No rules against eating junk food. Candy bars for breakfast and giant-size sodas when they stopped to fill the Peterbilt with diesel fuel. And tours of roadside attractions—places like the Jesse James Wax Museum and the world's largest ball of twine. One of Ruby's favorite pit stops had been Leila's Hair Museum, where she'd been in awe of the wreaths made from human hair.

Then there had been the afternoon her father had pulled off in Effingham, Illinois, home of the world's largest cross. Ruby had gazed up at the white monstrosity and asked, "Is God real, or did people make him up like Santa Claus and the Easter Bunny?" Her father had said, "God is real if you want him to be, and not, if you don't want him to be." And Ruby had taken him at his word.

In Indiana, they saw the Giant Lady's Leg Sundial in Roselawn, but her father wouldn't take her inside the resort because the people weren't wearing clothes. Then they visited the Backyard Roller Coasters of John Ivers in Bruceville. Mr. Ivers had let them ride the smaller one for free. Two weeks later her father would park the big rig in front of their trailer and Ruby would cry, sad to see their time together end. She and her father'd had a special bond, and that's why she'd been devastated the summer of her sophomore year in high school, when he'd canceled their road trip.

She closed her eyes against the memory—still painful after all these years. Her suitcase had been packed for days, and the list of roadside attractions was safely tucked inside her purse. The night before she and her father were to leave, her parents had gotten into a shouting match. Then the next morning her father had called off their trip. Her mother would say only that something had come up with her father's job and Ruby had to stay home. She didn't buy the lie for a minute, but each time she pressed for answers, her mother locked herself in the bedroom.

That morning was the last time she saw her father until Labor Day weekend. After that summer her relationship with Glen Baxter had gone downhill. He'd spent more hours on the road, adding extra deliveries to his schedule. Hurt and angry, Ruby had sought comfort elsewhere, which she'd found in the backseat of Dylan's car.

"How often do you see your dad?" Hank asked Mia.

"My mom said he used to stop by our trailer when I was a baby, but I don't remember that."

Thinking back on their relationship, Ruby conceded that she'd never been in love with Dylan—only the attention he'd given her. She'd put up with his sporadic visits after Mia was born because she'd wanted him to bond with his daughter. But Dylan had only dropped by when he'd wanted sex or money for cigarettes and booze. Once she'd booted him out of her life for good, she'd set her sights higher, determined to find a decent boyfriend—not an easy task when educated guys wanted nothing to do with a teenage mother.

"Does your mom have a boyfriend?"

"She just broke up with Sean, and he was really nice. He watched TV shows with me and helped me with my math homework. He didn't do anything wrong, but she made him move out of our trailer."

This was the first time Ruby had heard Mia voice an objection to Sean's leaving.

"Your mother must have had her reasons if she told him to go."

Hank's comment was hardly a glowing endorsement, but Ruby appreciated his support.

"My mom doesn't like you."

"I'm not surprised."

"When she found out you were her real dad, she called you a stupid old asshole."

"Girls shouldn't swear."

Why was Mia attacking her? Did she want Hank to hate Ruby?

"I earned that bad name because I gave your mother up for adoption. But she raised you. Made sure you had a roof over your head and food on the table."

"Once we leave here, my mom's never gonna visit you again."

"Maybe not."

"How much you wanna bet she won't let me visit you, either?"

"Mothers usually know best."

"Hank?" Mia's voice trembled.

"What?"

"Promise you won't let my mom keep me from coming to see you and the horses?"

"You'll always be welcome at the Devil's Wind." Hank stepped into view, pressing his shirtsleeve against his sweaty brow. He didn't act surprised when he spotted Ruby—maybe he'd known she was listening.

"If I don't like Elkhart, then I'll run away and come back here." Mia raked a pile of soiled hay out into the open.

"I see you're working hard," Ruby said.

Mia's eyes widened. "I'm mucking stalls."

"Nice of you to help." Ruby looked at Hank. "Did Joe mention you might have a visitor today?"

"He said the deputy was stopping by." Hank pushed the wheelbarrow farther down the aisle, and when he passed Mia, he said, "Will you finish up in here?"

"Okay."

Hank pointed a finger at Friend. "Stay." Then he left the barn.

Alone with Mia, Ruby said, "I'm surprised you like cleaning up after the horses."

"It stinks, but you get used to the smell."

This was her chance to discuss what happened with Sean. "Mia?"

"What?" Her daughter's glower siphoned the courage out of Ruby. They should have never gotten off the bus yesterday. If they'd gone straight to Elkhart, Ruby wouldn't have to compete for her daughter's attention with a grumpy old man, an ugly dog, and three nags. "Never mind." Mia wasn't in the right frame of mind for a rational conversation.

Ruby returned to the house, thinking that she'd stopped at the Devil's Wind to learn about Hank and her family tree, but none of that would matter if she couldn't fix things between her and Mia.

Because in the end her daughter was all the family Ruby had left.

Chapter 7

The shotgun was missing from the umbrella stand.

"Hank?" Ruby called up the stairs to the second floor.

"Out here."

A decade's worth of dust clogged the screen door, and she could barely make out his silhouette in the chair on the front porch. "You want a cup of coffee?"

"No."

Sheesh. Ruby was no Miss Manners, but she knew when to use *please* and *thank you*. She went into the kitchen, poured herself a mug of hot brew, then joined Hank. She nodded to the weapon resting across his lap. "The *deputy—not some outlaw biker*—is paying you a visit."

"Can't be too careful these days."

She squeezed past him and sat in the other chair. When he reached into his shirt pocket, she said, "You mind not lighting up?"

"It's my damned house"—he dropped his hand to the stock—"ought to be able to smoke if I want to."

Maybe he needed a reminder. "You invited me here."

A noise gurgled in his throat, but he left the cigarettes alone.

"I used to smoke," she said.

"Why'd you stop?"

"Too expensive." She'd quit cold turkey. And she'd fallen off the wagon only once—the afternoon she'd caught Mia and Kevin naked. Ruby had driven to the liquor store, bought the smokes, then burned through two packs until her lungs had caught fire. Thankfully she'd had no desire to continue smoking after that day. "I still get cravings once in a while." She stared at the pack of Winstons in his pocket. Unless she wanted her resolve tested, she'd better make her peace with him and head down the road sooner rather than later.

"Don't sit there with your wheels spinning. If you've got something to say, speak up."

"I irritate the hell out of you, don't I?" The question was intended to coax a chuckle or a smile from him, but he offered neither. She sipped her muddy water, waiting for the first jolt of caffeine to kick in. "I eavesdropped in the barn."

Hank's attention remained on the dirt road in front of the house. She doubted his cloudy eyes could see more than fifty yards from the front porch. She and Hank were little more than strangers, but she was hard-pressed to remain indifferent toward him. Maybe because they'd both been abandoned by Cora but more likely because every breath Hank took was one breath closer to his last.

"Mia exaggerated." She twisted her gemstone necklace. "I called you a stupid asshole, not a stupid *old* asshole."

Mouth twitching, he glanced at her. "What happened between you and Sean?"

Ruby didn't care to discuss her boyfriend troubles with Hank. She never entered into a relationship expecting it to end, but at the first sign of trouble, she dumped her boyfriend rather than wait for the whole affair to unravel.

She changed the subject. "I guess it's pretty obvious that Mia and I have some issues we're dealing with." Ruby hadn't told any of her friends or coworkers about what her daughter had done, but word had gotten around.

"Most mothers and daughters quarrel," he said.

This was more than a mother-daughter squabble. "I caught Mia in bed with a boy."

Hank's head snapped sideways so quickly Ruby marveled that he hadn't fractured a vertebra.

"Don't look at me like that. I don't condone sex at her age."

"I didn't say you did."

But the Pineville gossip grapevine had said . . . *That Mia will turn out just like her mother. Going from one man to the next.*

Like mother like daughter.

Wouldn't be surprised if Mia got pregnant before she was fifteen.

I bet Ruby will be a grandmother before her thirty-second birthday.

Fearing the town big mouths might be right, Ruby had packed their bags and gotten the hell out of Dodge.

"Is that why you're moving to Kansas?" Hank asked.

"Yes. It would have been tough for Mia to remain in school. I was hoping this move would help us grow closer." She swirled the coffee in her mug. "So far my plan isn't working."

"Give it time."

Interesting counsel from a man who'd turned his back on his own flesh and blood. "Thank you for being patient with Mia."

"She doesn't bother me."

But I do. "What's with the nursery on the second floor?"

"I told you to stay out of that room." Evidently he wanted to pretend he hadn't seen her footprints in front of the door. "Don't listen too well, do you?"

"Listening"—especially to her conscience—"has never been one of my strengths. After Cora left, did you remarry and have a baby with a different woman?"

"No."

Good. A couple who abandoned their child shouldn't be parents again.

As soon as the thought registered in her mind, Ruby flinched. How was she any different from Hank or Cora? She'd missed all the signs that Mia had been interested in a boy. If she'd been a better parent, her daughter might not have jumped into bed with the first guy who paid attention to her. *Like mother, like daughter.*

Why do you deserve a pass and not Hank?

Ignoring the voice in her head, she asked, "If you had no other children, why keep the nursery?"

When Hank remained closemouthed, Ruby lost her patience. "You didn't expect me to magically appear on your doorstep and act like we've always been family, did you?" To make clear he knew where she stood on that subject, she added, "Because we're not . . . *family*."

His gnarled fingers choked the shotgun—maybe his damaged heart had a little feeling left in it, after all. "Cora took off before the doctor released you from the hospital."

"Took off?"

"She was gone by the time I showed up to bring you both home."

Ruby couldn't imagine leaving Mia only hours after giving birth to her. "And you had no idea where Cora went?"

"I waited at the hospital all day, expecting her to come back."

But Cora hadn't. "And the police couldn't find her?"

"She up 'n' vanished into thin air." It suddenly occurred to Ruby that Joe Dawson had a lot in common with his boss—both had lost a child and their wives had left them. Maybe their wounded spirits had drawn them together.

"Did you bring me home from the hospital?"

Hank's shoulders sank into his chest, as if the memory were too heavy to bear. "No. I left you there."

"Someone would have been willing to help you with a baby."

"There weren't many women in the area."

"What about your parents?" she asked.

"I struck out on my own when I was fifteen."

Ruby's family tree wasn't looking so hot. "And Cora's parents?"

"She didn't remember her mother, and she hadn't seen her father in years."

Hank and Cora had experienced rough childhoods, but that wasn't a good enough excuse to abandon their baby.

Before arriving in Unforgiven, Ruby had been determined to hold Hank accountable for turning his back on her. But she struggled to hang on to her resentment after learning that Cora had made a deliberate decision to leave Ruby behind, knowing Hank hadn't been in a position to care for their baby. "So you called Social Services."

"The lady promised she'd find you a good home."

It occurred to Ruby that the reason Glen and Cheryl Baxter had moved from Oklahoma to Missouri a year after she was born hadn't been because of a job transfer like they'd told her, but to lessen the chance of Ruby coming into contact with Hank or Cora.

"Did you"—he cleared the phlegm in his throat—"get a good home?"

"I had a decent upbringing." Glen Baxter might have distanced himself from Ruby after her sophomore year of high school, but he'd never abused her. "My dad was a long-haul trucker and my mother cut hair in the back bedroom of our trailer."

"Your folks still alive?"

"They died in a car accident shortly after Mia was born." A truck driver had dozed off at the wheel and crossed the center line. Destiny had played a cruel joke; her father's life had been ended by a fellow trucker. "I was an only child, but I always wished I had siblings."

Hank scratched the silver stubble on his cheek. "You got any other relatives?"

"An uncle I met once." Ruby had been ten when her father's brother had passed through town. After the car accident, she'd searched her mother's address book but hadn't found his name or phone number. The only people who'd attended the funeral had been her mother's hair clients and a few of her father's beer-drinking buddies.

"Did you keep track of me?" she asked.

"No, but I insisted the adoption paperwork stated that if Cora wanted to find you, she could." He jiggled his knee. "Or if you wanted to find one of us . . ."

If Ruby had known she'd been adopted, she most certainly would have tracked down her birth parents, especially after the falling-out with her father. During the six-hour bus ride from Missouri to Oklahoma she'd examined her relationship with Glen Baxter but hadn't come to any conclusion as to why he'd turned his back on her practically overnight. Things between them had begun to get better before Mia was born, but the accident had robbed them of a reconciliation.

"Cora would have come back if she'd been able to."

Oh. My. God. How long had Hank held out hope that Cora would return to him?

"No regrets giving me up?" As soon as the question slipped from her mouth, Ruby silently cursed. It wasn't Hank's fault that her adoptive father had ignored her. And Cora wasn't without blame. She could have taken Ruby with her when she'd fled the hospital.

Hank swept his arm through the air. "This is a lonely place for a girl to grow up without a mother."

"You might have gotten married again."

His leg jiggled faster.

"How come you never tried to contact me before now?"

"Didn't see any point."

"You weren't curious about me?"

Silence.

Hank refused to give Ruby the affirmation she wanted . . . *needed* to hear in order to forgive him—not that *he* cared about forgiveness. But Ruby cared. A little regret on his part would be nice.

He might not be ready to open up to her, but Hank's crotchety personality and the crow baits in the corral had influenced Mia in a way Ruby hadn't or couldn't. It had been weeks since she'd seen her daughter excited about anything. When Mia was with the horses, her eyes sparkled, and for that reason alone, Ruby would cut Hank some slack.

"I'll help you turn the upstairs nursery into a proper guest bedroom." She hated that she felt like she had to do something nice for him before she and Mia left. She had no reason to feel guilty about leaving him so soon after they met.

He leaned forward in the chair. "We got company."

A dust cloud moved in their direction. "You're not going to shoot out the deputy's tires, are you?"

"Not unless he gives me a reason to."

The lawman parked, then stepped from his vehicle. "'Morning, Hank." He removed his mirrored sunglasses and dropped them into his shirt pocket. "Hello, Ruby."

"Paul."

"Didn't know you had a daughter, Hank." The deputy approached the porch.

"We're catching up after a separation," Ruby said. "Have you figured out who stole the Devil's Wind cattle?"

If the deputy was surprised she knew about the missing livestock, he didn't let it show. "'Fraid not. No witnesses have come forward." He propped a boot on the bottom step, then rested his forearms on his bent thigh. "Any chance Dawson is rustling your cows?"

"Joe didn't steal my cattle."

"You made up your mind yet about selling?" Randall picked at a piece of lint on his pant leg. "The buyer I mentioned is still interested in the property."

"You're selling the Devil's Wind?" Ruby asked Hank.

"Was thinking about it, if you didn't show up."

"What does Ruby have to do with deciding whether or not to put your ranch on the market?"

"She's my next of kin. When I kick the bucket, this place'll be hers."

"What's your daughter going to do with these badlands?"

"What do I care? I'll be dead."

Ruby grappled with the knowledge that her inheritance was the Devil's Wind and not a trinket Cora had left behind for her. Never in a million years would she have believed she'd own a ranch.

Randall tapped his finger against the brim of his hat. "Nice to see you again, Ruby."

"Wait." She set her mug on the porch floor and stood. "How

do you plan to catch the thieves who took Hank's cows? Have you contacted the authorities in other counties to see if they—"

"Cases like this take time." His smile slipped. "If we come up with a promising lead, I'll be in touch." The deputy drove off.

What the heck had gotten into Ruby—she'd acted like a mama bear protecting her cub. So what if Hank had lost a few bovines? "Were you kidding about leaving me the ranch?"

"Nope."

"Why?"

"It's all I've got to make up for the past."

Damn Hank McArthur. Ruby didn't want his stupid ranch. She'd answered his summons because she'd needed to know more about her birth parents and their medical histories. Accepting the house and property would mean that she forgave him for not raising her. And she didn't want to forgive him.

Not yet.

Maybe not ever.

Chapter 8

Joe spotted the patrol car speeding away as he pulled up to the barn and got out of his pickup. As soon as he finished mucking the stalls he'd find Hank and ask if Randall had any new information on the missing cattle.

"Where were you?"

He stopped midstride and glanced to his left, where Mia stood, holding a pitchfork. The fact that he'd walked into the barn and hadn't felt a presence proved Ruby and her daughter were interfering with his concentration. "What are you doing in here?"

"What does it look like?" Mia tossed a pile of soiled hay into the barrow. "I'm getting used to the poop," she said. "The barn smells like our old yard when the Lil' Stinky truck pumped out our septic tank."

"I'll finish up. You can go back to the house." He removed the pitchfork from her hand and stabbed the pronged tool into the dirty hay.

Mia jumped aside when horse dung sailed through the air, missing the barrow. "I picked out names for the horses," she said.

"Oh, yeah?" Apparently his boss had passed on his stubborn streak to both his daughter and his granddaughter.

"The black one is Pretty Boy, the gray one is Sugar, and the brown one is Lonesome."

Mia sprawled across the hay bales stacked in the corner. "Do you have any kids?"

Joe braced himself for the sharp pain that always pierced his heart when he thought of his son, but this time there was only a twinge. Until last night when he'd unloaded on Ruby, Joe hadn't spoken about Aaron to anyone—not even to Hank. "I don't have any children."

"I wish I had a brother or a sister," she said.

Joe had wanted more children after Aaron was born, but Melanie had said one was all she could manage. Would a second child have held their marriage together after they'd buried Aaron? Maybe not, but he'd have had a reason to wake up each morning. Another son or daughter wouldn't have erased the pain of Aaron's death, but it might have prevented Joe from shutting himself off from others. Having someone who depended on him would have encouraged him to at least give a damn.

"Have you ever been married?"

"Yes." Joe set aside the pitchfork, then broke open a fresh hay bale and spread it in the stall.

"I wanted my mom to marry Sean, but she broke up with him for no good reason."

So Ruby had been involved with a man before leaving Missouri. *It's none of your business*. Maybe not, but he'd spilled his guts in the bar, so he got a free pass to be nosy. "What happened to Sean?" When Mia didn't answer, Joe turned and came face-to-face with Ruby.

She struggled to keep a straight face. "What happened to Sean what?"

His gaze darted past Ruby—Mia had snuck off. "Sorry. Your

daughter mentioned him, but it's none of my business." He pushed the barrow to the next stall, which had already been cleaned.

"Sean and I were together for nine months before I ended the relationship." Ruby stared into space.

"Regrets?" he asked.

"Not really."

That wasn't exactly a *no.* "What happened with Mia's father?"

"We never married. I gave him a lot of chances to do right by me and Mia, but he blew us off."

"Hold still."

"What?" Ruby's eyes rounded.

Joe brushed his fingers against her shoulder. "Spider."

"Did you get it?" She swatted her hair and jumped around. "I hate spiders."

"You're going to break your neck if you keep flinging your head like that." He grinned at her antics.

She was halfway through the barn before she stopped and faced him. "I came in here to tell you that Hank made tuna sandwiches for lunch."

"What did Randall want?"

"The deputy was more interested in why I'm at the ranch than in finding cows."

"I figured as much."

"Are you busy later?"

"No."

"Would you mind giving me a tour of the ranch?" She spread her arms wide. "Apparently I'm going to inherit all this when Hank dies."

Joe hoped that day wasn't coming anytime soon. He liked working at the Devil's Wind—it was the first place that had felt a little like home since he'd left Tulsa.

"Sure. I'll show you the property." Joe stood by the doors and watched Ruby cross the driveway, then veer toward the corral, where Mia sat on the rails talking to Pretty Boy.

Maybe it was a good thing Ruby intended to leave next week. Since she'd arrived yesterday Joe swore the sun shone a little brighter and the air tasted a little less dusty.

And *he* felt a little more guilty because he'd noticed.

"Thought you were going inside to eat, Mia." Ruby stopped at the corral.

"She ate already." Hank ambled toward them. "This one is yours." After handing off the sandwich, he climbed the rails and sat next to Mia.

Ruby took a bite of tuna fish, perplexed when Hank and Mia just stared at the horse. "What's going on?"

"Shhh . . ." Mia pressed a finger to her mouth, then whispered, "Hank says the best way to make friends with a horse is to be quiet and wait him out."

Hank slid his fingers into his shirt pocket, but Mia nudged him in the ribs and he left the cigarettes alone.

"So all you have to do is sit there and the horse becomes your friend?" Pretty Boy answered Ruby's question when he moved within touching distance of Mia.

"Put your hand out," Hank said. "Nice and easy. Let him sniff."

Mia followed his instructions, and Pretty Boy dipped his head, bumping his nose against her palm.

"He's telling you it's okay if you touch him."

Mia rubbed her fingers over the gelding's nose. "I won't hurt you, Pretty Boy." She smiled at Ruby. "He likes me."

"I can see that." It had been forever since her daughter had smiled at her, and the sweet expression brought a lump to Ruby's throat.

"Look who's coming over." Hank stuffed his hand into his pants pocket, then handed Mia two sugar cubes.

The horse head butted Pretty Boy out of the way, and Mia giggled. "You're spoiled." She held out her palm, and Sugar lapped up the cubes. Then Pretty Boy bumped his nose into Mia's chest. Mia giggled and wrapped her arms around his neck.

"He likes the way you smell," Hank said.

"I know, Pretty Boy." Mia closed her eyes when the horse blew in her face. "You don't like Hank 'cause he stinks like cigarette smoke."

Hank chuckled. "You might be right about that, granddaughter."

"Go get Lonesome, Pretty Boy," Mia said. "He looks sad standing by himself."

"Maybe Lonesome just wants to be left alone," Ruby said.

"No, he doesn't." Mia tugged Hank's shirtsleeve. "Can I go over there with him?"

"Wait here." Hank climbed down off the rail. Lonesome stamped his front hoof, kicking up a cloud of dust as his owner drew close. When the horse stepped toward Hank, Mia's face broke into a wide grin.

Feeling like a third wheel, Ruby went into the house and finished her sandwich in front of the kitchen window. After several attempts, Hank got Lonesome to follow him over to Mia.

When Mia opened her arms wide, Ruby expected her to hug Lonesome—but she hugged Hank. His skinny arms patted her awkwardly on the back.

Ruby turned away from the poignant scene.

Chapter 9

"What are Hank and Mia doing this afternoon?" Joe steered the pickup west toward a sky full of dark clouds.

"I imagine they'll hang out at the corral."

"Has Mia always been interested in horses?"

"Nope. Just since we got here." She stared out her window.

Joe could take a hint. Ruby didn't care to talk about her daughter's infatuation with the ranch's equine boarders. Fine by him. He had other questions for her, which kind of surprised him, considering he'd become antisocial after Aaron's death.

"What made you decide to relocate to Kansas?"

She turned, her shoulders squaring off with him. He got the feeling just about everything in Ruby's life was a touchy subject.

"A job," she said. "I worked for the past three years as the assistant manager for the Booneslick Lodge. I told my boss that I needed a new challenge." Ruby faced forward in the seat. "She used her business contacts to help me land a position at the Red Roof Inn in Elkhart."

"Why transfer to another small town and not a city like Saint Louis or Chicago?"

Ruby pressed her fingertips into her thighs until the skin around the nail turned white. "I don't like big cities."

It wasn't any of his business what had driven Ruby and her daughter out of Pineville, Missouri. Whether a person remained in one spot or moved from place to place, everyone was running from something.

"Who named the rock Fury's Ridge?" she asked.

"The Osage Indians. It's rumored to be an ancient burial site."

"It looks like a final resting place for damned souls."

The pickup hit a bump and Ruby bounced off the seat. "Part of me wants to snub my inheritance."

He opened his mouth to tell her not to make any rash decisions but changed his mind. He didn't want to give her the impression that he came with the ranch. He'd already said too much at the Possum Belly. And because he'd opened up about Aaron, the choke hold his son's death had had on him loosened and he almost felt human again. He had Ruby to thank for the change in him.

He veered left, taking a fork in the road that led away from the churning sky. The wind blowing through his open window carried the scent of ozone from the lightning show miles away. He pressed on the accelerator and the speedometer edged toward sixty. Then he slammed on the brakes and put his arm out when Ruby flew forward. The truck skidded to a stop next to a stock tank riddled with bullet holes. Whoever'd used the metal reservoir for target practice had done so recently, because the ground was still damp.

"Wait here." He shifted into park, then got out of the truck. The wind roared in his ears and a violent gust pelted his skin with stinging bits of dirt. Thunder rumbled and the dark clouds overhead boiled and churned. If he didn't know better, he'd believe the Devil's Wind was a portal to hell—a fitting place for damned souls like his.

He crossed the soggy ground and peered inside the tank. Less than a foot of water remained. Shell casings littered the dirt. He picked one up and then returned to the truck and tossed the souvenir to Ruby before removing a pair of binoculars from beneath the seat.

"What's in that direction?" She wagged a finger at the barbed-wire fence stretching across the land.

"The Bar T."

She studied the bullet casing. "Maybe Hank's neighbor did this."

Joe surveyed the area before getting back into the truck and driving off. "After Hank returned from the hospital with his pacemaker, Sandoval showed up at the door and offered to buy the Devil's Wind."

"Hank wouldn't sell."

"No. A few days later a section of fence between the two ranches came down and cows went missing."

"Is Sandoval trying to intimidate Hank into selling?" she asked.

"Maybe. Maybe not."

"Are you going to contact the deputy and report the damaged water tank?"

"It won't do any good." Joe closed his window. "Sheriff Mike Carlyle is Sandoval's cousin. Unless Hank has concrete proof—which he doesn't—that the Bar T cowboys are vandalizing the Devil's Wind, the sheriff won't investigate."

"You haven't caught anyone trespassing?"

"No."

"Maybe I'll stop by the sheriff's office before I leave town." Ruby shouldn't care about Hank's problems—he'd never been there for her to lean on through the years. Still . . . the little girl inside her, who badly wanted a father's love, couldn't leave Oklahoma without conveying her concerns to the lawman. Besides, Mia would never forgive her if she didn't do everything in her power to help Hank.

"I don't see any cattle. Where's the herd?"

He pointed to a group of cows taking shelter in the underbrush.

"How large is the Devil's Wind?"

"A thousand acres—about one and a half square miles."

If Hank had had such a rough childhood and had run away as a kid, how had he ended up owning a ranch?

"Storm's getting close." Joe turned the truck around. "We'd better head back."

"Does Hank have a shelter?"

"There's a dugout on the side of the house."

Hopefully Hank and Mia had run for cover. By the time Joe parked next to the barn, the wind had picked up and Ruby had to use her shoulder to push the truck door open.

"Get in the shelter." Joe jogged to the corral, where Hank was attempting to rope Pretty Boy.

Ruby went in the opposite direction, toward the underground cellar. "Mia," she called into the dark hole.

"I'm down here, and so is Friend. Get Hank, Mom!"

Ruby wasn't surprised that Mia was more concerned with her grandfather's safety than her mother's. Shielding her eyes, she squinted into the blowing dust. Joe was guiding the horse to the barn, but Hank struggled to walk, the tempest shoving his old bones sideways. He stumbled and fell to one knee.

Ruby rushed to his side. "Give me your hand!" He pushed her away. Ignoring his protests, she hauled him to his feet. By the time they made it to the shelter, her mouth and nose were clogged with dirt and her eyes watered. Hank wanted her to descend the steps first, but she forced him through the opening.

"Hurry, Hank." Mia's voice spurred him forward.

The shelter door banged closed behind Ruby, and the roar of the wind faded to a loud hum.

Mia pointed the flashlight at her grandfather and laughed. "Your hair's standing up on your head."

Hank patted his shirt pocket.

"Don't you dare," Ruby said. "I didn't drag you down here so Mia and I could breathe in secondhand smoke."

"Sabrina smokes," Mia said. "She offered me a cigarette after PE class." Sabrina had been a best friend until she'd made the drill team and quit hanging out with Mia.

"Kids shouldn't smoke." Hank coughed, either to reinforce his point or because the dank air in the shelter hurt his weak lungs.

"Have you tried to stop smoking?" Mia asked.

"Nope."

"Why not?"

"I don't have a good reason to stop."

"What about me? Aren't I a good enough reason?"

The door above their heads opened, saving Hank from answering Mia. Ruby caught a glimpse of black sky before Joe descended the stairs.

"Are the horses gonna be safe in the barn?" Mia asked.

"Should be," Hank said.

Joe stood with his back to Ruby. She breathed in the scent of musty earth and hardworking male, then swallowed a moan at the rush of warmth pooling between her thighs. She shifted her feet, trying to ignore the tingling sensation.

Seconds turned into minutes, and just when Ruby thought she couldn't take the dark confined space any longer . . . *silence.*

"Is the storm over?" Mia whispered.

Joe climbed the steps and opened the door. "Coast is clear."

Friend bolted from the cellar first, and by the time she and Mia helped Hank navigate the stairs, Joe was halfway to the barn. Ruby surveyed the damage. The big cottonwood had lost a limb but remained standing. Smaller branches littered the yard. And the screen door from the back porch rested inside the corral. Ruby groaned at the thought of all the dirt that had blown into the house.

"I'm gonna check on—"

Ruby blocked Mia's path. "Let Joe take care of the horses. I don't want you getting near them until they've settled down."

"But—"

"Listen to your mother," Hank said. "The animals are spooked. Best leave 'em be for now." He walked off.

"Why don't you see what we can make for supper," Ruby said. For once Mia didn't argue. After she went inside, Ruby caught up with Hank in the front yard. She surveyed the house. "Looks like you lost a few roof shingles."

"Don't care about the roof."

He should. She eyed the puddles on the porch. There wouldn't be enough pots and pans to catch all the drips if it rained for hours.

Hank placed his hand against his chest.

"Are you feeling poorly?"

Ignoring her question, he took the pack of cigarettes from his shirt and crammed them into his pants pocket, then knelt on the ground in front of the raped rosebushes. In a trancelike state, he scooped up handfuls of the red petals and dropped them into his shirt pocket.

The man exasperated her. He nurtured abused and abandoned horses. Took in stray dogs. Treated his granddaughter kindly. And mourned battered shrubs.

Why couldn't he have found the strength and courage to take care of his own daughter instead of giving her away?

Hank called you home, didn't he?

Three decades later and with the threat of poor health hanging over his head. Even so, he looked feeble and small hunched in front of the thorny perennials.

The door to Ruby's heart inched open a little wider as she dropped to her knees and helped him gather the silky petals.

Chapter 10

"What are you going to do with these?" Ruby handed him the rose petals she'd gathered, and he slipped them into his shirt pocket.

"Save 'em."

She envisioned a heaping mound of shriveled petals hidden inside a shoe box stowed at the back of his closet. "Why?"

"They remind me of Cora."

That he doted on the stupid bushes after the woman had left him and his daughter was pathetic and touching at the same time. He eyed the petals that had blown out of reach, and she crawled across the ground to retrieve them. "How old are the bushes?"

"A couple of years older than you."

"I don't have a green thumb," she said. "Maybe you can share your secret on how you've kept them alive in this"—*bleak*—"climate."

Listening to Hank impart gardening tips wasn't how Ruby had envisioned her visit with him, especially when he hadn't said he was sorry for giving her away or waiting to contact her until after his health had grown frail. But the reality of his mortality weighed heavily on her. She curled her fingers over the petals in her palm. She could remain angry and resentful or . . . She unfurled her fingers. She could give Hank a chance to earn her forgiveness before he withered away and ended up in a box. She had to try, not for her and Hank's sake, but for her and Mia's.

"Looks like we got them all." Hank crawled to his feet. He stumbled, and Ruby grabbed his arm to steady him.

"Think I'll go rest." He climbed the porch steps, then stopped to catch his breath on the landing.

"Hold up." Ruby plucked a petal from the bottom step. "This one fell out of your pocket." He took the petal and disappeared inside the house. Assuming Mia would want an update on the horses, Ruby headed to the barn. "Joe?"

"In the storage room!"

The sound of his muffled voice sent a tingle racing down the back of her neck. She hurried her steps, then stopped when her conscience spoke.

What do you think you're doing?

She wasn't doing anything.

You're supposed to be focusing on Mia, not targeting your next boyfriend.

Just because she enjoyed Joe's company didn't mean she was looking to hook up with him before she left for Kansas. Right now he was the only one at the ranch who gave her the time of day. She felt sorry for him because he'd lost his son, and the last thing she wanted was to hurt him. The only way that would happen was if she let things go too far between them. And there was no chance of that.

Ruby had already been burned twice—the first time by Glen

Baxter and the second time by Dylan. Any idiot knew there were three strikes in baseball. The only way to protect herself was to run at the first inkling of trouble. So that's what she did—she left men before they could leave her. As long as she remained just friends with Joe, neither one of them would get left behind.

"Ruby?"

His voice jolted her back to the present.

"What's wrong?" He walked toward her, carrying a small chain saw in his hand.

"Sorry. I was lost in thought." She smiled. "Have the horses calmed down enough for Mia to visit them?"

"She can fill their grain feeders while I clear the debris out of the corral." He narrowed his eyes. "Are you okay?"

"Why wouldn't I be?"

"If you're not used to storms like this, they can be unnerving."

"Believe me," she said, "I've weathered worse storms than the one today." She went back to the house and surveyed the mess on the porch. Resisting the urge to stop and shake out the bedspread, she entered the kitchen and found Mia feeding Friend.

"When can I see the horses?" Mia asked.

"That's what I came in to tell you. Joe said you can fill their grain feeders if you want."

Mia made a dash for the back porch, then stopped. "You want to help me?"

Caught off guard by the invitation, Ruby was speechless.

"If you don't want to, that's okay."

"No, no. I'd love to go with you." She followed Mia back outside. Cleaning the house could wait.

"Is Hank okay?" Mia asked.

"Yes, why?"

"He acted like he didn't hear me a while ago when I asked why he was going upstairs."

"The storm tired him out. He'll feel better after he takes a nap."

Once they arrived at the barn, Mia went straight for Pretty Boy's stall. "He's your favorite, huh?" Ruby stood in the aisle and watched Mia pat the gelding's rump and then flip open the feeder attached to the side of the stall.

"Pretty Boy looks me in the eye. I think he can read my mind."

Ruby wished she could read her daughter's mind.

Mia walked over to a large blue barrel across from the stalls, grabbed the scoop sitting on the lid and filled it, then dumped the grain into the feeder. "You want to do Lonesome's?"

"Sure."

Ruby shoved the scoop into the barrel and poured the kernels into Lonesome's feeder. "You want me to fill Sugar's, too?"

Mia nodded, then slipped a grooming brush over her hand and gently worked the bristles across the jagged scars that marred Pretty Boy's hide. The frown that was usually present on Mia's face vanished. Her daughter seemed at peace around the horses. With Hank napping and Joe cleaning up the property, Ruby intended to take advantage of their privacy and Mia's calm disposition.

"Before we left Missouri you refused to talk about what happened between you and Kevin Walters. I think it's time, Mia."

The brush froze against the horse's neck. "It's not a big deal."

But it was. "Losing your virginity at fourteen is a *really* big deal."

Mia rolled her eyes. "It's not like other kids aren't having sex." Then she added, "At least I knew enough to use a condom and didn't get pregnant like you did."

Ruby pressed her hand to her warm face. Just once she wished her daughter would act like her age and not ten years older. "You were *lucky* you didn't get pregnant."

"No, I was lucky I listened to all your safe-sex lectures."

Ruby had begun talking about the birds and the bees when Mia had gotten her period at age eleven. At least she'd done one thing right in her daughter's eyes. "You're still too young for sex."

"Everyone's doing it, Mom. If they aren't taking their clothes off, then they're going down on their boyfriends beneath the bleachers in the football field."

Usually grown children complained that they didn't want images of their parents making out in their heads, not the other way around.

"How come you didn't tell me you were dating Kevin?"

"We weren't dating."

OMG. "So you don't even like Kevin?"

Mia dropped her gaze.

"Did Kevin pressure you into—"

"No. It was my idea."

"Did he know it was your first time?"

Mia wiped a finger across her eye, and Ruby's heart broke. "I wish you would have come to me first. We could have talked about it." *I could have talked you out of it.*

"There's no point in talking, Mom. You don't understand me. You don't even know me."

"Oh, c'mon. You're being unfair."

"I can't believe you even care."

"You're my daughter. Of course I care."

"Seriously?"

Ruby opened her mouth to protest, but Mia threw the grooming brush on the ground. "When are you going to call Hank 'Dad'? 'Cause he is, you know. Your real father."

She'd call Hank *Dad* if and when he earned the right to the title.

"And why are you so mean to him?" Mia asked.

How had this conversation become about Ruby? "I'm not mean to Hank."

"You never say anything nice to him."

That isn't true. "Hank and I are adults and—"

"You hate him 'cause he didn't want you when you were a baby."

Ruby hadn't thought there was anything Hank could say to convince her that he'd made the right decision in putting her up for adoption, but she understood now that he'd been in no position to raise a child on his own after Cora had run off. And Hank had never asked Ruby's parents to keep her adoption a secret. Maybe she was angry with the wrong person. But accepting Hank as her father was asking a lot when she'd already been let down by one father in her short lifetime.

"I don't hate your grandfather."

"He thinks you do."

"Did he tell you that?" When Mia looked away, Ruby knew her daughter was fibbing. "Hank might be my father, but he's still a stranger to me."

"It doesn't matter," Mia said.

"What doesn't matter?"

"You'll never let us be a real family."

Hank and his dusty ranch were hardly the symbol of home and hearth. "I don't know what you're talking about."

"Because you don't listen." Mia's upper lip quivered. "You only care about what *you* want. It's always been about you."

"That's not true. I took the job in Kansas because I was worried about *you,* not me."

"No, you're making us move because you're embarrassed by what I did."

Now Ruby couldn't look her daughter in the eye. She had been worried about people blaming her for Mia's poor judgment. They'd claim Mia didn't know any better because her only role model preferred live-in boyfriends to marriage.

"You're wrong," Ruby said, even though her daughter was right. She cursed when Mia ran from the barn. What good would leaving Pineville do if their problems followed them all the way to Kansas and wiped out their fresh start?

Chapter 11

"Feeling better?" Ruby eyed Hank closely as he shuffled into the kitchen.

"Are the horses okay?" he asked, ignoring her question.

"They're fine." But she was exhausted. Her confrontation with Mia had left her raw. When she'd returned to the house an hour ago, she'd made a fresh pot of coffee, needing a dose of caffeine before she tackled the dust that had blown into the house.

"I forgot to mention earlier that your stock tank is ruined," she said.

"Which one?"

She was terrible with directions—couldn't tell north from south or east from west. "It's near the area where your fence was torn down."

"What's wrong with the tank?"

"Someone peppered it with bullets."

The caterpillars above his eyes rippled across his brow.

"I put a frozen pizza in the oven for supper." The freezer was stocked with frozen meals, but there were no fresh fruits or vegetables in the house.

Hank removed paper plates from the cupboard, his crooked fingers trembling as he struggled to separate the stack.

"You need to report the damaged tank to the sheriff."

"Tomorrow," he said.

He didn't appear too concerned that his property had been vandalized again. "Why not now?"

"The sheriff's busy dealing with emergencies after the storm."

Ruby conceded that a damaged water cistern probably wasn't a priority after a major weather event. "Will your insurance cover the cost of a new tank?"

"Don't have insurance."

"Why the hell not?"

"You shouldn't cuss, daughter."

Ruby wanted to remind him that she wasn't his daughter in any true sense of the word, but she let it pass. "Why don't you carry insurance on the ranch?"

"Canceled my policy last year. Didn't see a point in spending the extra money."

Hank probably figured he'd be dead sooner rather than later, so why waste the money. "Do you have enough savings to replace it?"

"If you want to know how much money I have, why don't you ask?"

Fine. "How much money do you have?"

"Petro Oil owns the pump jacks on my property, and their leases bring in ten thousand dollars a month."

Hank earned $120,000 a year? "If you have that much money"—she gestured to the run-down room—"why do you live like this?"

"What's wrong with the way I live?"

Ruby wouldn't be human if she didn't admit that she'd love to get her hands on some of Hank's cash. She'd buy a new car and a two-bedroom house for her and Mia, so they wouldn't have to rent a trailer or a dumpy apartment in Elkhart.

"Tomorrow we'll drive into town and speak to the sheriff." Ruby's cell phone went off, and she recognized the Kansas area code. "I've got to take this." She retreated to the parlor, then a few minutes later returned to the kitchen.

"That was my new boss," she said. "The Red Roof Inn is opening two weeks ahead of schedule. I need to report early to the management training class." At least she had a legitimate reason to give her daughter for leaving the ranch sooner rather than later. "Mia and I will have to catch the Greyhound bus to Elkhart on Tuesday."

Hank's face turned pasty. The paper towel he was folding into a napkin fluttered to the countertop and then his legs buckled. Ruby sprang forward, catching him by the waist. They tumbled to the floor, her body cushioning his fall.

"What's the matter?" She pushed him onto his back and shook his shoulders. "Hank? Is it your heart?"

Mia waltzed into the kitchen, eyes widening when she saw her grandfather struggling to breathe.

"Get Joe. Hurry!"

Mia raced from the house.

Less than a minute later the back door crashed open. In one glance Joe assessed the situation. He removed a medication bottle from a cabinet and stuck a pill in Hank's mouth.

"What are you giving him?" Ruby asked.

"Valium." Joe grasped Hank beneath the armpits and hoisted him into the chair Mia had pulled out from the table.

Ruby got to her feet, wincing at the pain that shot through her tailbone. She dampened a clean dishcloth with cool water and placed it across Hank's forehead. He swatted her arm, but she held the rag in place.

"What does the Valium do, Hank?" When he remained mute, Ruby shifted her gaze to Joe.

"The pacemaker's rhythm can be disrupted if he becomes anxious. The pill calms him down."

Mia planted her hands on her hips. "What did you say to upset him?"

That Mia was accusing Ruby of causing her grandfather's collapse hurt like hell. She might not have formed a bond with Hank like Mia had, but that didn't mean she wanted something to happen to him. "I told him that you and I are leaving on Tuesday."

Mia gasped. "We are?"

"I have to report to my new job early."

"I don't want to go."

"We'll talk about this later." Ruby narrowed her eyes, warning Mia not to challenge her decision and upset Hank further.

Mia left the kitchen, slamming the door behind her.

Ruby removed the cloth from Hank's forehead, relieved the color had returned to his face. She brought him a glass of water, but he pushed it away. Not in the mood for his orneriness, she said, "Drink it, or I'll pour it down your throat."

While he guzzled the water, she eyed Joe. The fact that he knew right where Hank kept his pills and what to do with them proved he was more invested in his boss and his job than he pretended to be. She set the empty glass in the sink, but when she turned around, Joe was gone.

The timer *ding*ed and Hank shifted in the chair. "Stay right where you are." She grabbed a dish towel and removed the hot baking sheet from the oven, then cut the pizza into slices and placed one on a paper plate for him.

"You gonna shove this down my throat, too?" he asked.

She fought a smile. "Damn right."

"Your mother never swore."

"I wouldn't know that about her, because you don't talk about Cora."

"Fetch me a fork 'n' knife."

She'd forgotten about his missing teeth. She handed him the silverware, then opened the back door and poked her head outside. Mia had put Pretty Boy in the corral and was sitting on the top rail, gesturing wildly with her arms—probably bitching about her mother to the horse. No sense telling her supper was ready—she'd eat when she grew hungry. Ruby joined Hank at the kitchen table. "What time should we leave in the morning?"

"Don't matter to me." He got up from his chair, tossed his half-eaten meal into the garbage, and left the room, his footsteps echoing through the hallway and up the stairs. Then another door slammed.

The pizza in Ruby's mouth tasted like cardboard, and she forced herself to swallow. Hank acted as if he didn't want her to leave. He'd claimed he didn't have any regrets giving her up for adoption, but maybe he'd had to convince himself of that in order to live with his conscience all these years. But if he really wanted her to stay, why didn't he just say so?

She hadn't answered his summons because she'd wanted him to embrace her as his long-lost daughter. Well, maybe she had a little. But she'd come mainly because she'd wanted to learn who the real Ruby Baxter was. She'd never expected to want to know more about the real Hank McArthur—the man hidden beneath layers of dust and grit.

She stored the leftover pizza in the fridge, washed the dishes, then filled a bucket with cleaning solution and carried it into her and Mia's bedroom—she'd saved the worst mess for last. A half inch of grime coated the bed and rug. Once she wiped down the furniture and washer and dryer, she removed the comforter and went outside to shake the dust free. Joe had been busy. He'd reattached the porch door, then collected the fallen tree branches and piled them next to the barn. Dusk descended on the ranch, but Mia's backside was taking root on the corral rail.

Ruby grabbed her pajamas and went upstairs to shower. When she returned to the kitchen, she let Friend out in the yard to do his business. The dog came back in and settled down for the night on his pillow. A short time later Mia came into the house, sat at the end of the bed and pretended to watch the rotisserie oven infomercial on the TV.

"There's leftover pizza in the fridge, if you're hungry."

Mia ignored her.

"You were the one who said you didn't want to stay here after we got off the bus."

"That was before," Mia said.

"Before what?"

"I knew about the horses."

Ruby shoved a hand through her damp hair. "Mia, I—"

"And we can't leave Hank." Mia popped off the bed and paced across the carpet. "He's got a sick heart. Who's gonna help him if he has another attack and Joe's not here?"

Ruby envisioned Hank lying unconscious on the floor with Friend's head resting on his leg. It was possible his heart could give out at any moment, and once she and Mia left the ranch, it might be the last time they ever saw him alive.

"You go," Mia said. "I'll stay until school starts."

If Mia thought she could push Ruby away that easily, she'd misjudged her mother. But how could she take her daughter away from Hank and his horses when the Devil's Wind was the one place that made her happy? On the other hand, Ruby had to support them. If she didn't show up in Elkhart, her new boss might give her job to someone else. Then what?

But . . . maybe after another week or two at the ranch the shine would wear off Hank and the horses and then Mia might be open to moving on. Exhausted by the day's events, she decided to stew over the consequences later. "I'll notify my supervisor that I can't make the training session."

"Really?"

"I'll call her in the morning."

Mia's mouth curved into a genuine smile, and for once Ruby felt like she'd done something right in her daughter's eyes.

Chapter 12

When Ruby opened her eyes Saturday, she was alone in bed. Funny how a few horses had turned Mia into a morning person. Usually her daughter slept until noon on weekends.

Ready for whatever the day held in store for her, Ruby threw on a pair of jeans and a T-shirt, slid her feet into her flip-flops, and went into the kitchen. She poured herself a cup of lukewarm coffee, then gulped it down before going upstairs to comb her hair and brush her teeth. Five minutes later she grabbed her purse and went in search of Hank. She found him in the backyard, staring into the branches of the cottonwood.

"Did you love my grandma?" Mia sat on a limb, her legs dangling.

"Your grandmother was the prettiest woman this side of the Mississippi."

"What color was her hair?"

"Blond like yours."

"If she was so pretty, why'd she like you?"

Hank chuckled. "Are you saying I'm ugly, missy?"

"You don't have a lot of teeth."

"Had all my chompers when I was courting your grandmother."

"Do you think she would have liked my mom?"

"Cora loved everybody." The hollow ring in Hank's voice ached with tenderness. Thank God Ruby had ended things with Sean when she had. If this was what a person had to look forward to when they fell in love . . . *No, thank you.*

"Hang the feeder on the branch to your right." He pointed above Mia's head.

"I need help."

Ruby wasn't about to let her daughter fall and break her neck. She dropped her purse to the ground, climbed the stool next to the trunk, then snagged the lowest branch and hoisted herself into the crotch of the tree.

"Hold my leg," Mia said.

Ruby clutched the calf inches from her nose. "Be careful."

"How's that?" Mia asked.

"Good," Hank said.

"Move, Mom."

Ruby shimmied out of the tree, and when Mia's feet touched the ground, she said, "How would you like to go into town with me and Hank?"

"What are we going to Unforgiven for?" Hank asked.

Maybe his mind was growing as frail as his body. "We're reporting the damaged water tank to the sheriff."

"I wanna stay here," Mia said.

No surprise. "We'll be back soon." Ruby pulled Hank's truck keys from her pocket, then picked up her purse. "Ready?"

Hank patted his thigh, and Friend crawled to his feet from his spot in the shade.

"Stay." Ruby put her hand in front of the dog's face.

"He likes to go for a ride," Hank said.

"Friend stinks. And it's too hot for the dog to wait in the truck while we speak with the sheriff."

When they got to the front yard, Hank held out his hand. "Give me the keys."

"I'll drive," she said.

"I'm not an invalid."

She took the bottle of Valium out of her purse and shook it. "If your pacemaker goes crazy, I don't want you running us into a ditch."

He swiped the medicine from her hand, then got in on the passenger side.

Once he buckled his seat belt, she pulled away from the house. "No smoking," she said, when he made a grab for his Winstons.

He grumbled but left the cigarettes alone. The drive into Unforgiven took a half hour—plenty of time to interrogate him. "Where were you born?"

"Dumas, Texas."

"Never heard of the place."

"'Bout fifty miles north of Amarillo."

"Did you grow up there?"

"You gonna ask me questions all the way into town?"

"Yes."

"My father left when I was ten and my mother—" He coughed up phlegm, then unrolled his window and spit. "She moved us into a rent-by-the-week motel, and I hung out at the pool while she entertained men in our room."

"For money?"

Hank nodded.

How sad that Hank's mother had sold her body to support herself and her son.

"Were you an only child?" she asked.

"I was when my mother took off with one of her regulars."

Ruby's relatives were a bunch of losers. The fact that she shared their genes didn't bode well for her. "Did you ever see your mother again?"

"No."

She pictured a teenage boy returning to the motel after school and discovering his mother had vanished. At least Hank had spared Ruby that kind of hurt. A newborn couldn't know she'd been cast off. "You said you were on your own at fifteen. Wouldn't Social Services have—"

"I wasn't going to let them put me in a boys' home." He drummed his fingers against his thighs. "I worked odd jobs for food."

"What about school?"

"Dropped out."

She was surprised Hank didn't have a high school education. "How'd you end up with the Devil's Wind?"

"I'm tired." He slouched in the seat, then tipped his hat, shielding his face from view.

She'd hit a nerve when she'd asked about the ranch, which made her even more suspicious about how he'd come to own the Devil's Wind. She turned on the radio. Static poured from the speakers, so she shut it off and mulled over their brief conversation. Everyone who'd ever mattered in his life had left him. Maybe he'd turned his back on her not only because he couldn't take care of a newborn, but also because he didn't know any other way.

When Ruby had decided to answer Hank's summons, she'd had

no intention of establishing a relationship with him that went beyond a onetime visit. But learning about his unfortunate childhood changed everything. Now, when she left for Kansas, she'd be just one more person who'd deserted him.

How the hell was that fair? Her biological father was supposed to be the bad guy, not her. She should have thrown the lawyer's letter away. It would have been easier to live with her conscience if she'd never met Hank McArthur.

"We're here." Ruby applied the brakes at the four-way stop on the outskirts of town.

Hank popped into an upright position—the old fart had only been pretending to snooze. She pulled into a parking spot in front of the jail, then ushered him inside.

There wasn't much to the law office. A desk in the middle of the room with Deputy Randall's nameplate front and center. The placard on the door a few feet away identified the office as Sheriff Michael Carlyle's. And a man wearing nothing but boxers and cowboy boots snored off his drunk on the cot in the small holding cell.

"Hello?"

"Be right there," a muffled voice answered from behind the closed door.

She nudged Hank toward the chair across from the deputy's desk, then stood by his side.

The door opened and the sheriff stepped into view. If the lawman grew tired of chasing bad guys, he could pursue a career in the movies. A strong jaw, a jet-black mustache, and ebony hair threaded with silver would land him a role on a cop show. "'Morning, Hank." His smooth baritone voice added to his sex appeal. "You must be Ruby Baxter." He showed off his movie-star teeth. "I hear you're visiting Hank."

"News travels fast in a one-horse town," she said.

The sheriff sat in the deputy's chair and clasped his hands behind his head. "What brings you two by this morning?"

"Nothing," Hank muttered.

"The hell it isn't." Ruby ignored his grunt. "Someone shot up a livestock tank at the Devil's Wind."

The sheriff sat forward. "I'm listening."

Ruby recited an abbreviated version of her and Joe's tour of the ranch.

"Probably drunken cowboys firing off a few rounds for kicks," the sheriff said.

"A few rounds? The tank was riddled with holes, and most of the water leaked out."

"Were any cattle injured?"

"No. All the cows were accounted for except the ones Hank already reported missing." The sheriff didn't blink an eye at the mention of the ongoing investigation. "Your deputy stopped by the ranch yesterday and said he still has no idea who stole Hank's cows."

"These cases take time."

Ruby nodded to the holding cell. "If you're too busy rounding up drunks, maybe the police in Guymon would be willing to help with the investigation."

The lawman's mouth quivered—he found her amusing. "I'll advise the local ranchers to tell their wranglers to steer clear of the Devil's Wind."

"Will one of those phone calls be to Roy Sandoval? Maybe the person who took down the section of fence between the Bar T and the Devil's Wind is the same person who used the stock tank for target practice."

"I assure you, Ms. Baxter, that Deputy Randall is chasing every lead."

More like chasing his tail in circles. She placed the bullet casing found next to the tank on the desk. "You should ask your cousin if he owns a weapon matching this." The sheriff narrowed his eyes, but Ruby ignored the warning. "You and Roy Sandoval are related, right?"

Hank made a beeline for the door, but Ruby stayed put. "Were you aware that after Hank got his pacemaker, your cousin asked if he was ready to sell out?"

"Careful, Ms. Baxter. I don't care for what you're implying."

"And I don't like how you're investigating Hank's missing cows."

The jail door opened and closed, leaving Ruby to face off with the sheriff alone. Someone had to protect Hank from being bullied. She'd do it for Mia, because her daughter was worried about her grandfather, and for herself, because . . . well, just because.

"I'll discuss the case with—"

"Deputy Randall mentioned that someone else is interested in buying the ranch. Any idea why the Devil's Wind is so popular?"

The lines bracketing the sheriff's mouth deepened. "'Fraid not. Now, if that's all you came to discuss . . . I have work to do."

"Hank will need a copy of your report so he can settle with his insurance company." The report would be useless, since Hank had canceled his policy, but at least he'd know the complaint had been officially recorded.

"I'll see that Hank gets one." The sheriff walked across the room and held the door open for her. "When do you plan to leave town?"

"A week, give or take a few days." She held his gaze. "By then you'll have tracked down the owner of that bullet casing."

"Good day, Ms. Baxter."

Ruby joined Hank in the truck, and neither said a word as she drove to the mercantile. "You coming in?" she asked.

He shook his head.

"You'll suffer heatstroke if you sit out here." She walked around the hood and opened his door, then waited for him to unsnap his seat belt. He took his dang-tootin' time getting out. No wonder he and Mia got along—they were both ornery. She clutched a fistful of his shirtsleeve and dragged him inside the store.

She and Mia had visited the mercantile two days ago, yet none of the clothing racks or products on the shelves appeared disturbed. How did Big Dan make a profit if he wasn't moving inventory? Hank helped himself to a seat on the bench by the window.

"I'll be quick." She weaved her way across the floor to the shelf with personal hygiene products, then perused her two choices of sunscreen. "This is a rip-off."

"What is?"

She glanced down at the top of Big Dan's shiny bald head. "The cost of this sunscreen. Twelve dollars. Really?"

"Hello, Ruby."

Ignoring the greeting, she asked, "Do you have any body lotion?"

"Bottom shelf. How's your visit going with Hank?"

"Fine." Everyone seemed interested in her business with the cranky rancher.

"Are you planning to stay awhile?"

"I don't think so."

"A lot could happen to change your mind."

The man talked in riddles. "Change my mind about what?"

"Leaving."

Ruby examined the lotion bottle. "This is a rip-off, too." She called out to Hank, "Do you need anything?" When he didn't answer, she led the way to the checkout. "I didn't notice any damage in town from yesterday's storm."

Big Dan didn't ask if the Devil's Wind had survived the bad weather. Maybe all old men were grumpy on Saturdays. "What's the problem between you and Hank?"

"Don't know what you're talking about." He slipped the sunscreen and lotion into a plastic bag, then took Ruby's money.

Maybe she'd imagined the tension between the men. "In case I don't see you again, it was nice meeting you."

He ignored her outstretched hand and set her change on the counter. "You'll be back."

Not likely. If Hank missed her and Mia, he could visit them in Kansas.

Chapter 13

"What's your beef with Big Dan?" Ruby asked Hank after they left the mercantile.

"Don't know what you're talking about." That's exactly what Big Dan had said. There was definitely *something* going on between the men.

"Crap." Ruby stared at the flat tire on the truck. "Do you have a spare?"

"Nope."

"C'mon." She guided him across the street. "While I talk to a mechanic, you can wait in the air-conditioned diner." She stopped outside the Airstream. "How do you want to pay for this?" One of them had to cough up the money to fix the tire, and Hank had more cash in his bank account than she did.

He removed a credit card from his wallet and handed it to her. When he didn't go into the diner, she asked, "What's wrong?"

"Waiting for you to leave so I can have a smoke." He tapped the pack of cigarettes against the back of his hand.

If she continued to argue with him, he'd stand in the hot sun and smoke all twenty cancer sticks and then pass out from heat exhaustion. And her daughter would accuse her of bullying him. Mia blamed Ruby for a lot these days, but it hadn't always been that way between them.

"I quit cold turkey," she said.

"That right?" He pulled a BIC lighter from his pants pocket and lit the lung dart, then took a deep drag.

The sun glinted off the end of the lighter, reminding Ruby of the past and better times with Mia . . . Saturday mornings clipping coupons and then laughing when they couldn't figure out what to cook with all the mismatched bargains they'd hauled home from the store.

"Where's my chocolate cake?" Mia dragged a chair across the floor to the kitchen counter and climbed on, then began unpacking the groceries, lining the items up in front of her. A package of BIC disposable lighters, Bisquick mix, spaghetti sauce, green grapes, Wisk detergent, a bag of marshmallows, cheese puffs. She moved the box of chocolate cake closer to her. Her eighth birthday was two weeks away, but she'd been adamant that they buy the cake mix today because the coupon expired before her birthday. Ruby had allowed her to put it in the cart even though she'd already ordered Mia's cake—her first-ever bakery cake.

"What are we gonna make for supper?" Mia's blue eyes stared at Ruby.

"I was about to ask you the same question." The checkout lady had congratulated them on saving more than twenty-five dollars, but there was nothing in the four bags they could use to put a meal together.

"We can have pickles and some crackers." Mia lifted the can

at the end of the counter. "And sloppy joes." They hadn't bought any hamburger. She used both hands to move the liter of soda in front of her. "And this to drink."

If one of them came down with the flu, they'd have Sprite and soda crackers on hand.

Mia peeked up at her mother and giggled.

"We saved all that money and we have nothing to eat." Ruby laughed.

"I know what we can do," Mia said.

Ruby read her mind. "Put your coat back on."

"Yeah, McDonald's!" Mia jumped off the chair, hugged Ruby's legs, then raced from the room.

"You going to stand there grinning until I finish my cigarette?" Hank tapped the toe of his shoe against Ruby's sandal, and she blinked until he came into focus.

"At least take a break between cigarettes and cool off inside," she said, then left him to enjoy his vice. When she entered the gas station, she called out, "Anyone here?"

A grease monkey in gray coveralls pushed his creeper out from beneath a beige sedan and crawled to his feet. He was several inches taller than Ruby but stick thin. His round face was covered with acne. He couldn't have been older then twenty-one.

"Name's Kurt." He wiped his hands on an oil rag. "What can I do for you?"

"Hank McArthur's truck has a flat tire." She pointed down the block. "It's parked in front of the mercantile."

Kurt's gaze flicked between Ruby's face and her breasts. Years ago she'd given up objecting to men staring at her big boobs, because her complaints had only gained her more leers.

"Does he have a spare?"

"No, but would you mind taking a look to see if you can repair the leak?"

When they arrived at the truck, Ruby stood aside while Kurt examined the tire. "Did I drive over a nail?"

"The tire's been slashed."

"You mean like with a knife?"

"Yep."

First the missing cows, then the water tank, and now this. Someone had it in for Hank.

"It'll take me a week to get a new tire," Kurt said.

"You wouldn't happen to have a spare Hank could use until then?"

"I'll check."

After Kurt walked off, Ruby went back to the jail. If the sheriff was startled to see her again, he didn't show it. "Would you mind adding a slashed tire to the list of vandalism against the Devil's Wind?"

His eyes widened.

"The tire was fine when Hank and I arrived in town, but someone took a knife to it while we were in the mercantile."

"Do you need help?" he asked.

"The mechanic at the garage is putting on a spare."

"I'll find out if there were any witnesses."

"I wasn't joking when I suggested you contact the authorities in Guymon," she said. "This might be too much for your small department to handle." She left, slamming the door behind her. It was high time a woman stirred up a little dust in the Oklahoma outpost.

Kurt hadn't returned from the garage, so Ruby went into the air-conditioned mercantile to wait.

"Something wrong?" Big Dan stepped into the open.

"The tire on Hank's pickup was slashed. Did you see anyone loitering outside when we were in here earlier?"

"How would I see anything? I was helping you."

"You said you know everything that goes on in this town."

Big Dan peered at the wall of animal heads as if communicating with the stuffed beasts.

"Have you heard about the trouble out at the Devil's Wind?" she asked.

He wobbled over to a clothing rack of perfectly hung shirts and moved a hanger sideways a half inch. "I predicted you'd shake things up in town, but I didn't expect you to be so fearless."

"What's that supposed to mean?" The blasted men in Unforgiven were so frustrating. The sooner she left, the better. "Are you always this pleasant to newcomers, or do I get special treatment because you've got a grudge against Hank?"

He bent over and picked up a pebble off the floor. "Kurt's back."

Ruby glanced out the window. Sure enough, the mechanic stood next to the pickup. Forgetting about the miniature thorn in her side, Ruby went out to keep Kurt company.

"The spare's in decent shape." He jacked up the front end of Hank's truck. "You shouldn't have any problem with it."

A pickup with the Bar T logo on the passenger-side door passed by and parked in front of the jail. A tall, distinguished-looking man with gray hair entered the building. Maybe her threat had spurred the sheriff to have a chat with his cousin.

"Hank can pay for the new tire when he picks it up," Kurt said.

"What do we owe you for the spare?"

"It's on me." He packed up his tools. "Mind if I ask a personal question?"

"What?"

"Are you really Hank McArthur's daughter?"

"Yes."

He checked over his shoulder as if he was worried they were being watched. "Everyone knows the Devil's Wind is worth a fortune."

"Really?"

"They say there's millions in natural gas under Fury's Ridge."

Interesting how Joe had left out that fact when he'd talked about the Indian burial ground. "And you think I'm trying to swindle Hank."

"Seems like a coincidence . . . you showing up right after he had a pacemaker put in."

"Rest assured, I'm legitimate," she said. "If you need proof, talk to Hank's lawyer. He's the one who tracked me down."

Kurt's chin poked out. "You sticking around?"

"All you men in town can relax. I won't be calling Unforgiven home." She cut across the street to the diner. Hank was the only customer in the place.

"Hey, Ruby." Elvis lifted his hand in greeting. "We've been swapping cowboy and Indian stories."

She handed Hank his credit card. "Kurt had to order a new tire for your truck. In the meantime, he loaned you a spare."

"What happened?" Jimmy asked.

"I ran over a nail," Ruby lied. She didn't want to upset Hank after his pacemaker had shorted out yesterday.

"The offer still stands on the trailer out back."

"Thanks, Jimmy." She ignored Hank's puzzled expression and said, "Let's hit the road." He placed his cowboy hat on his head, and Ruby followed him outside. "Are you feeling okay?"

"Quit nagging me."

She managed to refrain from conversation for the first five miles, but then the silence got to her. "Tell me what's going on between you and Big Dan."

Hank's lips flattened.

"You don't like him and he doesn't like you. Why?"

He squeezed his knee until the bulging veins that crisscrossed the back of his hand turned dark blue. "Big Dan and Cora were friends."

Jealousy would definitely explain the testy looks between the men.

"Cora was lonely living on the ranch. She'd go into town when I was busy with chores."

When Hank didn't elaborate, she wondered how good of friends her mother and Big Dan had been. "That must mean women were once welcome in Unforgiven."

"Ladies used to come to town all the time until Guymon got the big Walmart and a fancy beauty spa."

It was reassuring to know the female population hadn't been chased out of town. Hank closed his eyes, and his shoulders hunched forward. He sure needed a lot of rest. It was a good thing Joe helped around the ranch; otherwise Ruby would have to battle her conscience when she said goodbye.

"Hank?"

"Hmm?"

"You told Deputy Randall that you were leaving me the ranch. Were you telling the truth, or did you just say that to piss him off?"

"I meant it."

"What if I don't want the place?"

His eyelids rolled back, and he looked at her. "Why wouldn't you want the land?"

Ruby might have been born there, but . . . "The Devil's Wind isn't home." She didn't have any ties to the property. And if she accepted her inheritance, Hank would assume she'd forgiven him for not keeping her after Cora had run off.

"I'll be dead," he said. "You can do what you want with the ranch; just find the horses a good home."

If Mia had her way, Hank's beloved four-legged misfits would end up in Ruby's backyard.

Once they arrived at the house, she offered to make lunch, then went inside to check on Mia, but her daughter was nowhere to be found. Ruby walked out to the barn. "Mia, are you in here?"

"She's with the horses in the corral." Joe stepped from a stall, wiping the sweat off his forehead with a blue bandanna.

"No, she's not." Heart pounding, Ruby left the barn. "Mia! Mia!" She stopped in front of the storm shelter and opened the door. "Mia? Are you down there?"

Hank came outside. "What in tarnation's got you all fired up?"

"I can't find Mia."

Joe jogged across the yard. "Pretty Boy's missing."

"Oh God." Ruby's voice shook. "I bet Mia took the horse for a ride." Channeling her fear into anger, she pointed a finger at Joe. "How could you not know she took off on one of the horses? Mia doesn't even know how to ride. She might have been thrown."

Miles of hostile emptiness stretched between the house and the horizon. This was Ruby's fault—not Joe's. She should have made Mia go with her and Hank into town.

"I'll find her." Joe got into his truck and backed it up to the horse trailer behind the barn, then hopped out and secured the hitch before speeding off.

"Mia will be okay." Hank's fingers curled around Ruby's arm, pressing into her flesh until they hit bone.

A wave of dizziness swept over her, and she covered Hank's hand with her own. She had to believe Mia would be fine. Nothing mattered but getting her daughter home safely.

Chapter 14

"You're gonna plow a furrow deep enough to plant corn in."

Ruby paced over to the cellar door, then spun and followed the worn path back to the cottonwood tree. "It's been an hour. Mia and Pretty Boy couldn't have gone that far."

"Depends on when she rode out after we left for town."

"Mia might be hurt or kidnapped or—"

"Don't think bad thoughts."

Ruby opened her mouth to argue—she had a host of fighting words stockpiled inside her—but she choked them back. A missing daughter was enough to worry about without having his heart attack on her conscience.

"Here they come," he said.

Dust billowed in the distance, and then Joe's pickup came into view. "Why's he driving so slowly?"

"I'm guessing he's got the horse in the trailer." Hank pushed himself away from the tree.

If Joe had Pretty Boy, he must have found Mia. Ruby wouldn't allow herself to believe otherwise. Her hammering heart didn't slow a beat as they hurried across the driveway to wait by the barn. When the vehicle drew near enough for her to see through the windshield, she spotted Mia and exhaled a sigh of relief.

As soon as Joe parked, Ruby opened the passenger-side door and tugged her daughter from the cab, then hugged her. "What the hell were you thinking, riding off alone like that?" Ruby's gaze roamed over Mia's sunburned face, arms, and legs. Thankfully, there wasn't a scratch or a trace of blood on her. "Are you okay?"

"Dehydrated," Joe said. "She drank a bottle of water on the way back." He opened the trailer doors and unloaded Pretty Boy, then escorted him into the barn.

"What happened? Did you get lost?" Ruby asked.

"No." Mia brushed away the sweaty strands of hair sticking to her face. "I wanted to check out Fury's Ridge, but when I got close, I heard a gunshot."

Ruby sucked in a quick breath. "Someone shot at you?"

"I don't know. I couldn't see anyone, but Pretty Boy got scared and he reared. I fell off, and he raced away."

Ruby envisioned her daughter flying through the air and hitting the ground hard. "You could have cracked your skull open."

"After I started walking home, Pretty Boy showed up again."

Home? How could Mia refer to the ranch as home after only a couple of days? Had she already forgotten the trailer she'd grown up in at the Shady Acres Mobile Home Park? The bedroom Ruby had painted pink, then aqua blue, and eventually mint green because Mia liked to change the color on a whim.

Ruby's heart, which had pounded with fear, now thumped against her ribs in pain. It wasn't the run-down house or the dusty Panhandle that symbolized home for Mia—it was Hank. And Ruby could hardly paint over him.

"Why didn't you ride Pretty Boy back?"

"He was limping."

"Taking off on your own was a foolish thing to do," Ruby said. The person who fired the gun was either a lousy shot or had intentionally missed his target. Regardless, Mia had been lucky she'd escaped without injury.

"I'm sorry for scaring you," Mia said, addressing Hank.

What about me? Ruby's hurt morphed into a fuming heap of pissed off. "Why are you apologizing to your grandfather? You should be begging me to forgive you for being irresponsible."

Mia's eyes narrowed. "You're irresponsible, not me."

Ruby didn't want to fight with her daughter, but Mia had scared ten years off of her life and she was ticked. "That's it. We're leaving on Tuesday for Elkhart."

Mia kicked the ground, sending a puff of dust into the air. "You're such a bitch!"

Speechless, Ruby stared, expecting tiny horns to pop through the top of Mia's skull.

"You always get your way. Like when you made Sean move out. You never asked how I felt about him going."

"That's not true." *Was it*?

"The only reason you want to leave the ranch is because you're jealous that Hank likes me better than you."

Ruby opened her mouth to dispute the charge, but the words got jammed up in her throat.

"You know what?" Tears dribbled from Mia's eyes, leaving muddy trails on her cheeks. "I slept with Kevin to hurt you because you only care about yourself. You don't pay any attention to me and what I want." Mia ran into the house.

The blood rushed from Ruby's head. Her gaze swung between the two men. Joe had the decency to look away, but Hank's rheumy-eyed stare socked her in the gut.

The miles of vast nothingness in every direction closed in on Ruby, and she fled to the front of the house. She sat for more than an hour, eyes dripping until Oklahoma's frickin' never-ending winds dried out her tear ducts. The sun had dipped in the sky when the front door squeaked open.

Hank lowered himself next to her on the porch step. "Thought you might be hungry." He offered her a bologna sandwich. "Mia said you like ketchup on your bread."

Ruby took a bite and chewed, barely tasting the food.

"Cora had a lot of boyfriends before me," he said.

After two swallows, the gummy lump landed in her stomach. "I'm not a whore."

"Some women can't commit to one man."

"That's not my problem." Or was it?

"What happened between you and this Sean fellow Mia liked so much?"

I slept with Kevin to hurt you because you only care about yourself.

Mia's admission screamed inside Ruby's head, threatening to deafen her. Learning her daughter had given herself to a boy she didn't love or care about in an act of revenge against her mother made the pain even worse.

"Did he mistreat you?" Hank wasn't going to drop the subject.

"Sean didn't return my text messages." Saying it out loud made it sound trivial, but it hadn't been. "I thought he was losing interest in"—*me*—"our relationship, so I ended it." If she couldn't trust him, why drag it out until he found someone else who made him happier?

"Did you ask him why he didn't return your texts?"

"He said the guys at work made fun of him because he was always checking in with me."

Ruby had yearned to give Sean the benefit of the doubt because he'd treated Mia like a daughter, but the agony she'd experienced when Glen Baxter had turned his back on her hadn't weakened over time—if anything, it had grown stronger. And Ruby knew that if she gave Sean a second or a third chance, it was still only a matter of time before he, too, turned his back on her.

Because that's what the men in Ruby's life did—they left her behind.

"Sometimes you have to take a leap of faith," Hank said.

"Like you did with Cora? Look how that turned out."

"I had two good years with her before she left."

Ruby'd had less than a year with Sean. She didn't want to consider it, but maybe she was just like Cora and wasn't capable of committing to one man. "What if Mia never forgives me?"

"She'll forgive you." He slid his arm across her back and clasped her shoulder.

Did he assume that all he had to do was wait long enough and she'd forgive him? Ruby wanted to lash out at Hank. Instead, she curled against his side and sobbed like a baby, because if anyone understood her fear of abandonment, it was him.

"Dusk'll be here soon," Hank called out as he approached the barn.

For the past two hours Joe had watched his boss sit on the front porch, staring at the road—as if he could will Ruby to return from wherever she'd driven off to. He doubted Hank had anticipated this kind of drama when he'd invited his daughter to visit. Joe had been surprised to learn that Mia had slept with a boy. He understood why Ruby would be upset that her daughter blamed her, but at least Mia was alive and healthy. He'd give anything to be in a similar situation with Aaron. "Did she say where she was going?"

"No."

Joe didn't want to get involved in a mother-daughter squabble, but he hated seeing Hank look miserable. "Do you want me to go after her?" Someone had to chase down Ruby before the old man shorted out his pacemaker again.

"If you wouldn't mind."

"Let me grab a quick shower." Joe went into the storage room for a change of clothes, then returned to the house with Hank. They parted ways inside the front door—Hank retreating to the kitchen and Joe heading upstairs to the bathroom. Twenty minutes later he climbed into his Dodge and drove off. After he crossed the cattle guard at the entrance to the ranch, he hit the brakes. Turning left would take him into town. Turning right would take him somewhere else.

He thought about Mia disappearing on Pretty Boy and how Ruby's accusing glare had reminded him that he'd failed his own son. He should have given in to Aaron that day and allowed him to stay home and play with his friend instead of insisting he tag along with Joe to check on the oil rig. The whole time Joe had driven around searching for Mia, he'd imagined the girl hurt or worse.

The relief he'd felt at finding Mia alive and uninjured had bled him dry, and he hadn't said a word to the teen during the trip back to the house, afraid the hurt and pain that had been bottled up inside for seven years would spill out and wound her.

He eyed the lonely stretch of highway leading away from Unforgiven. The white stripe down the middle of the road beckoned him. He could take the easy way out and keep running from his past, or he could turn left and face his demons.

Hank hadn't been the only one shaken by Ruby's and her daughter's visit. Watching the three get to know one another brought back fonder memories of Joe's past—the numerous fishing trips with his grandfather and father and the dinners on Sunday after church. Joe hadn't realized how much he missed being part of a family, and he was questioning his desire to go it alone the rest of his life.

He moved his foot to the accelerator and turned left. Twenty minutes later he arrived in town and parked next to Hank's truck in front of the Possum Belly Saloon. Ruby had the right idea—he could use a drink tonight, too.

He found her sitting at the bar, rolling an empty shot glass between her fingers. He slid onto the stool next to her and caught Stony's attention.

The bartender wandered over. "Hank driving you all to drink?"

"I'll take a beer." Joe would rather have a whiskey, but he'd better avoid the hard stuff if he intended to get himself and Ruby back to the ranch in one piece. Stony set a longneck in front of Joe and filled Ruby's empty shot glass with tequila.

She downed the liquor in two swallows, then grimaced. "How'd you know I was here?"

"Lucky guess." He studied her reflection in the mirror behind the bar. Aside from her blue eyes, he couldn't see much of Hank in her. Her tongue swept across her lower lip, and she exhaled a shaky breath. She looked like she hadn't a friend in the world, and he gripped his beer bottle with both hands so he wouldn't be tempted to hug her. "Hank's worried about you."

"Am I a horrible mother, Joe?" She clutched his forearm, her nails digging into his flesh. "I was trying to protect me and Mia from getting hurt when I sent Sean away." She released his arm, leaving four half-moon marks behind on his skin. "Is it too late for me and my daughter?"

"I'm the last person who should give parenting advice, Ruby."

"Aaron loved you, didn't he?"

"Yes." Joe envisioned his son's smiling face. "Every day he'd wait in the yard with his baseball mitt for me to come home after work."

Ruby pressed her knuckles against her eyelids. "I think Mia hates me."

"Mia doesn't hate you. She's an angry teenager." He swallowed a sip of beer.

"If she doesn't hate me now, she will when I make her leave the ranch."

"Then stay." The words slipped past his lips before they'd registered in his brain. "Stay until you work things out with Hank and Mia."

Ruby waved her empty shot glass at Stony—he ignored her. She turned pleading eyes on Joe. "Mia wants me to forgive Hank for giving me up for adoption."

"Do *you* want to forgive him?"

"Forgiving him won't make him love me."

"Hank hired someone to search for you, Ruby. That shows he cares."

"No, it proves he has a guilty conscience."

Joe knew all about guilty consciences. Maybe that's why he felt at home at the Devil's Wind—misery loves company.

"Does it matter if Hank loves you or not?"

"Yes, it matters. Hank might take his last breath at any moment and all I'll know the rest of my life is that he couldn't take care of me after I was born."

"Don't let fear control you." Joe was one to talk. His fears had sent him on the run for years. "Focus on your relationship with Mia. Once you two work through your problems, things between you and Hank will fall into place. The three of you are family now."

"A family for how long?"

No one knew the answer to that question.

"Losing Mia's love hurts more than not ever having had Hank's."

"Then fix what's broken between you and your daughter." He chugged the rest of his beer.

"Joe?" Ruby's hand covered his fist, and his fingers unfurled one at a time. He rolled his wrist sideways until their palms touched. "What?" he whispered.

"Thanks for caring."

He threaded his fingers through hers. He was beginning to believe Ruby was the kind of woman he could fall apart in front of and still walk away with his pride intact. "You ready to go home now?"

She pulled her hand free. "The Devil's Wind isn't *my home.*" She slid off the stool, and he followed her to the door.

"Hey, Ruby!" Stony's voice carried over the noise in the crowded bar. "You gonna pay for those shots?"

She flashed her middle finger. "Put it on my tab."

Once they stepped outside, Joe took her arm and led her across the street.

"I can drive." She stumbled. "Oops."

He helped her into his pickup, then slid behind the wheel.

"Thank you," she said.

"For what?"

"For coming after me."

"No big deal." But it was. For the first time since Joe had split with Melanie, he found himself concerned about another woman.

Chapter 15

"Thanks for giving Hank a lift into town to get his truck this morning." Ruby had taken three aspirin before she'd put on her sunglasses and screwed up the courage to face Joe.

"How are you feeling?"

"Like the worm at the bottom of a tequila bottle."

He grinned.

She pointed her finger at him.

"What?"

"I had no idea your teeth were so bright and straight." His pearly whites transformed his average looks into a face a woman wanted to stare at. "You should smile more often."

He frowned.

"The sheriff's deputy is on his way." Feeling light-headed, Ruby sat on the flatbed.

Joe loaded the last bale, then joined her on the trailer. "I'm surprised Randall's working on a Sunday."

It was tough to make eye contact with Joe after she'd bellyached in the bar. "He'll want to speak with you, too."

"I'll watch for his patrol car."

There was no denying that the charges Ruby's daughter had leveled against her were serious. And there was no going back and undoing what was done—Sean was history and so was Mia's virginity. She didn't need a therapist to explain that she had trust issues with men. Ruby had convinced herself that she'd sent Sean packing because she believed it was only a matter of time before he lost interest in her. But if she was brutally honest, she'd admit that she *looked* for a reason to send her boyfriends packing because she was afraid to put her heart at risk.

Then Hank had come into the picture, and years of guarding her heart made it difficult for her to give him a chance. But right now he was the only man Mia trusted and felt safe with. If Ruby didn't want to lose her daughter, she had to find a way to stop blaming Hank for things that had happened in the past.

"I'm here if you need to talk." Joe's voice drifted into her ear.

Ruby appreciated the offer. Back in Pineville she'd had a few meet-up-for-a-drink-once-in-a-while girlfriends but no one she talked with on the phone each day. After she'd given birth to Mia, she'd drifted apart from her high school friends. Her boss at the Booneslick Lodge had been the only person who'd given Ruby a send-off—a cake and a gift card to Walmart.

"Be careful. I might take you up on your offer." She hopped off the trailer, then went to the front porch to wait for the deputy. As soon as she sat in the chair, the door opened and Mia walked outside. If she'd had trouble looking Joe in the eye, it was magnified ten times with her daughter.

Mia plopped down on the steps. They needed to talk. No, Ruby needed to talk. She owed Mia an explanation for why she'd sent

Sean packing, but she worried her daughter would hate her even more when she learned her mother was a coward.

As Mia picked at her green nail polish, an idea came to Ruby. "How would you like to spend tomorrow in Guymon? We could get a mani-pedi and eat lunch out." She made a stab at humor. "I don't know about you, but I'm tired of Hank's sandwiches."

"I have to help with the horses."

Always the horses. "We don't have to be gone all day."

"I'd rather stay here." Mia wasn't making this easy.

"We could shop for school clothes." Classes in Elkhart began the Tuesday after Labor Day. She doubted Mia cared that they had only a month and a half to find a place to live and get settled. After Ruby had accepted the job at the Red Roof Inn, the manager had mailed her a packet of school and housing information for Elkhart and the surrounding area. There wasn't a whole lot to choose from in their price range, but she'd been looking forward to apartment hunting with Mia.

"Can Hank come with us?" Mia asked.

At first Ruby thought Mia was asking if her grandfather could move to Kansas with them, but then she realized Mia wanted Hank to go to Guymon—probably to act as a buffer. "I don't think he's a shopper." Any further discussion about tomorrow's plans would have to wait. "The deputy's coming."

The porch door opened and Hank appeared. Had he been watching for the lawman, or was he eavesdropping on her and Mia? Ruby doubted he had the nerve to kill anyone, but she wouldn't put it past him to fire off a warning.

The deputy got out of his car. "Howdy, folks."

"Deputy." Ruby left her chair and stood with Hank. Joe came around the corner of the house and nodded to the officer.

"You remember Mia." Ruby waved at her daughter.

Randall removed his mirrored sunglasses. "What's this I hear about you getting lost after going for a horseback ride?"

"I didn't get lost."

"Tell me what happened."

"Someone shot at me."

"Are you positive you heard a gunshot?"

Ruby jumped to Mia's defense. "She's not making this up. The sound of a gunshot excited the horse and she was thrown."

Mia scowled at Ruby. "I thought I was supposed to tell him everything?"

"I hope you weren't hurt," the deputy said.

"No."

"Where were you when you heard the shot?" the deputy asked.

"Out by Fury's Ridge."

Randall's gaze shifted to Hank. "You didn't warn your granddaughter to stay away from there?"

"Why do I have to stay away?" Mia asked.

"The ridge is a sacred Indian burial ground, and some people believe it's haunted," Joe said.

"You think a ghost shot at me?"

The deputy scowled. "Could you tell which direction the sound of the gunshot came from?"

"Behind me." Mia waved at the lawman. "How come you're not writing this down? The police in TV shows write down what the witness says."

Randall removed a notepad and a pen from his shirt pocket, then scribbled a few words to appease Mia. "Did you see anything suspicious out by the ridge? A pickup? Maybe an ATV or another horse?"

"Nope."

"What's your theory on what happened?" Joe asked.

"Probably a trespasser." He directed his words to Ruby. "Mia could have interrupted a Native American paying their respects to the dead and they fired off a warning to keep her away."

"What if the person wasn't trying to scare my daughter?"

"This isn't the Shady Acres Mobile Home Park, Ruby. People don't discharge their weapons for fun."

The only way the deputy could know where she and Mia had lived in Missouri was if he'd checked into their background. "Then you must disagree with the sheriff, who believes a group of inebriated ranch hands were blowing off steam when they shot up Hank's livestock tank."

"We questioned the Bar T hands, and they had nothing to do with damaging the stock tank."

"Maybe Roy Sandoval hopped the fence and took a stroll across Hank's property," Ruby said.

Randall shook his head. "The Sandovals have been ranching and drilling for oil in the Panhandle since the early 1900s. They're upstanding citizens." He flipped the page in his notebook. "After you fell off the horse, Mia, what happened?"

"I started walking home."

Like fingernails on a chalkboard, the word *home* grated on Ruby's nerves. The sooner Mia accepted that the Devil's Wind wasn't home, the sooner she'd embrace the idea of moving to Elkhart.

"Pretty Boy caught up with me, but he was limping."

"Pretty Boy?"

"My granddaughter named the horses."

"Is that so?" The deputy hid his smile behind a cough.

"I can drive you out to the area where I found Mia," Joe said.

"By now the blowing dust has concealed any footprints or tracks." Randall slid his sunglasses on. "No more horseback riding alone, young lady."

Hank set his hand on Mia's shoulder. "I'll make sure of that."

"What happens next?" Ruby asked.

"I file a report."

Ruby had her doubts about that.

"I'll be in touch." Randall got into the patrol car and drove off at a turtle's pace.

"A lot of good that did." Ruby's gaze tracked Joe back to the barn. Hank disappeared into the house, leaving her alone with Mia. The deputy's visit did nothing to reassure her that Mia or any of them weren't in harm's way. First the stock tank, then the flat tire on Hank's pickup, and now someone shooting at Mia. It all added up to get-the-hell-out-of-here. Boarding the Greyhound bus on Tuesday wouldn't just spare Ruby from having to reconcile with Hank, but it would protect Mia.

"I know you don't want to hear this, but it isn't safe for us to live at the ranch."

"We can't leave Hank alone," Mia said.

Guilt pricked Ruby. Okay, so the idea of deserting the geezer with trouble brewing on the horizon didn't sit well with her, either. But if they remained, she'd be forced to sort through her feelings for Hank. She hadn't expected to share a special moment with him after Mia had lashed out at her yesterday, yet he'd sensed that she'd needed comfort. And Ruby hadn't known how badly she'd yearned for his hug until he'd put his arm around her.

Mia shook her head. "The bad guys could hurt the horses, and we can't leave Friend behind." The mangy mutt must have heard his name, because he trotted into the front yard. When he saw Mia, he wagged his tail.

"I'm more worried about your safety than the animals."

"I never get a say," Mia whined. "You always decide everything."

That wasn't true.

You decided to kick Sean out. You *decided to pull up stakes and move.* And you *decided to stop in Unforgiven.* Mia was right—Ruby hadn't asked for her input on any of those plans.

"What if I promise to stay close to the house?"

Maybe Mia would give Ruby credit for meeting her halfway. "If we hang out here a while longer, you're going to have to follow some rules," Ruby said.

"Like what?"

"Like never going for a horseback ride alone."

"Okay."

"I mean it. I get that you're angry with me right now, but you care about Hank and you understand how fragile his health is."

"I know."

"So you agree not to take off anywhere without telling me, Hank, or Joe?"

Mia nodded.

"All right, then. I'll call my boss at the Red Roof Inn and inform her that we won't arrive until after Labor Day."

Mia's expression brightened. "C'mon, Friend, let's go tell Hank that I'm here for the rest of the summer." She raced into the house, and Ruby heard her yell, "Hank, we're not gonna leave for Kansas until September!" A moment later Mia ran to the barn, and Joe met her in the doorway. After Mia spoke to him, he looked Ruby's way and smiled. He approved.

Why that mattered so much, she had no idea.

Chapter 16

"Mia, let's go!" Ruby doubted her daughter would hear her through the closed bathroom door. She leaned against the stair banister and caressed the gemstone dangling from her neck. Although she was grateful Mia had agreed to spend the day with her in Guymon, Ruby assumed Hank had been the one to persuade her to leave the horses behind for a few hours.

Yesterday after supper Ruby had tackled cleaning the sticky kitchen cabinets. While scrubbing the grease and grime, she'd glanced into the yard and had caught Hank and Mia in an animated conversation. Actually, Mia had been the lively one—arms swatting the air as if a swarm of gnats were attacking her. Five minutes later Mia had entered the house and announced that she would tag along with Ruby to Guymon.

After Mia had returned to the corral to help Joe clean the horse trough, Ruby had phoned the hiring manager at the Red Roof Inn.

Martha Kendall had been more understanding than Ruby had expected. Although she couldn't keep the assistant manager position open for her until September, Martha had guaranteed Ruby a front desk job if she arrived on or before Labor Day weekend. Relieved that she'd have a source of income when they finally landed in Kansas, Ruby could now focus on Mia.

And Hank.

Not until Mia had dug in her heels had Ruby understood the real connection her daughter had with the ranch. Mia felt secure at the Devil's Wind. The ranch was old. Hank was old. The horses and Friend were old—too old to go anywhere.

The bathroom door creaked open and Mia appeared at the top of the stairs. No wonder it had taken her forever to get ready—her hair hung in soft ringlets down her back, and she wore eye makeup. She looked seventeen, not fourteen. Ruby hadn't given her daughter much in life, but she had passed on her looks. Mia was as beautiful and fresh-faced as Ruby had once been—before bad decisions had etched lines into her smooth skin.

In the grand scheme of things, all Ruby really wanted was to protect Mia and prevent her from making the same stupid mistakes she'd made. "Your hair looks pretty."

"Thanks."

"You still up for a manicure?"

Mia nodded to Ruby's fingers. "Your nails are too short."

Ruby let the necklace fall against her neck. "I don't mind waiting while you have yours done."

"That's okay. I'll just ruin them when I groom the horses."

The drive to Guymon was made in silence after Mia claimed she was tired and closed her eyes most of the way—like grandfather, like granddaughter. She didn't sit up straight until Ruby stopped in a strip mall an hour later. "Are you hungry? Hank suggested we try the Happy Days Pizza Parlor."

Mia checked the time on her iPhone. "It's too early to eat."

"I passed a Walmart on the way into town. Is there anything you need there?"

"Not really."

Ruby left the center. She drove several blocks, calling out store names, but Mia declined all offers to stop and shop. When Ruby saw a sign for Thompson Park, she turned down the road. Two miles later they arrived at the recreational area.

"What are we gonna do here?" Mia asked.

"Enjoy nature." Ruby parked near a pavilion, crowded with picnicking families. She and Mia entered the trail, which led through a wildflower exhibit that ended in front of a large pond. A concrete path circled the water and a handful of fishermen stood on the banks, casting their lines.

"Let's walk." Ruby waited for a couple to jog past, and then she and Mia stepped onto the path. "I spoke to my future boss at the Red Roof Inn and she's willing to hold a desk job for me until we arrive in September."

Mia's gaze followed a paddleboat on the water. "What happens if we don't make it by September?"

"I know you love the ranch, but it isn't practical to live there. I have to work and—"

"You could get a job in Guymon."

The hope shining in Mia's eyes almost blinded Ruby. Of course she could find a job in Guymon—that wasn't the reason she was eager to leave Oklahoma to its dust and move on. "I don't know if I want to live that close to Hank."

"Why don't you like him?"

"It's not that I don't like him. It's just . . ."

"You're never going to forgive him, are you?"

"I'm working on it." Ruby tugged one of Mia's curls, but Mia yanked her head to the side and Ruby released her hair.

"If you can't forgive Hank, then you probably won't forgive me for what I did."

"That's different. You're my daughter. I love you."

"You're Hank's biological daughter."

"Yes, but it's not like I've been aware of his existence my whole life."

"Hank says I should forgive you for breaking up with Sean."

Ruby was finding it harder and harder to keep pushing Hank away when he was trying to push Mia back to her.

"You could talk to Sean and see if he'll meet us in Elkhart," Mia said.

As much as she wanted to please her daughter, asking Sean for another chance was a waste of time. Any relationship she entered was doomed from the get-go until she figured out how to handle her fear of commitment. "Honey, it's over between us."

"Sean was like a dad to me."

"I didn't realize you'd grown so close to him."

"Because you only care about yourself."

Was Mia right? Ruby thought back to when she'd been Mia's age—half little girl, half grown woman. One day she wanted to be a kid, the next she wanted to be treated like an adult. And through all the angst and turmoil, Glen Baxter had been there for her—until their falling-out. He'd been a calm, constant presence in her life when she'd had trouble with friends at school or arguments with her mother over wearing too much makeup.

And you ripped that security right out from under Mia when you split with Sean.

"It doesn't matter." Mia wound a ringlet around her finger, twisting the curl until her finger turned blue.

"What doesn't matter?"

"I don't care how many boyfriends you have or if they stick around. I've got Hank now. He'll never leave me."

Mia was wise beyond her years. No matter how Ruby felt about Hank, he'd always be her biological father and Mia's grandfather. She couldn't kick *him* out.

"I know we talked a little bit about what happened between you and Kevin, but if you ever have any questions—"

Mia stopped walking and faced Ruby. "Did it hurt when you had sex with my dad the first time?"

"A little."

"Did you cry?"

Ruby shook her head. "No, but I remember saying the F word in my head." They moved aside so a pair of joggers could pass.

"It was kind of gross," Mia said.

"It's better to wait"—Ruby had been about to say until you fall in love, but that would be hypocritical of her when she'd had sex with guys she hadn't been in love with—"until you're older."

"Mom?"

"What?"

"I really don't want to move to Elkhart. I like it at the ranch."

"The ranch is isolated. A girl your age should have friends."

"I'll make friends at the school in Guymon."

Ruby racked her brain for a way to make Mia see how difficult it would be for her mother to live on the ranch with Hank.

"Never mind," Mia said. "You move to Elkhart. I'll stay with Hank."

Ruby opened her mouth to protest, but only air escaped.

"Hank said a school bus passes by the ranch every morning."

Mia had no qualms about living apart from her mother, which told Ruby how far she still had to go to make things right with her daughter. "Hank can't handle"—*you*—"raising a teenager."

"Well, I can't handle going back to the way things were."

"What do you mean?"

"I'm tired of all the boyfriends. It wouldn't be so bad if you just picked one, but you don't. Every time you let a new guy move in, I have to learn what he likes and what he doesn't like. When I have to be quiet and when I don't. I hate it."

Shame swelled inside Ruby until her chest threatened to crack open. She'd wanted things to work out with the boyfriends she'd invited to share their trailer, but until Sean, she'd never admitted to herself that she hadn't given any of them an honest chance. How could she when she'd always been on the lookout for a reason to break up with them?

She didn't want her daughter to grow up to be like her—making one bad decision after another because she was afraid to trust men. But until she overcame her fear of being left behind, Ruby would never experience a lasting relationship.

"Hank cares about me, and I'm not gonna let you keep me from being with him."

Ruby was on notice. From here on out Mia would decide who came and went in her life. That Mia had picked Hank over her own mother burned like hell.

"Mia, I—"

"You don't know what's best for me. You don't even know what I like."

Desperate to take back lost ground, Ruby joked, "You like purple Skittles and you like milk chocolate better than dark chocolate."

"That's not what I mean."

"Then make me understand."

"You think I'm stupid for spending so much time with Pretty Boy and the other horses."

"I never said you were stupid, Mia." *Argh!* "Tell me why you like spending time with the horses."

"When I'm around Pretty Boy, I'm not thinking about stuff in the future. I can relax."

"What's stressing you out?"

"School. I'm worried that someone will find out I slept with a boy and call me names."

Ruby shared her daughter's worries. "As long as you don't tell anyone, no one will guess."

"And what am I gonna do after I graduate?"

"You've got a few years to think about that," Ruby said.

"I'm not saying this to be mean, Mom, but I don't want to be like you. I don't want to work hard just to live in a dumpy trailer."

Ruby willed her eyes to remain dry. "You'll do better, honey. If you work hard in school, maybe you can go to college." Why hadn't Ruby enrolled in a few classes over the years and tried to better herself rather than rely on boyfriends to help pay the bills? Jeez, she'd been a sucky role model.

"I want to make enough money someday so I can have my own horses."

Mia couldn't be any clearer about her desire to remain at the Devil's Wind. Maybe if Ruby respected Mia's need to be with Hank and the horses, her daughter would return the favor and allow Ruby to work things out with Hank the way she saw fit. "I'll think about it."

"Me staying. Or you leaving?"

Ruby wasn't going anywhere without Mia. "*Us* staying at the ranch."

When they'd walked halfway around the lake, Ruby sat at a picnic table and Mia joined her. "I'll start looking for a job."

"What about the motel we passed on the way into Guymon?"

As Ruby suspected, Mia hadn't been sleeping during the drive. "That's a possibility." Not a good one. The Blowout Motel with its fake oil derrick out front looked as if it should have been condemned years ago.

"Are you gonna be nicer to Hank?"

"Yes." Didn't her concern for the Devil's Wind prove that she cared about him? Ruby was the one badgering the sheriff and his deputy to investigate the vandalism at the ranch.

"You're gonna do more stuff with him, right?"

Ruby nodded. She'd better get used to the idea that her daughter would hold Hank over her head until the day he died. "Are you ready to grab a bite to eat?"

"I'm not really hungry."

Ruby guessed her daughter's train of thought. "Me either. Let's head back to the ranch."

Mia gifted her with a wide smile. Ruby had never worked so hard to gain a smile from her daughter, and she intended to bask in her hard-won victory all thirty miles back to the ranch.

Chapter 17

Thursday afternoon Ruby stood on the front porch, eyeing the dark wall of clouds to the west. There had been a threat of a summer storm in the Panhandle every day since they'd arrived the previous week. A gust of wind churned up the dust in the yard and tiny bits of grit pelted her face.

How could Mia call this hostile land *home*?

Three days had passed since she and her daughter had visited Guymon, and each morning Ruby had woken with one thought in mind—she wanted to leave Oklahoma and Mia wanted to stay. Finding a compromise that would please them both was impossible when there was nothing between *stay* and *leave* but miles of brown, dead earth.

But if the Devil's Wind was the one place that would give Ruby a fighting chance to win her daughter back, then how could she force Mia to live somewhere else?

You can't.

Ruby went into the house, sat at the piano in the parlor, and tapped a yellowed key. She'd taken music lessons from first through fifth grade. Her parents hadn't owned a piano, but their next-door neighbor, Mrs. Olson, had allowed her to practice on her piano in exchange for a free haircut each month from Ruby's mother. Her fingers were rusty, but after two tries she stroked the right keys and sang . . . "Twinkle, twinkle, little star . . ."

"Didn't know you could play." Hank stood in the doorway.

"I took lessons when I was in elementary school."

"Cora taught herself." He wandered closer. "She'd play at night after the sun went down."

Ruby ran her fingertip over the edge of a key, imagining a connection with her birth mother that wasn't there—had never been there.

"I bought paint for the nursery."

"What color?" she asked.

"White."

"Would you like my help?"

"If you've got nothing better to do."

She choked back a laugh. He knew she was bored out of her mind. Maybe she'd win points with Mia for spending time with Hank. She followed him out of the room, noticing the way he swung his left leg out to the side when he climbed the stairs. "What's wrong with your hip?"

"Got a kink in it."

He must have a lot of kinks, because he teetered more than walked when he moved around. While he caught his breath on the landing, Ruby opened the nursery door. Hank had set the supplies in the corner next to a tarp and a toolbox. "What do you want to do with the baby furniture?"

"Store it in the attic. Mia might need it one day."

"Don't go marrying your granddaughter off and having her with babies anytime soon." She loved her daughter, but Mia hadn't been planned. Ruby shuddered to think about the decisions they would have faced if Mia had become pregnant after sleeping with Kevin.

Hank grabbed a screwdriver and began taking apart the crib. One by one Ruby carried the pieces into the attic. The top story was crammed with dusty boxes, mismatched furniture, a bicycle, and a leather trunk tucked away in the corner. The trunk wasn't large—maybe four feet by two feet. She dropped to her knees and peered at the faded gold letters across the front. C-O-R-A. What had her birth mother left behind? Photos, clothes, or family mementos?

Hank hollered into the opening, "You find that big rat that lives up there?"

"Ha-ha. Real funny." She descended the ladder. "There's an old trunk in the corner."

"Cora told me not to open it."

"And you never peeked inside?" His willpower must be as strong as the pump jacks that pushed oil out of the ground.

He opened the paint can and set the lid aside. "Figured she wouldn't have left it behind if she hadn't intended to come back for it."

Ruby's heart hurt for Hank. For the first time since she'd arrived at the Devil's Wind, she wasn't angry or pissed off at him—she was miffed at Cora.

What makes you think you're any better than Cora? You've been with lots of men.

But Ruby hadn't abandoned Mia after she was born.

"I'm sorry, Hank." Who better than Ruby to apologize for her birth mother—the apple not falling far from the tree and all that crap.

"You've got nothing to be sorry for."

She wouldn't say that. She'd done plenty during her thirty-one years that needed forgiveness. "Did you buy wallpaper stripper?"

"I picked out a new border to cover the old one." He handed Ruby the package.

"Zebra print?"

"The lady at the store said it was popular with teenage girls."

Hank was changing the room for Mia. Not Ruby.

"She'll be fine with it." He could do no wrong in his granddaughter's eyes. "Hand me the tarp."

While she spread the plastic sheet across the floor, Hank poured paint into a tray and began rolling a wall. Ruby filled a smaller dish, then dropped to her knees and cut in the baseboards. "When are you supposed to see the doctor again?"

"Don't remember."

The old coot needed someone to look after him.

"Mia said you two might not move to Kansas." Hank pushed the roller faster across the wall.

"My daughter informed me that she's not leaving here." *Ever.* "I can't very well go to Kansas without her."

"You're the mother. You should decide where you live."

"Mia forgets that I'm her mother." No one had to tell Ruby that she'd lost credibility with her daughter.

"You're welcome for as long as you both want to stay."

"We're stuck here until I come up with a plan Mia agrees to." She knelt in front of the closet door and painted around the trim. "In the meantime, I need a job, but I don't have a car to get to and from Guymon."

"You don't have to work."

Yes, she did. She couldn't stand around and watch Hank and Mia grow closer. Besides, being with her daughter 24-7 was stressful.

The other day they'd taken a big step in their relationship, but Ruby didn't want to push too hard, too soon.

"You can use my truck to go wherever you want whenever you want."

Speaking of the old jalopy, she should have purchased a new tire when she and Mia were in Guymon on Monday. "Has Kurt from the gas station called yet?"

"Nope."

"I'll drive into town in the morning and check on the tire, then see if anyone's hiring."

"You don't want to work in a town full of men."

"I'll be fine." Besides, any job in Unforgiven would be temporary, and she'd feel better staying close to the ranch in case anything happened to Hank. For someone who intended to keep her biological father at a distance, it was funny how he factored into all of her plans. She refilled the tray for Hank and added more paint to her bowl. "Can I ask a question that might make you uncomfortable?"

He nodded.

"Did you think of me through the years? Or did you just remember me on my birthday?" Assuming he remembered her birthday at all. He might have blanked out the date.

"Not a day went by that I didn't wonder how you were being treated. Or if Cora had found you."

"If she tried to see me, I never knew about it."

"The adoption counselor said we could ask your parents for permission to contact you."

"Did you try?"

"Didn't see any point."

Seriously? "I was your daughter."

"You had a new family and I didn't want to get in the way. Besides, when you turned eighteen, I figured you'd track me down."

But she hadn't, because her parents had kept her adoption a secret. None of this made sense—it just frustrated Ruby. "When I didn't find you, why didn't you look for me then?"

"I assumed you wanted nothing to do with me."

"Then why after so many years did you suddenly decide to search for me?"

Hank stopped rolling. "A scare with death makes a man think about his life. His regrets. I wanted to see you before it was too late." He dropped his gaze. "I wanted to apologize for not being able to keep you."

Ruby's lungs pinched closed. It would be so easy to say *I forgive you,* but then she'd have to accept that she was the only one responsible for the choices she'd made in the past.

"What were you like when you were Mia's age?" Hank asked.

"Better behaved."

"Doubt that. You two butt heads every which way you turn."

"I was a good kid until the age of sixteen. Then I began running with the wrong crowd. I skipped classes and got caught smoking in the girls' bathroom."

"What did your folks do?"

"My mother and I argued all the time about curfew and grades."

"Your father didn't step up and rein you in?"

What did Hank know about stepping up when all he'd done until now was step aside? "My dad worked overtime hauling construction materials all over the country. When he did come home, he hung out at a bar and drank with his buddies rather than referee fights between me and my mother." It hadn't always been that way. Ruby's father had been the one she'd listened to and turned to for advice. But they'd drifted apart after he'd canceled their summer road trip.

"Did you straighten out?"

"Not until I discovered I was expecting Mia my senior year. I don't know if it was pregnancy hormones or that Dylan refused to marry me, but I settled down."

"You didn't drop out of high school?"

She hadn't expected it to matter, but she was pleased he was interested in her childhood. "I graduated despite all the kids staring at my big belly."

"I regret not earning my diploma." At least the lack of a high school education hadn't prevented him from making a good living.

"It wasn't easy," Ruby said. The ridicule and pitying looks from her peers and teachers had stung, but she'd put on a brave face, determined to earn her diploma. Back then she hadn't realized her actions had made her parents the subject of gossip—especially her mother, who styled the hair of every Chatty Cathy in the town.

"What did your folks say when they found out about Mia?"

"They were disappointed. But when I quit my wild ways and hit the books, they grew excited about becoming grandparents. My father cut back on the overtime." Glen Baxter had spent a month of Sundays putting up a fence around the yard. He'd wanted to make sure his grandchild didn't wander into the road and get hit by a car. It was sad that Mia never had the chance to play in that yard. After Ruby's parents passed away, she'd been given two weeks to vacate the trailer.

"Hank?"

"What?"

"Now that you've seen how Mia has taken to the horses and Friend . . . do you think I'd have been happy growing up here?"

"Mia's a teenager, not a baby."

"I wouldn't have stayed a baby forever. Maybe I'd have learned to love this place." And the run-down house would have felt like *home.*

Hank set the roller aside. "You might have taken to ranch life, but . . . Never mind."

"What?"

He pressed his lips together, then opened his mouth and expelled a loud breath. "It would have pained me too much to look at you."

His confession stung.

"You're the spitting image of Cora. If I'd had to raise you and see your face every . . ."

His heart would break over and over. Day after day. Week after week. Month after month. Year after year.

Ruby had no idea what it felt like to love someone so deeply that in order to cope with the pain you had to give up your own child. "Do you regret loving Cora?"

Hank cleared his throat. "I'd rather live with heartache than have missed out on loving your mother."

It was one thing to make that choice for himself, but did he realize he'd also made it for her?

You did the same thing to Mia when you sent Sean packing because he failed to return your text messages.

Ruby was tired of the stupid voice in her head baiting her. "After Mia was born, I gave Dylan a lot of chances. When that didn't work out, I decided I was done trusting men."

Hank massaged his crooked knuckles. "How come?"

Did he really want to open that door? "It wasn't only Dylan walking out on me. My adoptive father gave me the cold shoulder after I turned sixteen." She pointed the paintbrush at Hank. "And you handed me over to the state." She didn't understand what she'd done to make them all turn their backs on her.

A shiny film covered Hank's eyes.

Horrified, she blurted, "You're not going to cry, are you?"

He turned his back to her.

Shit. "I didn't mean to hurt your feelings." *Yeah, right.* She'd wanted to lash out at Hank since he greeted her at the door with a shotgun.

"I'm sorry, daughter."

Hank might regret that his actions had caused her pain, but if he could go back in time, Ruby was positive he'd make the same choices again.

"You're a smarter person than I am," he said. "One day you'll find a man you can trust."

The simple statement hit Ruby square between the eyes. She admitted she'd never be able to commit to a man unless she trusted him, but how would he earn her trust if she never gave him the opportunity?

"What if I never do?" she asked.

"Then you've got me and Mia. We aren't going anywhere."

He made it sound so simple, but what if her problem wasn't trusting men—it was trusting herself not to panic when the relationship hit a bump in the road. All this self-analyzing was giving her a headache. "Do you think Cora knew you put me up for adoption?"

"I'd like to believe she cared enough to find out what happened to you."

So would Ruby. As a parent she struggled to understand how Hank could still love a woman who'd turned her back on their child.

Chapter 18

"Where were you?" Mia asked when Ruby crawled beneath the sheets late Thursday night.

"Cleaning the bathroom."

"That was nice of you."

Yes, it was. After Ruby and Hank had finished painting, Hank had gone outside to be with Mia and the horses and Ruby had embarked on a cleaning binge. She'd done a lot of thinking while scrubbing the toilet—mostly about her relationship with Mia. Ruby had come to the conclusion that she'd been naive to believe pulling up stakes and leaving Pineville was all she and Mia needed to get back on track with each other. She was relieved that Mia was talking to her again, but Ruby had made a lot of concessions to get to this point and she worried about the unforeseen consequences of delaying their departure from the ranch.

"How come you guys painted the bedroom upstairs?"

"Hank did it for you."

Mia turned onto her side, her gaze cutting through the dark, burning Ruby's face. "Why?"

"He wants you to have your own room when you visit."

"I won't need to visit if I live here."

If? Ruby took comfort in the two-letter word—at some point in the future Mia might entertain the idea of leaving the Devil's Wind. Ruby tried to view the ranch through her daughter's eyes but saw only blowing wind, dust, and an emptiness that stretched to the horizon. It was the vast nothingness she couldn't stop thinking about. There was something comforting in the lonely landscape—maybe because the bleak geography couldn't be choosy about whom it welcomed.

"I'm glad you helped Hank paint the room," Mia said.

"I am, too." Ruby's chat with Hank had brought her fears out into the open. For years she'd used anger and resentment to hide from the truth. Her distrust of men had begun with Glen Baxter, then had been reinforced with Dylan, and finally solidified by Hank—all three men had left her behind emotionally or physically. She'd shoved the hurt and fear so far down inside her that she'd almost forgotten it existed.

"Mom?"

"What?"

"I asked Hank why he never named the horses or Friend."

"What did he say?"

"That he was gonna die before the animals did and then someone else would give them a different name, like Grandpa and Grandma Baxter did with you."

If Hank hadn't liked the idea that her name had been changed, maybe that meant he'd bonded with her before he'd decided to give her up for adoption.

"I don't like it when Hank talks about dying," Mia said.

"How often has he mentioned it?"

"Every day. He says stuff like 'After I die, water the rosebushes if it hasn't rained in two weeks.' And 'After I'm dead, I don't want you to give the piano away.'"

Hank wanted someone to take his place and wait for Cora to come home.

"I think he's afraid if you leave, he'll never see you again," Mia said.

You . . . not *we.* Although Mia was no longer ignoring Ruby, her feet remained firmly planted in Hank's camp.

All the people closest to Hank had left him—his father, his mother, and then Cora. No one would blame him if he closed off his heart to others—but he hadn't. He and Mia were growing closer by the day, and that afternoon he'd opened up to Ruby. If Hank was willing to put his heart on the line, then she should be able to find the courage to do the same with hers.

"You're not gonna leave Hank, are you?"

Mia might act like she didn't need Ruby because she had Hank, but the tiny tremble in her voice said otherwise.

"Not anytime soon." Ruby grasped a strand of Mia's hair and rubbed it between her fingers. "I'm surprised you enjoy hanging out with an old person."

"Hank likes me the way I am."

Meaning Ruby didn't?

"And he never gets mad, even if I hurt his feelings."

"Did you hurt his feelings?" Ruby asked.

"Maybe."

"What did you say?"

"That it wasn't nice of him to give you away."

"Really?" This was the closest Mia had come to acknowledging Ruby's right to feel hurt.

"Hank said his mom had a lot of boyfriends, too."

Ruby opened her mouth, then snapped it closed. There was nothing she could say in her defense, but she didn't appreciate Hank comparing her to his mother.

"I'm going to look for a job in Unforgiven."

"Doing what?"

"I'll ask Jimmy if I can take orders at the diner. Or maybe Big Dan could use help in the mercantile." She doubted the miniature entrepreneur would hire her when few customers shopped in the store. "I could waitress at the bar."

"What about finding a job in Guymon?"

Why did Mia care where Ruby worked? "I'll try Guymon if I strike out in town."

Just when Ruby thought her bed partner had fallen asleep, Mia whispered, "Joe was really quiet today. Is he mad at me because I rode off on Pretty Boy?"

"I don't know."

Mia poked Ruby's thigh. "He likes you and not just as a friend."

"Don't be silly." The tiny quiver that spread through Ruby's heart mocked her denial.

"I'm serious, Mom. He watches you all the time when you come outside."

The decision to stay at the ranch didn't just affect Ruby's relationship with Hank and Mia. It left the door wide-open for her and Joe.

"Sean used to look at you the same way."

"Mia?"

"What?"

"I liked Sean. A lot."

"Then why did you make him leave?"

"I got scared."

"About what?"

"That he'd get tired of being with me." She didn't want to go into too much detail because she already looked weak in front of her daughter. But a little truth might go a long way with Mia.

"Your father had said he loved me, but when I became pregnant, he changed his mind. I loved Dylan and I gave him a lot of chances." Ruby had even looked the other way when he'd slept with girls behind her back.

"I'm glad my dad isn't part of my life."

"People can change, honey." She sure in hell was trying to. "One day you might want to get to know your father."

"Maybe," Mia said. "Did Grandma and Grandpa Baxter get along?"

"Most of the time." Until Ruby's sophomore year of high school. Then things had become strained between them. She'd assumed it had a lot to do with her rebellious behavior and the bad crowd she was running with at the time. And now she wondered if her parents had regretted adopting her. Maybe they'd blamed her wild ways on her birth parents.

The answer might be in the diary.

Ruby wasn't ready to learn the truth.

"Mom?"

"What?"

"Are you positive it's too late for you and Sean to get back together?"

"Yes."

After only a few minutes, the sound of chirping crickets and Mia's even breathing echoed in the bedroom.

Ruby clasped her necklace between her fingers and closed her eyes. Maybe her decision to give Hank a chance and Mia's decision to give Ruby a chance would gift her with her first good night's sleep since she'd arrived at the ranch.

"Where'd you get the paper?" Hank asked Friday morning.

"Joe brought it back from town earlier." Ruby nodded to the coffeemaker. "If you need caffeine, I made a fresh pot five minutes ago." The importance of coffee in Hank's daily routine hadn't escaped her. She equated the dark beans to a Native American peace pipe. Instead of smoking, she and Hank practiced the ritual of drinking the hot brew together. They shared a love of the drink, which brought them together at all different times of the day.

He poured himself a cup and joined her at the table. "What are you reading?"

"The job ads." But she'd gotten sidetracked when she'd run across postings for livestock sales. She pointed to the type she'd circled in blue ink, then pushed the page toward Hank. "Check out this ad from the Humane Society."

He held the paper inches from his eyes.

> **Need foster families willing to care for confiscated horses in county animal cruelty case. Old horses suffer from malnutrition and need extra TLC. Humane Society will pay vet and food bill for first month. Minimum six-month commitment.**

He handed the paper back, then blew across the top of his mug. "Didn't think you were interested in horses."

"I'm not, but I thought Mia might like to pick one of her own to rescue."

"You fall and hit your head this morning?"

Her mouth twitched. "Maybe." She stared out the window. Mia was in the corral, trying to coax Lonesome to join Sugar and Pretty Boy at the grain feeder.

"Once Mia brings the horse home, she's not going to let you take it back," Hank said.

"I know."

"That's a long-term responsibility."

"Not if you encourage her to pick the oldest nag."

Hank chuckled, and then his wrinkles settled back into place. "What happens when you move?"

"We'd take the horse with us." They'd have to rent a trailer in the country where they could keep the animal, or she'd have to pay to have it boarded. She hated asking him for anything, but she'd do it for Mia. "I might need help with the expenses."

"I'll pay for its keep."

Hank hadn't made her beg. That he was offering his financial help even if she and Mia left the ranch put another chink in the armor around her heart.

"I want to show Mia that I accept and respect the bond she has with the horses and that I admire her for wanting to take care of them."

"You're doing a good thing, Ruby."

She hadn't asked his opinion, but she appreciated his approval. "Will you come with us to the Humane Society? Mia trusts your judgment, and you'll make sure she picks the right one."

"When do you want to do this?"

"How about tomorrow morning?"

Hank nodded. "As long as we're back before my date."

"What date?"

"A date with my bed."

"I won't let you miss naptime." Ruby carried her empty mug to the sink. "Do me a favor and don't say anything to Mia. I'd like to be the one to tell her."

Hank made the motion of zipping his mouth, then handed his empty cup to her and went out to the corral.

By the time Ruby entered the Jailhouse Diner, the breakfast crowd had already cleared out. "Hey, Jimmy."

"Be right with you." He disappeared with an armload of dirty dishes.

She smiled at the two men sitting in the booth next to the air conditioner. They nodded, then resumed their conversation—beef cattle. Ruby slid onto a stool at the counter. Jimmy reappeared, carrying plates piled high with eggs, bacon, and hash browns. He delivered the food to the ranchers, then stopped at her side. "What can I get you?"

She eyed his outfit. He must own several pairs of white T-shirts and black jeans. "I need a job."

"Thought you were heading to Kansas."

"Change of plans. Mia and I will be staying at the Devil's Wind the rest of the summer. Could you use a waitress or a dishwasher?"

"Sorry. I don't make enough money to put anyone on the payroll but me."

"Mind if I ask how you"—she waved her hand—"became a restaurant owner?"

"When the oil companies started drilling on the reservation, my great-grandfather invested his royalty checks. Others used their money to buy new cars and houses. My mother said if I went to college and earned a degree, she'd let me cash in my inheritance early."

"You majored in business?"

"Earned a bachelor of science in dietetics and nutrition."

"I guess that fits."

"I'd help you out if I could, but I'm barely making ends meet."

"I have a lot of waitressing experience. If things change, let me know." Ruby had landed her first job at sixteen, taking orders at a pizza parlor. The following year she'd worked at a chain restaurant. After Mia was born, she'd changed jobs and waitressed at Carmen's Chicken Fry, working her way into a hostess position. And when she could get a babysitter, she'd served drinks on weekends at a dive bar, where she made as much in tips in one night as she did all week at Carmen's.

"You might stop by Petro Oil and see if they need an office assistant."

"Thanks." She hiked across the street, but the door to the oil company was locked. She eyed the mercantile. Big Dan was odd but interesting.

She went into the store, ignoring the stuffed animal heads leering at her, and walked back to the cash register. "Big Dan?"

"Hello, Ruby."

Her pulse jumped when he appeared behind her. "I'm looking for part-time work. Any chance you need help watching the store or stocking shelves?"

"If I did, I wouldn't hire you."

"Why not?"

"Wouldn't want Hank coming in here and reading me the riot act."

"Hank doesn't have the stamina to read anyone the riot act." She expelled an exasperated breath. "What's the deal between you two anyway?"

"You wouldn't be interested."

Oh, yes, she would. "Where I work is none of Hank's beeswax."

"Maybe. But I don't want the aggravation."

Damn Hank and his orneriness. "I guess I'll see if the bar needs a waitress."

"That's no place for a lady to work."

Ruby wasn't a lady, and no one had ever accused her of being one. "Thanks for your concern, but I've been looking out for myself since I was eighteen."

"You're as tough as your mother."

Since he'd brought up Cora . . . "Hank said my mother spent a lot of time in your store."

"She loved rearranging the shelves. Had the place looking like a women's boutique."

"What was she like?"

"Pretty." His gaze dropped to Ruby's hands, and he frowned. "She had the daintiest fingers."

Embarrassed by her hangnails and rough skin, Ruby shoved her fingers into her jeans pockets. "What else?"

"She liked to read."

Finally, one thing Ruby didn't have in common with her mother. "What did she read?"

"Magazines and newspapers. She read the *Guymon Daily Herald*."

Ruby had a million more questions she wanted to ask but didn't feel right going behind Hank's back. "I better take off."

"Ruby."

She stopped at the door. "What?"

"Cora wasn't happy here. You won't be, either."

Ruby let the door slam shut behind her. She was tired of people who didn't know her comparing her to Cora. She walked over to the gas station. Kurt stopped texting on his phone when he noticed her. "Did the new tire for Hank's truck come in?" she asked.

"Yep."

"When did it get here?"

"A couple days ago."

"You could have called."

"I've been busy."

She glanced at the empty bay. *Yeah, real busy.* "The truck's parked in front of the diner." She tossed him the keys. "I'll be back in a half hour. Be sure you tighten the lug nuts. I'd hate to have to sue you if the tire comes off after I leave town."

"The tire's not free."

"Mail the bill to Hank. You know he's good for the money." Ruby cursed the dimwit and cut across the street to the saloon—her last hope of landing a job in Unforgiven.

Chapter 19

When Ruby walked into the Possum Belly Saloon, Stony was seated in the shadows, holding a shot glass in one hand and a bottle of booze in the other. "A little early in the day to start drinking, isn't it?" she asked.

He tossed the scotch back, his lips flattening before he expelled a loud hiss. "What do you care?"

Stony's hypnotizing eyes—caramel colored with a copper rim around the iris—glowed like a lion's. "Are you drunk?"

"Just getting started, darlin'."

She didn't blame the women for avoiding this town if all the men did was drink. "Are you married?" She couldn't imagine any female wanting to wear Stony's ring.

"Twice married. Twice divorced."

"Any kids?"

"Hell no." He poured a refill. "Heard you have a teenage daughter."

"I do."

"No husband?"

"Never been married."

"Figured as much."

"What do you mean by that?"

He grinned. "You look like a handful."

"Right back at you."

He chuckled and slid the liquor bottle toward her. "You here to drink or chat?"

"I need a job. Are you hiring?"

"My clientele wouldn't approve of a woman invading their territory."

"The men didn't seem to mind when I was in here a few nights ago."

"Oh, they minded. But I assured them you'd be leaving soon." He drained a third shot.

"Plans change. We're staying."

"For good?"

She shrugged.

"There are plenty of jobs for women in Guymon."

"I don't want to drive that far for part-time work."

"What do you need a paycheck for? Hank earns a decent living off his oil leases."

"I pay my own way." Ruby might invite boyfriends to move in with her to share expenses, but she'd always covered her half of the bills. Irritated by Stony's questions, she lost her cool. "You want to know why I need a job?"

He dipped his head.

"Because I'm bored out of my mind. And if that's not a good enough reason, then how about the fact that my daughter is happier when I'm not around? Mia would rather spend time with her grandfather than with me."

Stony's mouth curved upward. "Sounds like happy times out at the Devil's Wind."

"I know my way around bars."

"I bet you do."

Ignoring the snide remark, she said, "I can take care of myself."

"Does that mean you'll keep your hands off my customers?"

"Roughnecks and cowboys aren't my type."

"What is your type, Ruby?"

"If I knew, I'd be married. Will you give me a job or not?"

"Part-time. Afternoons. I open at one."

"You want me to work when no one's here?" And make nothing in tips.

"Take it or leave it."

"What employment forms do I need to fill out?"

"I'll pay you cash under the table."

Figures. The men in Unforgiven followed their own laws.

"You look like your mother," he said.

Who would have guessed her mother had been so popular in this town?

"I saw Cora come and go. She spent a lot of time in the mercantile."

So I heard. "When do I start?"

"Whenever you want."

"Are you open on Sundays?" Tomorrow was Saturday, and she and Hank were taking Mia to the Humane Society.

"Open seven days a week."

"See you on the Sabbath."

"You gonna pay for that tequila you drank the other night?"

"Deduct it from my earnings." When she left the saloon, she spotted Hank's truck at the gas station. "Thanks for putting on the new tire," she said when she reached the business.

Kurt scribbled on a piece of paper, then handed it to Ruby. "Give that to Hank."

She shoved the bill into her pocket.

"And tell him that he should replace the other three tires soon."

"I'll give him the message."

A half hour later Ruby parked in front of the ranch house. Joe's pickup was gone and the horses were in the corral, but there was no sign of Hank or Mia. When she entered the house, she heard voices coming from the second floor.

"Mom can buy me an air mattress in Guymon."

"I want my granddaughter to have a proper bed. I'll order a new one from Sears. They'll deliver it."

Ruby inched closer to the stairs.

"Can I use the dresser for my clothes?"

"You can use whatever you want."

Hank must have emptied the drawers.

"You think my mom will mind if I move up here?"

In a way Ruby did mind Mia sleeping upstairs. She'd miss their nightly chats. It was easier to talk about sensitive subjects in the dark than the broad daylight.

"Your mom wants you to be happy."

"She says she does, but I'm not sure."

"She cares."

"Did she say that?"

"Your mother's giving me a chance like you asked her to."

"She wasn't supposed to tell you that."

"I admire your mother's honesty."

"Hank?"

"What?"

"Do you think my mom will forgive me for . . . you know . . . ?"

"Your mom already forgave you."

Ruby pressed her hand against the nauseous feeling flaring up in her stomach. That Mia was still uncertain of her mother's love shamed her.

"Will you go for a horseback ride with me later? I need more practice."

"These old bones don't stick so good to the saddle anymore."

"We don't have to go far."

"Maybe Joe will take you for a ride. Think I'll lie down now."

Ruby hurried over to the front door and closed it loudly. "Anyone here?"

Mia came to the top of the stairs. "Did you just get home?" There was that four-letter word again . . . *home.*

"Yep. What have you been up to?" Ruby asked.

Mia descended the stairs. "Hank said I can use the bedroom now that the paint is dry."

"I think it's nice that you'll have your own room."

"If anything happens to Hank in the middle of the night, I'll probably hear him," Mia said.

"It's good that you'll be close by."

"Did you get a job?"

"I did."

"At the diner?"

"I'm waitressing at the bar."

"Oh."

Not caring to talk about the saloon or her new boss, she said, "I was thinking maybe it's time I learned more about the horses since we're not leaving." Yet.

Mia's eyes widened. "Are you serious?"

"You could go over the basics with me." Ruby set her purse on the stairs. "Like teach me how to climb on and steer."

Mia laughed. "Let's go."

"What about Friend? Isn't he coming?"

"He's taking a nap with Hank."

Ruby followed Mia outside. When she cut across the driveway, Ruby said, "Aren't we going the wrong way? The horses are in the corral."

"First you have to learn about the tack. That's the ropes and saddle and stuff."

Ruby knew what tack was but allowed Mia to ramble on and share what Hank had taught her when they went into the equipment room in the barn.

"This is called a bit. It's the part that goes into the horse's mouth." Mia removed the harness from a peg. "Pretty Boy doesn't mind his, but Sugar doesn't like the bit and backs up when you try to put it on her."

"What's this?" Ruby ran her fingers over a leather strap.

"The lead rope. Hank attaches it to the halter. It's kind of like a dog leash." Mia brought Ruby a piece of rope. "This one's called a war bridle. It's made of hemp, not leather."

"I'm really impressed that you know what all this stuff is used for." Ruby was more confident than ever that she'd made the right decision to allow Mia to have her own horse.

"I think you should try riding Lonesome first."

"Why's that?"

"Because Sugar doesn't like anyone to ride her, and Pretty Boy likes to run."

"What does Lonesome do?" Ruby asked.

"I don't know. I haven't ridden him."

"Maybe we should wait for Joe—" Ruby stopped talking when Joe waltzed into the barn.

"My mom wants to ride Lonesome."

Joe's mouth stretched into a slow, easy smile. "She does, huh?"

"I don't think she can handle Pretty Boy, and Sugar hates people riding her."

"Mia's right. Lonesome is your best bet."

Her daughter's eyes lit up at Joe's praise. Until just now Ruby hadn't realized that in her determination to protect herself, she'd denied Mia what she'd needed most—a man to look up to. Sean had been the closest Mia had come to experiencing a father-daughter relationship, but Ruby's self-doubts had ripped that away from her. If Mia latched on to Joe and Hank, Ruby would never convince her to leave the ranch.

All these years a promise had held Hank prisoner at the Devil's Wind—his vow to wait for Cora. And Ruby suspected Joe stayed because the barren land asked so little of him and nurtured the hurt and pain of his son's death. As for Mia's infatuation with the bleak landscape . . . it had more to do with Hank than the horses. The old nags were only a means of communication between grandfather and granddaughter. Hank provided Mia with a sense of security that Ruby had never given her.

"I guess I'll ride Lonesome," Ruby said.

"I'll bring the saddle and meet you girls at the corral."

"No laughing at me," Ruby warned.

"I'm gonna wake up Hank." Mia veered toward the house. "He'll want to see this."

Chapter 20

"When are we going to get there?" Mia asked. She and Ruby sat in the backseat of Joe's truck. He drove and Hank rode shotgun.

"We're almost there," Joe said.

As far as Mia knew, they were visiting the Humane Society to make a donation. If her daughter thought it odd that the horse trailer was hitched to the back of Joe's truck, she hadn't said anything. Ruby had changed her mind about telling Mia she could foster a horse. She'd decided it was best to see the condition of the horses before agreeing to bring one back to the ranch. If the animals were too bad off, Ruby didn't want to chance one of them dying in Mia's care and leaving her heartbroken. Ruby had put Hank in charge of making the call after they assessed the boarders.

"Here it is." Joe slowed down, then turned left at the entrance to the facility. There were several corrals, a metal barn, and two smaller buildings.

"Look." Mia pressed her face to the window. "They've got goats, a cow, and a two sheep in that pen."

Joe parked, and they piled out of the pickup. A young woman met them outside the barn. "Howdy." Her smile widened when she noticed Joe. "Welcome to the Humane Society. I'm Ellen. What brings you by today?"

"Hank is gonna make a donation," Mia said. Before she caught her breath, she asked, "Do you have any horses here?"

Ruby tried to make eye contact with the woman, hoping to convey a silent message to speak with her in private, but the brunette batted her eyelashes at Joe and asked, "Is this your daughter?"

"I'm her mother, Ruby Baxter, and this is her grandfather, Hank McArthur." She nodded to Joe. "He's the ranch hand." She ignored the twinkle in Joe's eyes—he knew she was jealous.

"We have five horses boarding with us. All are geldings between the ages of fifteen and twenty-two."

"Where's the twenty-two-year-old?" Ruby asked.

"Follow me." Ellen led them into the barn, where large industrial fans circulated the warm air. She stopped in front of a stall with a sliding door. "This is Hombre. He's a Thoroughbred. He's been bought and sold his whole life. I think he's tired of moving and just wants to stay in one place." She clicked her tongue. "Say hello, Hombre."

The horse spun away from the door, sticking his rump in their faces. Ellen laughed. "Takes a while for him to warm up to people."

They moved to the next stall. Two tan horses with white patches shared the space. "These guys are brothers and escape artists," Ellen said. "Their owner couldn't keep them contained."

"Why are they so skinny?" Mia asked.

"The last time they ran off, they got lost for three months and didn't have much to eat." Ellen waved them to the next stall. "This is Bob."

Bob was black with a large white spot across his back.

"I'll show you how he got his name." Ellen clapped her hands. "Hey, Bob, are you hungry?" The horse moved his head up and down. "Do you want to eat?" More bobbing. "Is it okay if I give all your food to Hombre?"

"I get it." Mia laughed.

"Bob's not very social. He kicks if you get too close to him. We can't adopt him out to just anyone."

"You said there were five." Mia hadn't appeared impressed with any of the horses.

Ellen walked to the rear of the barn. "This is Poke. Because he loves to poke his nose in everyone's business."

Mia gasped. "It's a baby horse."

"He's a miniature pony. He's sixteen, and you can't ride him because his leg is deformed."

"What happened to him?" Mia stuck her hand between the bars, and Poke nuzzled her fingers.

"Got his leg caught in a fence, and the broken bones didn't heal properly."

"He's a boring color," Mia said.

"I don't know," Ruby said. "He looks like a big Nutter Butter cookie."

"It's a good thing his personality isn't boring." Ellen's gaze swung to Joe. "How would you like a tour of the vet clinic?"

"Mia and her grandfather would love to see where you treat the injured animals," Ruby said. She nodded to Hank. "We'll wait out here for you."

"The clinic is this way." Ellen smiled at Joe before she walked off.

Ruby stabbed the toe of her athletic shoe against the cement floor.

"What's the matter? Can't decide which one Mia should pick?"

Ha-ha. He knew darn well why she was agitated. "Ellen sure seems fascinated with you."

"I know."

He could have pretended to deny her charge. "What are you going to do about her?"

He leaned against the stall door, crossed his boots at the ankles, then shoved his fingers into his jeans pockets. "Why are you asking?"

Why was she doing this? "You know what?" She waved a hand in front of her face. "Never mind." She had no claim on Joe. Besides, why would he want to become involved with a woman who was just waiting for him to slip up? She should leave the barn, but Joe's stare held her captive.

He pushed away from the wall and moved closer, forcing her head back to meet his gaze. "I'm a grown man, Ruby. I know when a woman is interested in me."

Could he tell *she* was testing the waters with him?

"But I'm not looking for a young girl."

Don't ask. "Are you looking at all?"

His eyes focused on her mouth. "Maybe."

His honesty earned him a token of Ruby's trust, and she wanted to see how things played out between them.

"Mom."

Ruby stepped away from Joe and met Mia at the entrance of the barn. "How was the tour of the clinic?"

"Okay. Hank's filling out paperwork to make a donation and

I wanted to see Poke one more time." Mia walked over to the stall and rubbed the pony's nose.

"He seems like a sweet horse," Ruby said.

"He's not that much bigger than Friend."

"I was thinking," Ruby said. "You've learned a lot about horses from Hank. I bet you could take care of one of your own."

Mia whipped around. "Are you saying we can take Poke home?"

"Yes."

Mia threw herself at Ruby, almost knocking her down.

"What's all the excitement about?" Hank shuffled toward them.

"Mom said Poke can come home with us."

"Is that right?" Hank cleared his throat. "You want a horse you can't ride?"

"I don't care." She looked at Ruby. "Will Poke like Pretty Boy, Sugar, and Lonesome?"

"I think your grandfather can best answer that question," Ruby said.

Mia tugged Hank's shirtsleeve. "I want Poke, but I don't want Pretty Boy to be mad at me, either."

Poke stuck his tongue between the bars and licked the back of Mia's arm. "Eew!" She laughed.

"Poke's a charmer," Hank said. "He'll do fine with the other horses."

"I'll back the trailer up to the barn." Joe and Hank left Ruby and Mia alone.

"Did Joe bring the trailer because he knew you were gonna let me get a horse today?" Mia asked.

"I wanted to be prepared in case you saw one you liked."

"Why are you letting me have a horse?"

"Because you've proven that you're responsible enough to care for one." *And I'm trying to show you that I respect the young woman you're becoming.*

"What happens if we move?"

"Wherever we go, Poke goes."

Mia gave her another hug, and Ruby savored the sweet feeling of knowing she'd made her daughter happy.

Chapter 21

"Am I doing it wrong?"

Stony's deep chuckle pissed Ruby off. Her new employer sat on his butt with his boots propped on a table, his golden eyes watching her sweep the floor.

"Or maybe you just like staring at my boobs."

"You got your mama's figure, all right."

As long as the only things she shared with her birth mother were the woman's looks and big bosom, Ruby could live with that. She set aside the broom, then sprayed cleaner across the top of a table and wiped the stickiness away.

An hour had passed since she'd arrived at the Possum Belly and not one customer had walked through the door. "Why are you open on Sundays if no one comes in here to drink?"

"The men gotta go to church and repent before they start another week of boozing it up."

She pulled out a chair and sat across from him. "Enjoying yourself, aren't you?"

"What do you mean?"

"You're doing your best to make me feel uncomfortable."

He waggled his eyebrows. "Is it working?"

"Not a chance. Don't get your hopes up that I'll quit anytime soon."

Ruby thought she saw a glimmer of respect in his eyes, then decided she was mistaken. Men like Stony appreciated women for only one thing—sex.

"I'm surprised you came home after all these years."

"The Devil's Wind is not my home." What did she have to do to make people understand that?

"Touched a hot button, did I?"

"Stating a fact, is all. Hank never brought me to the ranch after I was born."

"I didn't realize that."

Why not? He and everyone else in this town acted as if they knew all about her past. "How old are you?"

"Why? You gotta thing for seasoned men?"

"Seasoned? Is that what they call middle-aged males these days?"

"Fifty-four."

"And you've lived in Oklahoma your whole life?"

"Grew up in Guymon. I bought the bar three years ago, after I quit the oil fields."

Ruby nodded. "Brothers or sisters?"

"An older half brother."

"He wouldn't by chance work in law enforcement, would he? I'm not happy with the way Sheriff Carlyle and Deputy Randall are handling the investigation into the vandalism at Hank's ranch."

"Heard you've had problems out there."

"I think Roy Sandoval is behind the trouble."

"Really?" Stony sat up straight. "Why's that?"

"After Hank got his pacemaker, Sandoval offered to buy him out."

"Sounds like something my brother would do."

Brother? "Your last name is Sandoval?"

"Davis. My mother had an affair with Benson Sandoval after his wife died. The old man refused to tie the knot with her after she became pregnant with me."

"What's the age difference between you and Roy?"

"Fifteen years."

"Maybe you can convince your brother to quit harassing Hank and leave the Devil's Wind alone."

"Can't help you there. Roy doesn't acknowledge my existence."

Ouch. Ruby finished cleaning the tables, then swept the pile of dirt across the floor, opened the door, and sent the clumps of dried mud flying. When she stepped outside to whisk the dirt into the street, she noticed Big Dan keeping company with the Indian statue outside his store. She waved, but he turned his head and stared off into space.

God, the men in this town were strange.

To pass the time Ruby dusted the liquor bottles behind the bar and washed shot glasses by hand. At four Stony turned on the sound system and country music rumbled through the speakers mounted on the walls. The first wave of muddy, smelly roughnecks flooded the bar, the men ignoring Ruby as they requested their drinks. While Stony filled the orders, she paid close attention to what each man was drinking.

"What's she doing here?" a guy the size of Paul Bunyan asked.

"Ruby's my new waitress." Stony's announcement quieted the crowd. "Treat her right or go somewhere else to drink."

She jutted her chin. "If you tip well, you won't go thirsty."

Paul Bunyan offered a yellow-toothed grin. "Okay, sister. You gotta deal."

Ruby set his empty shot glass in front of Stony. "He's drinking whiskey—Ten High." Her gaze traveled through the crowd. "I'm not your sister, mother, aunt, or girlfriend." She pointed to the shit-kicker at the end of the bar. She'd confiscated the old cowboy boot when she'd searched the utility closet for the spray cleaner. "If I fetch you a drink, you tip me."

A resounding "Yes, ma'am" reverberated through the group. The men resumed their conversations, and Ruby zigzagged among them, delivering drinks.

"Maybe I should hire a second waitress," Stony said when she called out for six more longnecks.

"You're smoking crack if you think any waitress can bring in drink orders like me." Ruby wasn't cocky—she was smart. She never asked a man if he wanted a refill. Instead, she delivered each drink with a smile and a hand on his shoulder. Rarely did a customer object to her VIP treatment or their growing tab. By the end of the evening, she'd earned the bar a lot of money and herself a nice bonus. She nodded to the cowboy boot, where dollar bills stuck out of the shaft. "It's almost full."

"You'll need a pair of ropers next time," he said.

"Speaking of next time." She glanced at the clock on the wall—six o'clock. "I'm done for the day."

"You're leaving already?" Stony asked.

"Yep." She wanted to check in on Poke and Mia and see how they were doing. She dumped her tips into her purse. "Maybe you'd like to change your mind about me coming in early to clean?" She pressed her lips together to keep from laughing at his grumpy face.

"Come in when you want. Take off when you want. I don't care."

"Okay, see you whenever." Ruby stood on the sidewalk for a full minute after leaving the bar in case one of the men followed her out, thinking he'd help himself to her tips. She had plans for the money—school clothes for Mia.

A shadow swept past the window of the mercantile, and without knowing why, she crossed the street and entered the store, almost bumping into Big Dan.

"You shouldn't carry all that money in your purse," he said.

The psychic had X-ray vision. "If this stupid town had a bank, I wouldn't have to haul my tips home and hide them under my mattress."

His gaze roamed over her. "You don't look any worse for wear."

She laughed. "Did you expect the men to behave like animals?" She curled her nose at the stuffed carcasses mounted on the wall. "Where did you get those things?"

"Souvenirs from my carnival days." He picked up an empty box. "I was stocking shelves."

Ruby pressed her hand to her chest, baffled by the odd sensation she experienced when she made eye contact with Big Dan. Had Cora felt the same pull around the man?

"Be right back." He disappeared through the doorway behind the checkout.

Her gaze shifted to the counter, where a handful of photos was strewn across the surface. She went to take a look.

Oh, my.

The town seer had a fetish for scantily clad blondes. Make that one blonde—the same woman was in every photo.

When Big Dan returned from the back room, Ruby held up a snapshot. "Old flame?"

"No." He climbed onto the stool behind the counter and opened his tobacco pouch. "That's your mother."

Ruby drew in a quiet breath and studied the images a little closer. Stony was right. She did look like Cora. Why had her mother posed for the photos? "Where did you get these?"

He selected the snapshot of Cora wearing red panties and a matching bra. "Your mother gave me the photos for safekeeping. She didn't want Hank to see them."

"Why not?"

"She was afraid he'd throw them away." Big Dan cleared his throat. "Cora and I became friends." He shrugged. "We were both misfits in this town of brawny beefcakes, and we understood each other."

Ruby eyed the black fishnet stockings attached to a red garter belt. She'd always wanted to buy herself trashy lingerie, but there had never been enough money.

"You two have the same hair color," he said.

True. Her mother's hair appeared as wavy and thick as Ruby's. Since Big Dan was willing to discuss Cora and Hank hadn't opened up much about her, Ruby asked, "How old was she when these were taken?"

He flipped over a photo. "This one says seventeen."

Seventeen? Ruby had been pregnant with Mia at that age.

"She's twenty-eight in this one." Big Dan held out the photo. Still beautiful, still slim. No visible baby pouch. "What age was she when she had me?"

"Thirty-six or thirty-seven. She was younger than Hank by a few years."

"Who took these pictures?"

"Probably one of the girls at the ranch."

"What ranch?"

"The Love Ranch Cathouse in Crystal, Nevada."

"Cora worked in a brothel?"

"Thought you knew."

Good Lord. Her mother had been a prostitute.

"Why would she keep these if she was starting a new life with Hank?"

"Cora came down here and tried to be someone else, but I think she felt lost and maybe a little scared. The snapshots reminded her of home. A place where she was accepted."

Maybe after watching his mother turn tricks, Hank had sympathized with Cora's plight and offered her a way out of the profession. Still, Ruby thought it was odd that he'd been attracted to a woman who sold her body for money.

And what about Ruby's parents? Had they known about Cora's background? Maybe Cheryl Baxter had mentioned it in her diary.

It was bad enough Ruby had to worry that her parents hadn't loved her as much as they might have had she been their biological daughter, but now she wondered how they could have loved her at all knowing she'd inherited the genes of a prostitute.

"Was everyone in town aware of Cora's profession?"

"She didn't brag about it, if that's what you're asking."

Since when was whoring something to boast about? "But the men found out."

Big Dan nodded.

Ruby had gone through her share of boyfriends, but at least she'd felt *something* for them before she'd jumped into their beds. Had Cora loved Hank—really loved him—or had he been nothing more than her ticket to a new life?

Do you care?

Yes, she did care. Even though she'd been given up after birth, it would be nice to know she'd been conceived in love.

"Hank must have taken flack for being with a woman like Cora."

"Some."

"Was she faithful to Hank?"

"Tried to be."

Empathy for Hank filled Ruby. If he hadn't handed her over to the state, how would she have survived her mother's reputation in a town like Unforgiven? Suddenly it was easier to forgive Hank for leaving her behind than to forgive him for not tracking her down until he'd become old and ill.

"Who did Cora have an affair with?"

"Roy Sandoval."

Nice neighbor.

"I thought Roy might have been trying to shame Hank into selling the Devil's Wind," Big Dan said.

"And Hank forgave her?" It might have taken Ruby a while to see the light, but at least she'd screwed up the courage to finally shut the door in Dylan's face after she'd accepted that he'd only wanted money and sex and not a permanent place in her and Mia's lives.

"Things were never good between Roy and Hank, but they grew worse when Hank found out about the affair."

Big Dan dipped his head, and the shiny bald spot spattered with freckles glinted in the overhead lights. "Did you sleep with my mother?" Ruby asked.

"It wasn't like that between us." He gathered the photos, plucking the one from Ruby's fingers and then dropping them into a Priority Mail envelope and shoving it into the drawer.

One more question before she left. "Did Cora run off with a secret lover after I was born?"

"Don't know. She never said goodbye." Big Dan's eyes glistened. Cora's departure had blown a hole in his heart—one that rivaled Hank's.

Her mother had left behind a trail of broken hearts as she'd made her way through life, and Ruby hated the thought that she might have more in common with her birth mother than she'd first believed.

Chapter 22

Ruby left the mercantile and got into Hank's truck. At the four-way stop she remembered she wanted to check in with the sheriff, so she made a U-turn and parked at the end of the block near the jail. Leaving the engine running, she went inside. The front office and the holding cell were empty. "Anyone here?"

The sheriff's door opened, and the instant he saw her, the smile slid off his face. "Ruby."

"Sheriff." She didn't waste her breath on pleasantries. "Any idea yet who shot at my daughter?"

"We're still interviewing people."

"Which people?" She'd like to know the names of those suspected of foul play.

"That's confidential. I'll call Hank as soon as we have any news."

"In case you haven't heard," she said, "I'm working at the saloon. I'll keep my ears open for any gossip about the Devil's Wind." There was a chance one of the roughnecks might drink too much and let something slip.

"You're staying, then?" The muscle along his jaw bunched.

"I'm worried about Hank's safety, and I'm not leaving until you've caught whoever's responsible for all these incidents."

"I don't believe Hank's in any danger."

"You better be right." She left the jail and drove back to the ranch. After she parked in the yard, Joe signaled to her from the backyard. The lines across his brow deepened, and she picked up the pace.

"What's wrong? Is Mia okay?"

"She's fine."

Right then Mia walked Poke out of the barn and waved at Ruby as she led the pony to the corral where Hank waited.

"Why the frown?" she asked.

Joe shoved his fingers through his sweaty hair. "How come you didn't tell me you'd gotten a job at the Possum Belly?"

Actually, it hadn't occurred to her to inform him. She didn't think he cared where she worked. "I guess I forgot."

He stared into the distance, his shoulders stiff, hands clenched. Then his gaze swung back to her. "It's a rough place for a woman to work."

Her heart tripped, then picked itself up and raced inside her chest. Was he worried for her safety, or more worried one of the roughnecks would make a play for her?

He opened his mouth to speak, then changed his mind and walked off. Halfway to the barn, he stopped and turned, his long strides bringing him back to her.

"What is it?" she asked.

"I'd finally gotten used to the idea of being alone the rest of my life, and then you and Mia showed up. Watching you two and Hank work things out reminds me of what it was like to have a family."

The intensity of his brown-eyed stare sent a jolt through Ruby.

"I don't know what's happening with me. And it doesn't seem to matter that I don't *want* this."

"Want what?"

"Want to care about you."

Ruby's pounding heart insisted she was attracted to Joe and interested in seeing what developed between them. But caring was a big step. That involved trust, and it was way too soon to place any faith in him.

"I've been hollow inside for so long I didn't expect to miss the emotional mess that comes with being part of a family. But you, Mia, and Hank have me thinking twice about wanting to live on the outskirts of people's lives."

Emotions were messy. She wasn't ready to go that far with Joe. What if she screwed up again? He'd suffered enough pain after losing his son and wife. She didn't want the responsibility of protecting his heart when she could barely protect her own.

"I admire you for trying to work things out with Hank." His feet shuffled, kicking up dust. "You want to forgive him, but you don't know how."

So much for believing she'd successfully hidden her feelings from others.

"And you're not giving up on your daughter. It takes guts to watch Mia grow closer to Hank when you wish it was you."

She appreciated that he recognized what she was up against. Most days she felt like a one-man army waging a battle to gain a foothold with Mia and Hank. "What are you asking of me?"

"I'm worried about your safety and I don't want you to work at the bar."

"I can handle myself."

"Maybe, but what if a drunk cowboy gets out of line?" He nodded to the corral. "What are they supposed to do if something happens to you?"

Feeling cornered, she lashed out. "I'm not your responsibility."

"I know that, Ruby." He inched closer. "But I want to be someone you can lean on. If you'll let me."

Ruby had no experience depending on anyone but herself. Joe was asking a lot—could she deliver? The ranch was where she, Mia, and Hank were working out their issues. But what if it was also the right place and this was the right time for her and Joe to explore a relationship?

What if he was *the one* who wouldn't leave her behind?

"Okay."

"Okay what?" he asked.

"I'm not quitting my job at the bar, but I accept your invitation to be there for me."

Joe brushed his mouth across hers in a quick kiss. Then he walked off with a smile on his face.

She waited for the doubts to creep in and change her mind, but they never materialized. Feeling proud of herself, she went into the house and was met in the kitchen by Hank and Mia. She hadn't noticed the pair go inside while she and Joe talked.

"How was work, Mom?"

Ruby upended her purse on the table and all her tips spilled out.

"Holy moly, that's a lot of one-dollar bills." Mia began counting them.

"Since I have a job, I'll pay you an allowance to help Hank with chores."

"How much?"

"A hundred dollars a week."

Mia's eyes lit up. "Seriously?"

"You're going to need money to care for Poke and to put toward school clothes."

"Hank said he'd buy my clothes." Mia separated the bills into ten-dollar piles.

"I can afford to buy my daughter clothes, Hank."

"Thought you might want to save for a car," he said.

She needed transportation, no doubt about that. Hank offering to help with the cost of Mia's wardrobe would allow Ruby to save for a vehicle. But she'd wanted Mia to understand that she'd taken the job in town so she could support her daughter—not so she could buy *herself* a new car.

"Hank said there's a carnival next weekend. Can we go?" Mia asked.

"Unforgiven has a carnival?"

"Halfway between the ranch and Guymon," Hank said.

"Please, Mom."

"Sounds like fun. I'll leave work early on Friday."

"Joe's gonna help me give Poke a bath." Mia ducked out of the house.

"You have to stop this, Hank," Ruby said.

"Stop what?" Gnarled fingers gripped the coffeepot tighter as he poured the remaining inch of sludge down the kitchen sink.

"Trying to get one up on me with Mia."

He gave her a blank look.

"If I'm going to get back on better footing with my daughter, I can't have you doing all these nice things for her, like paying for school clothes and new bedroom furniture."

"If you don't want me to buy her clothes, say so."

"Okay, I don't want you to buy her clothes." Why was everything so trying between them?

"How was work?" He filled the pot with fresh water.

It took a few seconds for her brain to switch gears. "I said it was fine."

"Stony treat you right?"

"He didn't step out of line, if that's what you're asking." Hank's hand shook when he lifted the pot, so she took it from him and poured the fresh water into the reservoir. "You add the coffee grounds." Once he did that, she flipped the switch. "I learned something interesting about my new boss."

"Oh?" He removed two mugs from the cupboard.

"He's Roy Sandoval's half brother." Hank didn't seem impressed with the information. "Do you know who Stony's mother is?"

He shook his head and sat at the table. He wasn't interested in the bar owner, so she changed the subject.

"I stopped at the mercantile before I left town." She rubbed her achy calves. "How come you never mentioned that my mother worked in a brothel?"

"Big Dan should know better than to shoot off his mouth."

"Were you ever going to tell me?" Maybe he hadn't wanted her to learn about Cora's past. The timer beeped on the pot. Ruby waved Hank back to his seat and filled their mugs, then waited until he took his first sip before talking.

"Big Dan didn't tell me about her profession. I came across photos of her wearing skimpy lingerie."

Hank's gaze flew to hers. "What photos?"

"Pictures taken of her when she was younger. She gave them to Big Dan for safekeeping." Ruby blew on her coffee.

"Don't think poorly of your mother. She did what she had to in order to survive."

Until Hank in his dusty armor rescued her.

"Cora was very beautiful. I can see where you'd be attracted to her, but I don't understand how you could want to be with a prostitute after growing up with a mother who sold herself to men." *Then ran off with one of her clients, leaving you behind.*

"I didn't know she was a prostitute when I met her."

Ruby held her tongue and allowed Hank to take his time explaining.

"I pulled off the highway for gas in Crystal, Nevada. Cora was sitting outside in the hot sun. She looked tired and thirsty. I bought her a Coke." He stared across the room as if watching their first meeting unfold live before his eyes. "I offered to give her a ride and she accepted."

"Where did you go?" Ruby asked when he didn't elaborate.

"Spent the rest of the day driving around. We stopped for lunch at a country store. Sat on the tailgate of my truck and ate sandwiches. Ended up putting a hundred miles on the pickup that day. Then it got dark and we pulled off the highway to gaze at the stars."

Their day sounded romantic, and she had trouble reconciling a much younger Hank with the one sitting across the table from her. Then again, thirty-one years of being alone would change anyone.

"Cora said it was time for her to go home and I asked if I could take her out again. She said I wouldn't want to after I found out where she lived."

"The Love Ranch Cathouse," Ruby said.

He nodded. "I was disappointed that she worked there."

"I still don't understand why you wanted anything to do with her."

"When I dropped her off at the Cathouse, she had the same haunted look in her eyes that had been in my mother's every time we walked into our motel room."

Hank hadn't asked for Ruby's sympathy, but it was difficult not to feel empathy for him.

"I invited her to live with me at the ranch and promised to take care of her."

Hank had wanted to do for Cora what he'd been too young to do for his mother—he'd wanted to rescue her.

"But she wasn't ready to leave the bawdy house." He rubbed his fist against his pacemaker.

All this talk about Cora was upsetting Hank. Still, she'd answered his summons, and that entitled her to the truth about her birth parents' relationship—even if the truth made him uncomfortable.

"After all you did for Cora, how can you keep loving her when she deserted you?" *And me.*

"You can't choose who you love, Ruby."

She didn't want to believe she had no control over the person she gave her heart to, but what if Hank was right? When Joe had said he cared for her, Ruby's gut instinct had been to flee. But she wasn't the same woman she'd been when she'd first arrived at the Devil's Wind. The closer she grew to Hank—and there was no use denying that she felt something for the old man—the less scared she was of a long-term commitment, which was a good thing, because she didn't want to end up like Hank—a dusty shell with a shattered heart.

Chapter 23

The greasy smell of funnel cakes and fried okra on a stick socked Ruby in the nose Friday night as she passed through the gates of the Texas County, Oklahoma, fair.

"Let's move before we're trampled." Joe grasped Ruby's hand and pulled her after him, bypassing the group of teens hanging out near the entrance. "What rides do you want to go on, Mia?" He nodded to the growing line at the ticket booth.

Ruby pulled money from her pocket and handed it to Joe. "See how many tickets fifty dollars will buy."

After Joe walked off, Mia opened her mouth, then snapped it shut.

"What is it?" Ruby asked.

"Nothing." Mia tugged Hank's shirtsleeve. "Will you go on the Ferris wheel with me?"

"I think I can handle that."

"What about you, Mom? Are you gonna go on any rides?"

"Nope," Ruby said, hurt that Mia didn't want to ride the Ferris wheel with her. "I'm more interested in eating funnel cake."

"Mom's got a sweet tooth."

"Me too." Hank flashed his gums. "That's the reason I'm missing half my teeth."

"A dentist will make you false teeth," Mia said.

"I don't care to have anyone stick their fingers in my mouth."

As Ruby listened to Mia and Hank's banter, she found it difficult to believe that only two weeks had passed since she and her daughter had arrived at the Devil's Wind. The emotional toll their visit was taking on Ruby made the fourteen days feel like fourteen months.

"The concert's at ten o'clock," Hank said. "We'll want to get out of here before then."

Fine by Ruby. She could use a decent night's sleep before she went into work tomorrow. "Let's meet back here at nine." She caught her daughter's eye. "Text me if *anything*"—meaning if *Hank*—"happens."

Mia nodded in understanding.

"Here you go." Joe handed Mia a roll of tickets.

"That's more than fifty dollars' worth," Ruby said.

"I bought a few extra." He tore off a strip and said, "In case you and I want to go on any rides."

"Have fun, you two." Ruby meandered off, and Joe followed her.

"Are you okay?" he asked.

"Why wouldn't I be?"

"You seem upset."

"I am." They got in line at the cake stand. "Mia and I always ride the Ferris wheel together, but Hank won the honor tonight."

Joe's hand slid inside hers, and he gave her fingers a gentle squeeze. "You're a good mother, Ruby."

No one had ever said that to her before. "Nice of you to think that, but—"

"I don't think it. I know it. Even though you and Mia are going through a tough time, she wouldn't test you the way she does if she didn't trust that you love her."

Trust that you love her. How was it that a fourteen-year-old knew more about trusting another person than a thirty-one-year-old?

"If my son were alive today, I'd hope he'd feel secure enough in my love for him that he could challenge me the way Mia's challenging you." Joe's gaze shifted to the big wheel turning circles behind them.

She slid her arm through his. "You rode the Ferris wheel with Aaron, didn't you?"

"Yes." They moved forward in line. "Melanie was afraid of heights."

Had Ruby known the carnival would bring back painful memories for Joe, she wouldn't have coaxed him to come along. He stepped up to the window and ordered a funnel cake and a bottle of water. Ruby let him pay.

"Thanks." She tore off a piece of the sweet dough and offered it to him. They ambled past the gaming booths, stopping to watch a little girl toss Ping-Pong balls into goldfish bowls filled with colored water.

"My parents took me to the 4-H fair every year," Ruby said.

"Mia mentioned her grandparents died in a car wreck."

"It was the craziest thing. My father made a living driving a long-haul truck, and he and my mother ended up getting killed in a head-on collision with a semi that crossed the center line."

"How old were you?"

"Eighteen. Mia was three months."

"That must have been rough."

"It was." But she'd had help from her mother's hair clients. Several ladies had volunteered to babysit Mia while Ruby worked. Then, when Mia turned two, Ruby left her with a friend who ran a daycare in her house. Ruby had been so exhausted from work and taking care of a toddler that she hadn't had time to properly mourn her parents' deaths. "What about your folks. Are they alive?"

"My father died of cancer before Aaron was born. I'd like to believe he's looking after my son." Joe watched his feet as they walked. "That is, if there is a heaven."

Heaven. Aside from baptizing Mia in the First Congregational Church, Ruby hadn't spent much time pondering religion. Her mother had placed a cross above the door inside their mobile home, but they'd attended church services only on Christmas Eve and Easter Sunday. When Ruby entered middle school, they'd stopped going to Sunday services altogether.

"I've never been a religious man." Joe placed his hand against her back and guided her away from a group of teens congregating in the middle of the runway. "But after Aaron died, I needed to believe that he was still a breathing, thinking, feeling . . . being. I couldn't wrap my head around the fact that he didn't exist anymore."

She understood. Only in death would Ruby find out if she'd be reunited with her adoptive parents. If there was life after death—a meet-and-greet somewhere above the clouds—then she'd ask her folks why they hadn't told her she'd been adopted.

Read the diary. Ruby would never know if her mother had written about her adoption unless she opened the journal. "What about your mother, Joe?"

"She lives with my sister and her husband on their farm in Nebraska."

"How often do you see your family?"

"I talk to my mom once a month and I spend a few days with them at Christmas."

They left the games behind and took a path that led to the carnival sideshows. She pointed to a sign outside one of the colored tents. "We can see the world's hairiest man or"—she wagged her finger at the red canvas—"have our fortunes told."

"How about neither."

"Don't be a chicken." She stopped in front of the red tent. "Let's have our palms read."

"No, thanks. The last time I went to a fortune-teller, she said I'd marry Becky Montrose."

"When was that?"

"Fifth-grade spring-fling fund-raiser at school."

Ruby laughed. "Who did Becky end up marrying?"

"My best friend."

"Really?"

"Jared and Becky dated their senior year of high school, then got hitched right after graduation."

"Do you mind waiting for me?" she asked.

"Don't forget I warned you." He released her hand when the tent flap opened and two giggling teenage girls stepped into view.

"I've been expecting you, Ruby." Big Dan wore a black cape and a purple turban on his head.

Why wasn't she surprised that Unforgiven's soothsayer worked at the fair? "I thought your days as a carnie were behind you."

"I have friends who travel with this company and they invite me to perform every summer."

"How did you know I'd be here?" She hadn't told Stony her plans for the night.

"Everyone loves a carnival." He held open the curtain.

Ruby glanced at Joe. "Still want to sit this one out?"

"Yep. Have fun."

She slipped inside the tent, where two oscillating fans moved the air around. Big Dan lowered the flap, then nodded to the table covered in white fabric. A shiny crystal ball and a deck of tarot cards awaited Ruby. She pulled out a chair and he sat across from her.

He pushed the ends of his cape aside. "Give me your hand."

She rested her forearms on the table, palms facing up.

He gripped Ruby's fingers with his pudgy digits, then leaned over and studied her palms. Tiny puffs of air escaped his nose and tickled her skin. "The left hand shows potential and the right hand reveals what you've done with that potential." He peered up at her. "The left are the gifts God gives you. The right is what you do with those gifts."

Oh, brother.

"Your hands are clammy." His snowy eyebrows twitched. "Do I make you nervous?"

"No. It's hot in here."

"People with clammy hands are lazy and unstable but well intentioned."

She wasn't lazy. She'd been employed most of her adult life.

"You're a Pisces. Your zodiac element is water." He shook his head and the turban wobbled. "But your hands are air."

"I don't understand."

He ignored her and said, "You have rectangular palms with long fingers. And your skin is dry."

Of course it was dry—she had the hangnails to prove it. He tightened his grip. "You have toxic levels of nervous energy."

That didn't surprise her, seeing how her life had been no walk in the park.

"You hide your true feelings from others and you don't trust easily." His stare unnerved her. "And you have trouble with relationships."

Big Dan was creeping her out.

He traced a wrinkle that cut across her palm. "The head line is straight, which means you're practical and a realist."

Amen to that.

"But there's a circle in your head line."

She held her breath—so far his analysis of her personality was hardly flattering.

"You're experiencing an emotional crisis."

That was a no-brainer. Anyone could make that assumption if they knew she'd traveled to Oklahoma to confront her biological father. "What else can you see?"

"The heart line . . ." He made a clucking sound. "You're selfish when it comes to love, Ruby." He ran his finger across the skin below her pinkie. "The heart line breaks here."

"And that means what?"

"That you've suffered an emotional trauma in the past."

Ruby considered how her relationship with Glen Baxter had changed overnight and attributed that to the break in her heart line. If the falling-out with her adoptive father wasn't enough to sever the line completely, then learning she'd been adopted had finished the job.

"I'll read your life line and fate line together." He pulled in a deep breath. "The life line swoops in a generous curve, which means you're stronger than you think. This break"—he pressed down on her palm—"shows that you will experience a major change in your life."

Big deal. Life was all about changes. So far Ruby wasn't impressed with the seer's reading.

He flicked the tip of his finger over her jagged nail. "Short nails are not good."

She couldn't remember the last time her nails had been long—probably high school, when she'd dated Dylan.

"You're distrustful and sarcastic."

Darn, he was blunt.

But it was true. She was suspicious of every man that came into her life.

"Maybe I have good reason to be wary." She'd liked to see Big Dan walk a mile in her shoes.

"Cora never had a bad word to say about anyone."

"Yeah, Cora was perfect. So perfect she abandoned her baby." Ruby yanked her hands free and crossed her arms over her chest, as if the action would block Big Dan from seeing into her soul.

"We're not finished," he said.

She was tempted to end the session, but his compelling gaze kept her fanny glued to the chair and she gave him her hands again.

He frowned.

"Now what?"

"Your Venus mount is flat."

She smiled. "That sounds X-rated."

He didn't find her sense of humor amusing. "The flesh at the base of your thumb is level, not puffy, which means you have little or no interest in family."

"Now I know you're full of shit." *Family* was the reason Ruby had changed her plans and stopped in Unforgiven. *Family* was the reason she'd turned down the job in Elkhart and was serving drinks to a bunch of randy roughnecks at the Possum Belly Saloon. *Family* was the reason she was giving Hank a chance to be a father and a grandfather.

Big Dan tapped the area beneath her index finger. "This is even. You have no self-confidence."

Like an old-fashioned movie reel, all of Ruby's exes played through her mind.

He rubbed his thumb over the base of her middle finger. "I'm not surprised the skin is higher here." His gaze pinned her. "You're stubborn and you like being alone."

What did he mean—being alone? She'd never gone more than a couple of months between boyfriends. But if Big Dan referred to the fact that she'd rather keep her heart to herself, then she couldn't deny that.

"What do you see in here?" Ruby stretched her fingers toward the globe, but he blocked her hand.

"Do you have a question for the crystal ball?"

"Yeah. Who shot up Hank's stock tank and tried to scare my daughter?"

He rubbed his hand over the polished quartz and peered into the reflective glass. "My mother was a clairvoyant."

Of course he wouldn't answer her question. "Did she travel with a carnival?"

"No, but her grandmother did." He leaned forward, squinting at the ball. "I see a tree with lots of branches. And a mushroom."

Ruby didn't see a darn thing. "What does that mean?"

"Someone in your family needs your help. A mushroom has to feed on things and a person close to you may become dependent."

Hank. The old coot had waited until his twilight years to reveal himself and then expected Ruby to be there for him.

"There's a hammer, which indicates a need to build stability. Perhaps you began something in the past that you didn't finish."

What had she started, then stopped? *The diary*.

"A bird is flying to the right—the right means the future."

"Where's the bird going?"

"It's circling the tree. It can't make up its mind."

Kind of like Ruby hovering over the Devil's Wind, uncertain which direction to go in next.

"The sailboat means you need to have a heart-to-heart with someone close to you. You can't move on with your life until this talk takes place."

Big Dan's reading was nothing more than a hoax—a way for him to encourage Ruby to patch things up with Hank. But why did he care? Did he believe Cora would want her to forgive Hank? "I've heard enough." She tossed a five-dollar bill down, then left the table.

"Ruby."

Her fingers clutched the tent flap.

"What you want in life may not be what you need."

Chapter 24

Good grief. If Ruby had wanted a therapy session she'd have gone to a shrink, not a fortune-teller. When she stepped outside the tent, Joe emerged from the shadows.

"How did it go?" he asked.

"Be glad you didn't have your palms read."

"That bad?"

She reached for his hand, unclear if she needed reassurance or if she just wanted to touch him. Maybe a little of both. "I won't bore you with the details."

Joe leaned in and whispered, "Did he predict anything about your love life?"

"I don't have a love life."

His lips brushed her ear, and she shivered. "Maybe we can change that."

"Don't make promises you can't keep."

"Nothing I like better than a challenge."

If she had to pick one adjective to describe herself, it would be *challenging*. "Want to check out the fun house?" She needed a good laugh after the depressing reading. Big Dan was a master at cutting people down to his size.

They made their way to the fun house, which was located at the end of game alley. The line was short, and Ruby wished the wait was longer, especially when Joe stood behind her with his hands on her hips.

"The ride operator looks bored to death," Ruby said. And as old as Hank. A high-pitched scream rent the air, followed by loud laughter.

"He's probably deaf; that's why they put him in charge of the fun house." Joe handed the operator their tickets when they reached the front of the line.

"No food or drink allowed." The man opened the gate, and Ruby stepped onto the platform first. "Keep moving along. Don't want a traffic jam in there."

She climbed the swaying stairs, stumbling once. Joe gave her a gentle nudge onto the landing. "Thanks."

"My pleasure," he whispered in her ear.

She baby-stepped across the moving ramp, laughing when Joe lost his footing and stumbled to one knee. "Not too coordinated, are you?"

"Make fun of me all you want." He swatted her fanny playfully. "Your turn is coming." Sooner than Ruby expected.

When she walked around the next corner, the floor dipped and she landed on her butt, legs sticking up in the air. Joe hauled her to her feet, then tucked her close to his side as they crossed the suspension bridge.

"My superhero." She smiled at him.

When their feet touched solid ground, he said, "I'm no Captain America, Ruby."

"I'll be the judge of that." She stood on tiptoe and kissed him. Not a chaste kiss, but an open-mouth-taste-of-tongue exchange that left them both breathing hard.

He brushed his finger across her cheek. "It's been a long time since a woman kissed me like that."

"Really?"

"Yes, ma'am." Joe led the way to the barrel of love. It took several tries, but eventually they kept pace with the turning cylinder. "We make a great team."

It had taken a coordinated effort to keep moving without falling—perhaps a signal that it was time Ruby stopped believing she had to do everything on her own. If she found the courage to allow herself to connect with Joe on a deeper level, maybe the trust part would come naturally. "Wanna see if we can kiss without falling?"

He pressed his mouth to hers, but the kiss lasted only a moment before their feet tangled and their arms windmilled.

"Try again." Ruby pursed her lips, but before Joe's mouth touched hers, she pitched forward. Clutching a fistful of his T-shirt, she pulled him down with her as she fell. Laughing, they tumbled on top of each other, body parts bumping in places that hadn't been touched in a long while. After several unsuccessful attempts to stand, Joe set his hands against her rump and pushed her toward the opening. Ruby crawled from the barrel and he landed on top of her.

They ended their adventure in the hall of mirrors, laughing at their three-foot-wide images before they left the fun house and found Hank and Mia waiting in line.

The last thing the geezer needed was a busted hip to go along with his pacemaker. "Hank's too old for the fun house," Ruby said.

Joe pointed to the games. "I'm pretty good at throwing a baseball."

"Can you win me a stuffed animal?" Mia asked.

"I'll give it a try." The group walked over to the milk-bottle toss and the operator handed Joe three softballs. "Knock 'em all down and you win the giant panda." He waved a hand at the humongous bears hanging on the sides of the tent.

Joe threw all three balls but only two bottles fell from the pyramid.

Mia laughed. "You suck, Joe."

"Sorry, kid. I tried."

"Bet I can knock 'em over." Hank handed the man more money and picked up the first softball. "Everyone watching?"

Amused, Ruby said, "Our eyes are glued to you."

He wound up his arm like an airplane propeller, clearly hamming it up for his granddaughter. He let the first softball fly. It slammed against the sweet spot in the middle of the stack and the wooden bottles exploded into the air, tumbling off the stand.

Joe stuck his fingers into his mouth and whistled.

"You did it, Grandpa! You did it!" Mia hugged Hank.

The blood drained from Ruby's face. Mia had called Hank *Grandpa*—and in the process had sealed Ruby's fate. The question wasn't where Hank would fit into her and Mia's relationship but where Ruby would fit into theirs.

"You want the panda, kid, or something else?" the operator asked.

"The black teddy bear. It matches the zebra-print border in my room."

The game attendant handed Hank the bear and he turned it over to Mia. She hugged the stuffed animal, then balanced the bear on top of her head and danced in a circle.

"We should get out of here before the concert begins," Joe said.

"Can I get a soft pretzel?" Mia asked.

They stopped at a concession stand near the gates and purchased drinks and snacks for the drive home. As they crossed the parking lot, Ruby noticed that Hank was moving a lot slower than he had earlier in the evening. He'd probably pushed himself too hard—not that it mattered. The look on his face after Mia had called him Grandpa made all his aches and pains worth it.

Joe got behind the wheel, and Ruby found a country music station on the radio. Ten minutes into the drive, Mia rested her head against the teddy bear and slept. Then Hank's snores filled the cab.

Joe glanced at Ruby. "I had a good time tonight."

"Me too." She'd been envious of her daughter and Hank going off together at the carnival, but she was proud of herself for stepping aside and allowing them to have fun. And it wasn't as if she hadn't enjoyed herself with Joe. The last time she'd acted so silly had been back in high school before Mia was born.

It was almost eleven p.m. when they drove beneath the entrance to the Devil's Wind. The bumpy road woke the backseat passengers, and Mia yawned loudly. "I get first dibs on the bathroom," she said.

"Something's not right." Ruby leaned forward and peered through the windshield when Joe parked in front of the house.

"What's got you spooked?" Hank said.

Ruby's gaze moved from the steps to the chairs on the porch to . . . The screen door was partially open. "I know I closed the door all the way when we left this evening."

"Stay here." Joe unsnapped his seat belt.

"Hank's shotgun is in the umbrella stand at the bottom of the stairs," Ruby said.

"No, it's not. I put it under my bed."

"Why'd you do that, Grandpa?"

"If someone breaks in while we're sleeping, I can protect you and your mother."

"Did you lock the door when we left?" Joe asked.

Ruby nodded.

"The horses," Mia said.

"I'll check on them after I look around inside the house." Joe climbed the porch steps. When he turned the knob, the door swung open.

"I knew it," Ruby whispered. "Someone broke in." She left the pickup, listening for sounds of a confrontation. She didn't know how much help she'd be if Joe got into a scuffle with a burglar, but she could smash the umbrella stand over the intruder's head if she had to.

The lights inside the house came on and Joe stepped outside, almost bumping into Ruby. "Coast is clear."

She signaled to Mia and Hank and then all three entered the house. Nothing appeared disturbed.

"They probably gave up when they discovered I don't hide my money in the house." Hank grabbed ahold of the stair banister, but Ruby's voice stopped him on the second step.

"Who opened the hall closet before we left?"

"Not me," Joe said.

"Me neither," Mia answered.

Ruby looked at Hank and he backpedaled down the steps, then peered inside the closet. "It's gone."

"What's gone?" Ruby asked.

"The cash box on the shelf."

"I thought you didn't keep money hidden in the house," Ruby said.

"I don't."

"Then why would you hide a cash box in plain view?"

"It's not in plain view if the door's closed."

"What was in the box?" Mia asked.

"My oil papers."

"The leasing agreement between you and Petro Oil?" Joe asked.

Hank nodded.

"Better check your other valuables," Ruby said.

"I don't have other valuables."

"Are you sure you haven't hidden money somewhere in the house?" A man his age was entitled to forget a few things.

"Petro Oil deposits my monthly stipend into my bank account." Hank climbed the stairs. "I'm going to bed."

"You need to call the sheriff and report the break-in," Ruby said.

Hank paused on the landing. "The next time you work at the bar you can talk to Sheriff Carlyle."

Just what she looked forward to—another productive chat with the lawman.

"Stop by Petro Oil and ask for a copy of my lease." Hank went into the bathroom, closing the door behind him.

Mia slumped on the stairs. "Guess Grandpa doesn't know what 'first dibs' means."

Chapter 25

"I'll take a look outside and make sure whoever helped themselves to Hank's oil papers didn't decide to hang around," Joe said.

"Can I go with you?" Mia asked.

"You better stay here with your mom." Joe left through the front door.

"It's kind of creepy that a stranger was in the house." Mia hugged the black teddy bear. "Mom?"

"What?"

"We had fun tonight, didn't we?"

"Yes, we did." Ruby sat next to Mia on the stairs and brushed a strand of hair off of her forehead. That her daughter didn't jerk away made up for Mia not asking her to ride the Ferris wheel with her.

"We should do more fun stuff with Hank and Joe."

"Maybe we will." Ruby waited with Mia until they heard Hank's bedroom door close.

"Guess it's my turn to use the bathroom." Mia stood. "Will you please check on Poke for me?"

"I'll do that right now." Ruby left the house, then cut through the yard to the barn. "Joe? Are you in here?"

He came out of the storage room. "Whoever broke into the house opened the stall doors before they left."

"Are the horses okay?" Mia would be inconsolable if one of her beloved pets had been harmed.

"They're fine."

"I'm glad they didn't escape," she said.

"The old nags have it good here. They're too smart to run off."

"Joe?"

"What?"

"I'm worried for Mia's and Hank's safety. Do you think we're in real danger?"

"No." He slid his arm around Ruby's shoulders, then pulled her close.

"It's obvious whoever is doing this wants Hank to sell," she said.

"They'll give up when they realize they can't push him off his land."

Ruby peered past him. "Where's Friend?"

"Snoozing on my cot." His gaze traveled over her face, his eyes softening. "I enjoyed being with you tonight."

"Me too." She kissed his prickly cheek. "I'll take Friend into the house. He can sleep with Mia." She entered Joe's quarters and flipped on the light. The dog lay curled on the bed, loud snores escaping his snout. Some watchdog. Joe had shoved the cot against the wall, and a battery-operated lantern sat on a hay bale that served as a nightstand.

"All the comforts of home," she said. What a pair they made.

He'd left his home years ago. Ruby was in search of a new home. And they'd both ended up at the Devil's Wind.

Friend opened one eye.

"C'mon, ugly mutt. I'll take you to your master."

The dog jumped off the bed, trotted past Ruby and out of the barn. "I swear that canine is smarter than he lets on." She turned to leave, but Joe blocked her path. He looked as if he wanted to say something right before he brushed his mouth over hers. "Sweet dreams, Ruby."

Her dreams would definitely be sweet tonight. Back inside the house, Ruby led Friend to the foyer. "Mia's up there." After the dog climbed the stairs, she went into the kitchen, drank a glass of water, and then got ready for bed.

She lay in the darkness, listening to the frogs croak and the crickets chirp. Her thoughts drifted to Joe. How had he known his kind words and reassurances had been exactly what she'd needed tonight? In the back of her mind, Ruby had always believed she'd fallen short in her parenting abilities, but maybe she wasn't giving herself enough credit. Despite her mistakes, she and Mia had made it this far together. There was no reason to doubt Ruby would find a way to forgive Glen Baxter. Forgive Hank. Forgive Mia.

And maybe even forgive herself.

"Mom?" Mia appeared in the doorway. "Are the horses okay?"

"They're fine. I thought you were sleeping; otherwise I would have told you."

Mia crawled beneath the covers.

"What's wrong with your new bed?"

"Friend's hogging my pillow and his breath stinks."

Ruby smiled into the dark.

"I'm worried about Grandpa."

"So am I."

"Do you think the person who broke into the house wants to hurt him?"

"Joe says they'd have done so already if that was their goal."

"I'm glad Joe's here. He won't let anything happen to Hank." Mia wiggled into a more comfortable position. "Mom?"

"What?"

"Are you mad that I called Hank 'Grandpa'?"

Ruby's throat tightened. She wished she knew why it was so easy for Mia to love the old man but so hard for her. "I'm not mad."

"I think he liked winning the bear for me." Mia propped her head on her hand. "Did my dad ever win me anything when I was little?"

"Not that I remember."

"You won me a goldfish at a carnival once."

"You were only four. I can't believe you remember that far back."

"Maybe we could see a movie next week," Mia said.

"That would be nice."

"I bet we could get Grandpa to go with us."

"I bet you're right." Hank would agree to a movie because he could sleep through it if he wanted.

"Besides the fun house, what else did you and Joe do?" Mia asked.

"I saw a fortune-teller."

Mia sat up and crossed her legs. "What did the gypsy lady say?"

"Big Dan was the gypsy lady."

"That's weird. Did you ask if we're going to live at the Devil's Wind forever?"

"You don't get to ask questions," Ruby fibbed. "The fortune-teller does all the talking."

"So what did Big Dan see when he read your palms?"

Too much of Ruby's character. "Nothing exciting."

"Oh."

Ruby waited for Mia to bring up the real reason behind her late-night visit. When she didn't, Ruby said, "Something's on your mind. What is it?"

"Grandpa wishes he had kept you after Cora left."

"Did he tell you that?"

"Not exactly, but—"

"Honey, it's okay. I've accepted that Hank couldn't raise me." But forgiving him was tricky. "Things worked out the way they were supposed to. If I hadn't been adopted, I wouldn't have lived in Missouri and I wouldn't have met your father and I wouldn't have had you."

"Sometimes I bet you wish you hadn't had me."

Ruby tickled her daughter. "You got that right."

"Stop!" Mia swatted Ruby's hands away.

After the giggling ended, Mia said, "It's okay if you want to be Joe's girlfriend."

It wasn't any surprise that Mia knew her mother and Joe were interested in each other.

"I like Joe," Mia said. "He's nice and he helps take care of Grandpa."

Any man who watched over her grandfather would be a winner in Mia's eyes.

"Do you like Joe, Mom?"

"Yes, I like him, but you shouldn't get your hopes up that it'll become a permanent thing."

"It doesn't matter. I have Grandpa now." Mia rolled onto her side, and a few minutes later soft snoring sounds drifted into Ruby's ear.

She and Mia were making progress. She and Hank were making progress and she and Joe were making progress. The only person Ruby wasn't making enough progress with was herself.

It was time to read the diary.

She would never be able to put the past behind her and move on until she learned what her parents really thought of their adopted daughter. If it wasn't what she hoped, then so be it. She'd focus on the future and only look forward. Now she just had to find the courage to follow through.

Saturday afternoon Ruby parked next to a patrol car in front of the jail and went inside. The place was deserted. Maybe the lawmen had stepped out to grab lunch. In no hurry to start her shift at the bar, she decided to wait. Her bottom had barely touched the seat of the chair across from the deputy's desk when a feminine giggle drifted from beneath the door of the sheriff's office.

The polite thing to do would be to leave, but Ruby was dying to know who the sheriff was entertaining—especially when women weren't welcome in town. A few minutes later the door opened and an attractive brunette with swollen lips and messy hair appeared. She froze when she saw Ruby.

"What's the matter, Leona?" Deputy Randall nudged his sex kitten out of the way, then stepped into view, his fingers fumbling with his pants zipper.

Ruby's gaze dropped to his open fly, and she quirked an eyebrow.

Avoiding eye contact with Ruby, Leona scurried out the door.

"What the hell are you doing here?" Randall glared at Ruby for a second, then returned to the boss's office.

Curious, she poked her head through the doorway and caught Randall picking up files scattered across the floor. He stacked them on the desk, then gathered the spilled pens and dropped them into a cup holder.

"Nice to know Hank's tax dollars are being put to good use," she said.

The deputy didn't have a chance to comment before the jail door opened and the sheriff escorted Leona back inside.

This ought to be interesting.

"Just took a phone call for you, Mike." Randall closed the sheriff's office door.

"Who was it?"

"Wrong number."

That was brilliant.

"Hello, Ruby." The sheriff nodded to the woman next to him. "This is my wife. Leona, this is Hank McArthur's daughter, Ruby Baxter."

The woman's eyes begged Ruby even as she smiled. "Nice to meet you."

"I thought you were heading out to Optima Lake," Randall said.

"On the way I got a call from Fish and Wildlife. They caught the guy who set the illegal traps." The sheriff nodded to his wife. "Good thing I wasn't needed out there or I'd have missed Leona's surprise visit."

If the sheriff had arrived a few minutes earlier, he would have received an even bigger surprise.

"We're going to grab a bite to eat at the diner. Can you handle things here?"

"Of course." Randall tapped a pen against the notepad on the desk.

The sheriff's eyes narrowed. "Everything all right, Paul?"

"Actually, it's not," Ruby said, amused by the alarmed look Randall and Leona exchanged. "I'm here to report a break-in at Hank's house."

"When?" the sheriff asked.

"Last night while we were at the carnival."

"Take Ruby's statement. I'll be back soon." The sheriff escorted his wife outside.

"Wow, you have some big cojones," Ruby said.

Randall glared at her. "How do you know someone broke into Hank's house?"

"Well, for one thing, the idiot left the screen door open. I shut it all the way before we took off for the evening."

"Anything else?"

"Yeah, the guy didn't shut the closet door, either, so naturally Hank looked in the hall closet, where he stores his cash box, and it was missing, along with his Petro Oil lease."

"What makes you think the culprit was a man?"

"Men don't pay attention to details." Her gaze flicked to the sheriff's door, then back to Randall. "You know it smells like sex in there, don't you?"

His face reddened.

"Men never think they'll get caught." Ruby enjoyed taunting Randall, especially since he'd proven he wasn't the helpful officer he'd portrayed himself to be when she'd first arrived in town. "Will you be filing a report?"

His eyes darted to the door behind him. "I'll take your statement later."

No doubt he was debating whether or not to fumigate the room with disinfectant spray before the sheriff returned with his wife.

"I intend to follow up with your boss about this, so you might want to at least call Sandoval and ask his whereabouts last night."

"You're barking up the wrong tree, Ruby."

Maybe, but Sandoval had not only offered to buy Hank out,

but the man had had an affair with Cora. And as long as the earth turned on its axis, men would do stupid things because of women.

"When did you say you were leaving Unforgiven?" Randall asked.

"I'm not."

Randall balled his hands into fists. "What do you mean, you're not?"

"Mia and I are staying indefinitely."

"That's a bad idea."

"Oh?"

He pointed out the window. "Working at the Possum Belly will cause problems with the oil workers and—"

"What? You and the sheriff might have to keep the peace in this town?" Ruby left the jail, closing the door hard enough to rattle the windows. She walked to the Petro Oil office.

"Hello, Ruby." A tall, balding man with a potbelly stepped from behind his desk and offered his hand. "Steward Kline. I've heard a lot about you."

Since she and Mia were the only females within shouting distance of the town, she wasn't surprised they were the topic of conversation. "I stopped by on Hank's behalf to ask for a copy of his lease."

"Why does he need a copy?"

"Someone broke into his house and stole the original one."

"I'll have to check with my supervisor before I print off a copy."

Ruby thought it strange that he didn't ask about the break-in or if anyone had been hurt. "I'm working at the saloon until ten tonight. You can drop off a copy there."

Ruby went outside and moved Hank's truck across the street. "Stony, I'm here!" she shouted when she entered the bar. "Stony?" She hung her purse on a hook, found the spray cleaner and a rag, then went to work wiping down the tables.

Ten minutes later Stony came through a side door that led from the Dumpster in the alley. "You're early." He grabbed a beer from the cooler and sat on the bar. "Heard you went to the carnival last night."

She exhaled loudly. "The men in this town act like a bunch of clucking hens."

He chuckled.

"If everyone knows we went to the carnival," she said, "then everyone must know that Hank's house was burglarized while we were gone."

Stony nodded. He'd probably heard about the break-in before she'd even left the jail.

"Don't know why anyone would want to rob Hank. The only thing worth any money on his ranch is the oil being pumped out of the ground."

"I'm certain Sandoval is behind this." She moved to the next table and cleaned the surface. "If your brother believes a piece of paper will make it easier for him to steal Hank's ranch, he's got a screw loose."

The saloon doors opened and the first rush of patrons pushed their way into the bar. Ruby didn't make eye contact with the men and their glances bounced off her. She and the roughnecks had struck a silent truce—she pretended to be invisible and they left generous tips in the shit-kicker.

The bar grew crowded and the hours passed in a blur. Ruby was considering quitting early when she heard someone call her name.

"Ruby Baxter!"

A hush fell over the room. She stepped from the shadows, where she'd just delivered a round of tequila shots to three rowdy cowboys. "I'm Ruby."

The man looked familiar. Then he removed his cowboy hat,

revealing a full head of steel-gray hair. *Sandoval.* Her first impression of him hadn't been wrong—he was an attractive older gentleman. His lean face was wrinkled like Hank's, but his height and broad shoulders made him appear younger and healthier. He dressed the part of a wealthy rancher—Western shirt with black pearl snaps, gray slacks, and freshly shined black boots.

No surprise that her birth mother had strayed. Even in his prime, Ruby doubted Hank could have measured up to Sandoval. The rancher pointed his Stetson at her. "I haven't touched a hair on Hank's head. Nor have I instructed my men to destroy his property. You've got no proof and no right to accuse me of any wrongdoing." He shoved the hat on his head and left the bar.

Ruby's gaze swung through the room. "Quit ogling me." Conversation resumed, and she kept busy delivering drinks. At nine the place cleared out.

"Where's everyone going?" she asked Stony after the last customer left.

"Next door. Once a month Dwayne sponsors a billiard tournament."

"Do you want me to take the trash out to the Dumpster?"

"I'll get it later." Stony poured a glass of cold tea and brought it to Ruby. "Sit down and take a break before you head home."

"Thanks." After she guzzled the liquid, she asked, "Did you happen to see Steward Kline come into the bar tonight?"

No sooner had Ruby spoken than Kline opened the saloon door. The oil agent sent Stony a quizzical look before handing Ruby an envelope. "A copy of Hank's lease." Kline left before she could thank him.

Ruby fetched her purse and collected her tips. "I won't be in tomorrow."

"Why not?"

"I want to spend time with my daughter." She skirted the tables.

"Hey, Ruby?"

"What?"

"Hank ever tell you why he and Sandoval don't get along?"

"It's obvious they both wanted the same woman."

Stony shook his head.

"Cora's not the only reason. You should ask him."

Maybe I will.

Chapter 26

Ruby turned the pickup onto the gravel road leading to the ranch house. The drive back from the bar took forever—too many jumbled thoughts racing through her mind. Unforgiven would make the perfect backdrop for a male-only soap opera—lies, cheating, deceit, corruption, intimidations, and grudges threatening to snuff out anyone who dared to challenge the status quo.

Well, screw that. It was only a matter of time before the male morons figured out Ruby Baxter didn't back down from a fight or scare easily.

Except when it came to relationships.

The headlights swept across the front porch and she caught a glimpse of Hank sitting in the chair. What was he doing up past his bedtime? She set the parking brake, then took her purse and got out of the pickup. At the bottom of the steps, she caught a whiff of tobacco smoke.

"I thought you were giving up cigarettes." She claimed the seat next to him and propped her sore feet on the rail.

"Tough habit to break." After one last drag, he flicked the butt over the rail and it landed in the dirt, the red embers winking in the dark like a bewitching siren.

"Where's Mia?" she asked.

"Listening to music in her room."

"And Joe?"

Hank looked sideways at Ruby. "Something going on between you two?"

"Maybe."

"Joe's a good man."

She knew that. "He's got a lot of baggage."

Hank's caterpillar eyebrows inched up his forehead. "You got a few suitcases in your closet, and the biggest bag is sitting right next to you."

Time to change the subject. "How did you end up owning the Devil's Wind?"

His shoulders stiffened. "Did someone tell you this place doesn't belong to me?"

"No, but Roy Sandoval came into the bar and insisted I stop spreading rumors that he's after your ranch." When Hank didn't comment, she pressed him. "If I'm inheriting this land, I deserve to know how you came by it."

He leaned forward and rested his forearms on his bony thighs. "I won the ranch in a poker game."

He might as well have told her it had dropped out of the sky and landed on his head. "You're joking, right?"

"I was thirty-six when I hired on as a wrangler for the Bar T. Roy and I rubbed each other wrong from the get-go."

No surprise that the son of a wealthy rancher would have nothing in common with a drifter like Hank, a man who hadn't even finished high school.

"I was a good poker player. Learned a few tricks from Mr. Charleston, one of my mother's regulars."

Without a male role model in his life, Hank would undoubtedly look up to any man who showed him attention.

"Mr. Charleston said I needed a way to support myself if I was ever on my own. When I was old enough to gamble, I spent my paychecks at the casinos, practicing tricks. One day I got wind of a high-stakes poker game Roy had signed up for, and I wanted in."

"Was Roy surprised when you sat down at the table?"

"He acted like he didn't know me."

"Don't keep me in suspense. What happened?"

Hank cleared the phlegm from his throat. "The pot grew, and one by one the players dropped out. Came down to me and Roy. I won."

Hank had beaten the boss's son. "But you cheated."

Cricket chirps filled the silence until Hank spoke. "I paid the dealer to turn a blind eye."

Ruby's stomach twisted. Just when she was opening her heart to him, he had to go and make it more difficult to trust him. "No one in the poker game accused you of cheating?"

"Roy did, but the dealer kept his mouth shut."

"How much was the pot worth?"

"Two hundred fifty thousand."

She whistled. "I'm guessing Roy's father didn't take the news well." Ruby had caused her parents plenty of grief growing up but had never committed an offense that had taken a chunk out of their pocketbook.

"Instead of paying me, Roy's father offered me a thousand acres of the Bar T. I put up a fence and called my side the Devil's Wind." He swept his hand in front of him. "The house and barn once belonged to Roy's grandparents. After they died, the place sat vacant until I moved in."

"Why would Benson Sandoval give you land with oil on it?"

"He'd had the property tested a decade earlier, but they didn't find enough oil and gas worth drilling for. Benson figured he was gifting me acres of worthless scrub."

"Did the oil company botch the tests?"

"No, but they didn't test all the land or Fury's Ridge."

"Because it's an Indian burial site?"

He nodded. "Benson didn't want to mess with it, but I wasn't afraid of ghosts. I gave Petro Oil permission to explore the ridge and the other areas. They struck pay dirt."

"Then why don't you have pump jacks on Fury's Ridge?"

"I got enough money coming in from the other ones. No need to be greedy."

Ruby mulled over the fact that her biological father was a cheat. If she accepted the Devil's Wind as her inheritance, did that make her a cheat, too?

She was no saint. There were days when the fridge in the trailer had been empty and she'd snuck food home from Carmen's Chicken Fry without paying for it so she and Mia wouldn't go to bed hungry. Other times she hadn't reported all of her tips to the boss, because she'd needed the extra money for cigarettes. And once she'd siphoned gas from her neighbor's car so she could make it to and from work.

But Mia had placed Hank on a pedestal and worshipped the ground he shuffled across. What would happen to that love if she learned her grandfather was a swindler? Part of Ruby—the part still jealous of Mia and Hank's closeness—wanted to expose him for the fraud he was, but she didn't dare. Ruby's relationship with her daughter might be on the mend, but bad-mouthing Hank would turn Mia against her. Besides, exposing his faults was just a cheap way for Ruby to get back at him for abandoning her. And since Hank had hinted to Mia that he wished he hadn't put Ruby up for adoption, no good could come from holding on to the hurt and anger.

"When we painted the nursery, you asked a lot of questions about my adoptive parents."

"Can't blame me for wanting to know who took care of my little girl."

Little girl sounded like an endearment. "My mother kept a diary, but I haven't read it."

His slumped shoulders straightened. "Why not?"

"I forgot about the journal until Mia and I"—Ruby mostly—"planned our move to Kansas."

"What's keeping you from reading it now?"

"Whatever my mother wrote isn't going to magically erase my anger at her and my father for not being honest with me about my adoption." And what if her mother confessed that she'd regretted adopting Ruby and wished she'd brought home a different baby girl?

"Maybe they had a good reason to keep your adoption a secret." Hank's stare pierced her—was he hoping she'd share the journal entries with him? Was he looking for redemption after choosing not to raise her—assurance that he'd made the right decision? What if neither of them found what they were looking for in the journal?

"Be right back." Ruby went into the house and fetched the diary from the nightstand, then returned to the porch and dropped the leather notebook in Hank's lap. "Since you're so nosy, you read it first." She'd taken a big step, trusting Hank with her mother's thoughts and allowing him a glimpse into the life he'd chosen for her. But it was best this way—she wouldn't feel pressured to pick and choose the details she believed he should know. He'd read the raw, uncensored version, and in doing so maybe he could help her see her way through the hurt and pain.

His gnarled fingers caressed the leather cover. "Did you get a copy of my oil lease?"

"I did." She removed the envelope from her purse and handed it to him.

"Turn on the porch light," he said.

She reached around the screen door and flipped the switch.

"The date's wrong," he said. "It says the lease terminates on September thirtieth of this year. It should be September 2050."

"Simple mistake?"

"Maybe." Hank didn't sound convinced.

"Does your lawyer have a copy of the original lease?" she asked.

"I didn't have a lawyer look over the paperwork before I signed it."

"What happens if they refuse to fix the date?"

"Then I'll lose my income."

"Will you be able to afford to keep the ranch if you don't have money coming in from the lease?" If the Devil's Wind went on the auction block, she and Mia would have no choice but to move somewhere else.

"I've got enough money in savings to keep this place going until . . ."

You die. "How much money do you have in the bank?"

"Little over a million."

A million dollars and he lived like a pauper. If there was ever a man who embodied the saying "Money doesn't make you happy," it was Hank McArthur. Ruby was positive he'd give away his fortune to bring Cora home.

She left him alone on the porch and retreated to her bedroom, where she sat in the dark, listening to the wind rustle the tree branches. When she'd first learned the ranch was her inheritance, she'd wanted nothing to do with the miserable place.

But a million dollars went a long way in saying *I'm sorry.*

Sunday morning Ruby pulled the string hanging from the naked bulb in the attic ceiling. Ever since she'd discovered Cora's trunk, she'd wanted to investigate the contents. The gold latches winked at her from the corner, beckoning her closer. The room was hotter than Hades, and sweat beaded across her brow.

Her mouth went dry when she knelt before the trunk. She knew what she wanted to find inside—something that would represent one single redeeming quality that Cora had passed down to her. She opened the lid—lace bras, panties, and corsets. The sexy material held Cora's secrets—maybe the ones she didn't want Hank to discover. Ruby buried her nose in a satin camisole, but there was no hint of perfume—just a musty smell.

Along with the photos of herself, Cora had left her costumes behind. Was she trying to outrun her past? Ruby pushed the clothing aside and found a pair of jeweled slippers. Tucked inside one of the shoes was a velvet pouch. She dumped the contents on the floor and stared at the earrings and bracelet that matched the teardrop ruby around her neck.

Now she knew why Hank had asked where she'd gotten the necklace when she'd first arrived at the ranch—he'd known it had belonged to Cora.

If only she understood what had been going through Cora's mind the day she'd fled the hospital. Maybe then Ruby could make sense of every wrong turn she'd made in life.

She placed the jewelry back in the pouch, then hid it in the slipper. When she tugged the silk lining at the top of the chest to close the lid, the thin material tore, exposing a packet of letters held together by a faded blue ribbon.

There were six letters in all, showing the Devil's Wind as the return address. Ruby shouldn't read Hank's private messages to Cora, but that didn't stop her. She slid the first letter out of its envelope.

Dear Cora,

Got another check from the oil company and bought twenty-five head of cattle. I'm a real rancher now. Wish you'd come see the place.

~Hank

Dear Cora,

I planted red rosebushes in front of the house. Say the word and I'll come get you.

~Hank

Dear Cora,

Bought a used piano at an estate sale. It's sitting here waiting for you to play it.

~Hank

How many letters had Hank written to Cora before she'd finally shown up at the Devil's Wind? Ruby closed her eyes and imagined a much younger Hank standing in front of a mailbox, full of hope and excitement as he dropped his love letter inside.

A surge of protectiveness toward him filled Ruby, and she wished she could throttle Cora for her insensitivity. She returned the letters to the compartment behind the lining, then closed the lid and left the attic, her heart swelling with more compassion for the old man than she believed possible.

Chapter 27

Wednesday morning Mia burst into the back porch, where Ruby was tossing a load of dirty clothes into the washer. "Can I go with Joe to fill the new stock tank with water?"

"What new stock tank?"

"The one Grandpa ordered. They delivered it yesterday."

"I thought I was going to help you make an obstacle course for Poke to play on." Hank had suggested that Mia put some objects in the corral to keep Poke busy; otherwise he pestered the bigger horses, testing their patience.

"Hank and I did that yesterday when you were at work and Poke didn't care about the stuff, so we put it back in the barn."

She considered reminding Mia that she'd taken another day off work to hang out with her but didn't want to put her on the defensive. Still, it rankled that she sat at the bottom of Mia's list of people she wanted to be with. "Just be—"

"Careful, I know."

Ruby removed Hank's bedding from the dryer and stood at the window, mindlessly folding a sheet while she watched Joe lift Friend into the truck bed. The dog was more attached to Mia now than Hank. As the pickup grew smaller in the distance, her thoughts shifted to Joe. He'd been avoiding her since the carnival and she didn't know why.

Before she'd arrived at the ranch, Ruby would have jumped to the conclusion that she'd done something wrong or Joe had lost interest in her because another woman had caught his eye. But she shoved her fear aside, telling herself that if Joe had changed his mind about wanting to be a part of her, Mia's, and Hank's lives, that was on him, not her.

Maybe the carnival had brought back too many sad memories of Joe's previous life and he wasn't ready to move on. Whatever his reasons, it made her sad. She'd connected with Joe in a way she hadn't with any of the other men she'd dated and had found comfort in knowing that, like her, he'd made mistakes with his child.

Have a little faith, Ruby.

A sliver of panic worked its way inside her head. What if Joe turned out to be like Glen Baxter? Or Dylan. Or Hank all those years ago?

Mia approves of Joe. Ruby was grateful for her daughter's blessing, but Mia was motivated by the hope that her mother's relationship with Joe would keep them from leaving the Devil's Wind.

Hank appeared in the doorway. "Where are Joe and Mia going?"

"To put water in the new stock tank."

"You hungry?"

Ruby checked the display on her cell phone. "It's only eleven."

Hank's mouth twitched. "Been up since five."

"I'll fix lunch as soon as I finish the laundry." After he went into the kitchen, she called out, "Hank!"

He came back to the doorway.

"Don't you have a doctor's appointment this afternoon?"

"Two thirty."

"Want me to go with you?"

"I can drive myself."

"I know. I thought you might like company."

"Suit yourself."

Okay, she would.

"That doesn't look good." Joe stopped the pickup and got out. Mia and Friend followed him over to the windmill. "What's wrong?"

His gaze climbed upward. "The sails are barely moving."

"Sails?"

"The blades." He examined the gearbox, squinting against the blowing dust.

"You look mad," Mia said.

He was mad. Someone had put a hole in the oil reservoir. The round-the-clock wind had burned up the gears and destroyed the motor. "The oil leaked out." Another attempt to sabotage the Devil's Wind.

"Can you fix it?"

"It'll have to be replaced." Next he checked the connector and the pump rod—both were loose. Maybe the person had been interrupted before they'd finished the job. He fetched a screwdriver from the toolbox in the truck bed and tightened the parts. "We're done here. Let's go." He whistled to Friend, and the dog leaped into the truck bed.

When the water tank came into view, Joe kept his eyes peeled for anything that appeared unusual or stood out against the barren land.

"Where's the one with all the bullet holes?"

"Is that why you're tagging along with me?"

"I wanted to find out if my mom exaggerated. She said there were like a hundred holes in it."

"Not sure about a hundred, but it was close." He backed up the truck. "The company that delivered the new tank hauled the old one to a salvage yard." He unrolled the hose and draped it over the side of the tank, then opened the valve.

Mia shielded her eyes from the sun. "I don't see any cows."

"Once they catch the scent of water, they'll head this way." Joe inspected the base of the tank for leaks.

"You kissed my mom."

He'd known if he waited long enough, Mia would divulge the real reason she'd accompanied him this morning.

"I told my mom it was okay if you wanted to be her boyfriend."

He was glad to have Mia's blessing, but he wondered how she really felt about him, especially after she'd thought of Sean as a father. "Why is it okay for me and your mom to be together?"

Mia tapped the toe of her sandal in the dirt. "I've got Hank now, and my mom doesn't have anybody."

"Your mother has you."

"That's different. It's not like I can just leave her."

Kids didn't have to run away to leave their parents. Aaron had been here one minute and gone the next. "It's good that you and your grandfather hit it off." He'd rather keep the conversation on Mia than on him and Ruby—mostly because he felt like an ass for telling Ruby he missed being part of a family and then, like a coward, he'd shut her out after the carnival.

"Hank gets me," Mia said.

"Gets you how?"

"I don't know." She shrugged. "He understands me."

Joe opened a second valve on the potable water tank.

"Are you going to ask my mom out?"

He hadn't thought to take Ruby on a date.

"Don't you think she's pretty?"

"Your mother's very pretty." Ruby's tangled blond hair was sexy, and although the lines fanning from the corners of her eyes gave her age away, her smile reminded him of a willful teenager. She looked as wild and untamed as her spirit.

"Are you worried she might dump you because she's dumped all of her other boyfriends?"

Joe coughed to cover his smile. If only Mia knew that he was worth dumping.

"She hasn't slept with that many guys. There were lots of times growing up that I can't remember a boyfriend living with us."

He didn't care how many guys Ruby had invited into her bed. He wasn't qualified to stand in judgment of anyone.

"I know you like my mom." Mia raised her arms in exasperation. "I've seen the way you watch her when she leaves for work. You don't want her to go."

That was true. He didn't want Ruby working at the saloon because he worried that one of the rowdy customers would step out of line and make a pass at her. And yeah, he liked believing she was his.

"We're gonna stay at the ranch," Mia said. "At least I am. My grandpa said I can take the school bus into Guymon when classes start in a few weeks."

"What does your mom have to say about that?"

"She told the boss lady at the motel in Kansas that she's not coming. I guess that means she's gonna stay, too." Mia dropped her gaze. "I kind of get why my mom was so hurt when she found out my grandpa didn't want to raise her."

"Your mom and Hank will work things out."

"I know." She peered over the rim of the water tank. "How many trips will it take to fill it all the way?"

"Three." Joe sat on the tailgate next to Friend and avoided Mia's stare, baffled that the teen had unnerved him—like mother, like daughter.

"My mom told me that you had a son."

Oh, man, he did not want to talk about Aaron.

If you want to be with Ruby, you can't pretend the past never happened.

"What was his name?"

"Aaron. He was six years old"—he forced the words out of his mouth—"when he died."

"What happened to him?"

"He got run over by a car."

"That's sad."

S-a-d—a three-letter word packed with enough emotion to choke a person to death. "Aaron would have been close to your age if he'd lived."

"How did he get hit by the car?"

"It was an accident. He rode his bike into the street without stopping to check for cars. And he wasn't wearing his helmet because he was mad at me."

"Why was he mad?"

"I told him he couldn't play video games with a friend."

"I did something stupid because I was mad at my mom."

Joe patted the teen's back. "Everyone makes mistakes. Sometimes all we can do is say we're sorry." Joe accepted that he hadn't failed Aaron completely—he'd loved his son unconditionally. No amount of guilt or pain would convince him that Aaron hadn't been aware of how deeply he'd been loved by both his parents.

"Can I see a picture of him?"

Joe pulled his wallet out of his back pocket and removed a school photograph of Aaron.

"He looks like you." She held the picture up to his face. "He's got your eyes and mouth."

What kind of man would his son have grown up to be, if he'd had the chance to become an adult? He studied the heavens, searching for Aaron's shadow in the moving clouds, hoping that wherever he'd ended up, he could still feel his father's love.

Mia handed over the photo, then jumped to the ground. "Will you ever get married again? Maybe have more kids?"

A pain sliced through him—the sting sharp, but the throb afterward sweet. If he'd been asked that question a few weeks ago, he'd have said *no way.* But today . . . "Maybe."

Because Joe wanted to believe Ruby, Mia, Hank, and all their problems could sway him not to spend the rest of his life alone.

Chapter 28

"Hank, are you ready to leave?" After lunch he'd gone into his bedroom to nap and Ruby worried that he'd forgotten his doctor's appointment.

"Be right there!"

She went outside to wait on the front porch. When he joined her, he asked, "Is Mia coming?"

"No." He didn't protest when she slid behind the wheel and he had to sit in the passenger seat. "She wants to stay with Poke."

Once Ruby turned onto the highway, Hank spoke. "I've been reading your mother's diary."

So that's what he was doing every day instead of taking his nap. Her fortune-telling session with Big Dan came to mind. *Perhaps there's something you began in the past that you need to finish.* Was she ready to find out what her mother had written?

"You want to know what she said?" Hank asked.

"Is it bad?"

"No."

Whew.

"Your folks agreed they'd tell you about your adoption on your eighteenth birthday."

So her parents hadn't intended to keep the truth from Ruby forever. As if someone stuck a pin in her heart, the anger she'd harbored toward her folks suddenly burst, leaving her chest deflated. "Why didn't they tell me on my eighteenth birthday?"

"You'd just given birth to Mia a few weeks earlier and your mother didn't want you getting upset, so they decided to wait a little longer."

Too bad they hadn't followed through. "Mia was already three months old when my parents died in the crash and they still hadn't said a word to me."

"Your father wanted you to know the truth when you were sixteen."

That was a tough year for Ruby and her parents. She'd caused her mother numerous headaches—breaking curfew, skipping classes, smoking pot, and then her father had canceled their summer trip.

Hank removed the pack of Winstons from his shirt pocket and tapped the end against his palm. Ruby wouldn't object if the cigarettes kept him talking. He took a deep drag, then lowered his window and exhaled.

"Did she say why my father wanted to tell me sooner?"

"Cora wanted to see you."

Shock robbed Ruby of her voice.

"A social worker called your mother, asking permission for Cora to visit. She said Cora might be moving to Missouri and wanted to establish a relationship with you."

"Don't leave me hanging. Why didn't my parents let me meet her?"

"Your mother didn't want Cora influencing you." Hank drew

in another lungful of tobacco. "You were a hellion. 'Rebellious' was the word your mother used."

"It's true." Ruby guided the truck over to the shoulder and allowed the vehicle riding their bumper to pass. "But that wasn't a good enough reason to keep me from seeing my birth mother."

"She was afraid you'd run off with Cora because you two weren't getting along."

If Cora had tried to talk Ruby into leaving Pineville, there was no doubt in Ruby's mind that she would have gone just to piss off her parents. She wanted to resent them for keeping Cora's request a secret, but the mother in Ruby understood Cheryl Baxter's fear of losing her child. Ruby had felt that same anxiety when she and Mia first arrived at the Devil's Wind and Mia had latched onto Hank. Fortunately for Ruby, Hank didn't want to steal Mia away. Cheryl Baxter had no way of knowing Cora's intentions. Ruby took some measure of comfort in learning that her mother had loved her despite her being Cora's offspring.

"Your father hoped Cora might be able to straighten you out."

Ruby's throat tightened and her thoughts drifted back to the day Glen Baxter had turned his back on her . . . "Why can't I go with you?"

"Because I said so." Her father wouldn't look her in the eye.

"Are you punishing me for the D I got in health class?"

"No, Ruby. Something else has come up," he said.

That something else had been Cora.

Ruby pulled a notebook out of her overnight bag. "I already marked which roadside attractions we're going to see." This was the year her father had scheduled a run through Texas. "First we're stopping at the Houston National Museum of Funeral History. Then, the next day, it's Barney Smith's Toilet Seat Art Museum in San

Antonio. And before we come home, I want to take pictures of the Cadillac Ranch in Amarillo." Her father opened his mouth, but Ruby talked over him. "And if we have time, we can stop in Lubbock and see the thirteen-ton boulder with John Wayne's head carved in it."

"Not this year, Ruby."

Tears filled her eyes. "What if we go a different week this summer?" She desperately needed this trip. There were a million questions she wanted to ask her father about boys and sex. Ruby's mother wasn't comfortable talking about the birds and bees with her.

"I said no."

Her father stormed out of the trailer and her mother fled to her bedroom. Ruby stood in the living room, her gaze swinging between the closed doors, trying to digest what had happened. She waited all evening for her father to phone and reassure her that everything was okay. When he didn't call, she left several voice mails, but he never answered them. She didn't speak to him again until he came home in September.

Knowing that her father had disagreed with her mother's decision to reject Cora's plea made it all the more clear why he'd scratched the road trip at the last minute—he was afraid he'd let it slip that she'd been adopted.

What had made Cora believe she could waltz back into Ruby's life without there being consequences? If she'd waited to make contact until after Ruby had turned eighteen, then Ruby and her father wouldn't have had a falling-out. And maybe she wouldn't have developed such a deep mistrust of men, which resulted in Ruby kicking Sean out and had led to Mia losing her virginity to Kevin.

Why not blame Cora for all of it?

Hank helped himself to a second cigarette, his fingers trembling when he held the lighter. Her anger turned into empathy for him. "Are you upset that Cora tried to contact me?" *And not you?*

"No."

"What do I do now?" she asked. "Go look for her?"

He let the lighter flicker out, then removed the unlit cigarette from his mouth. "Whatever you decide, I don't want to know if Cora's dead or alive."

"Why not?"

His bony shoulders lifted an inch, then settled back into place.

Neither spoke the remainder of the drive into Guymon. Ruby mulled over what she'd learned, feeling a measure of relief that Glen Baxter hadn't stopped loving her—he just hadn't known how to handle the situation with Cora. And Ruby understood her mother's fear of losing her daughter, but she was sad that Cheryl Baxter hadn't put Ruby's interests ahead of her own.

So much hurt and pain . . .

And there was nothing Ruby could do to change the past.

"You want a cup of coffee?" Ruby asked Hank when he appeared in the kitchen Saturday afternoon.

He sat at the table and she placed a mug in front of him. "Thought you were working today."

"Stony closed the bar. He's in Dallas, visiting a friend."

Hank sipped the hot brew. "Charles called. He's still checking into my lease with Petro Oil."

"Good." Ruby was glad Hank had gotten his lawyer involved. She hadn't forgotten the strange look Stony and Steward Kline had exchanged when the oil agent had dropped a copy of the lease off at the bar. It was probably nothing, but after Big Dan's claim that

Unforgiven was a town full of secrets, Ruby wouldn't be surprised if the two men had shady pasts.

"Be right back." Hank left the kitchen, returning a few minutes later with the diary. "Finished it last night."

Ruby didn't want to talk about the journal entries. She hadn't yet processed the knowledge that Cora had attempted to contact her. She couldn't summon up a kind thought for her biological mother after the woman had thrown Ruby's family into chaos and destroyed her relationship with her father.

"You should read it," he said.

"I will." *Eventually.*

"Your mother's favorite color was yellow."

"I knew that." Her father had given her mother a dozen yellow roses each Valentine's Day.

"Do you know your mother's favorite dessert?"

"Lemon Bundt cake." A pang of longing hit Ruby. Her mother hadn't been perfect, but Ruby had loved her.

"Your parents were good people."

Glen and Cheryl Baxter had always been there for Ruby—until Cora had interfered. Ruby wished her adoptive father were alive to reassure her that she and Mia would grow close again. Each night she crawled beneath the covers with the same fear—if push came to shove, would Mia choose Hank over Ruby?

"I'm real proud of you," Hank said.

Where had that come from? "Why?"

"You did what I didn't have the guts to do. You raised a fine daughter by yourself."

The sincerity in his voice shoved Ruby's heart into her throat. Why had he made this confession today—when his dry, wrinkled skin appeared paler and the charred bags beneath his watery blue eyes reminded her that the grim reaper stalked him?

"Has the doctor's office called with the results of your blood tests?"

"Yesterday. I'm fine."

Fine was not an adjective a doctor would use to describe Hank's health. She opened her mouth to ask for details, then changed her mind. They both knew his days were numbered. She'd rather pretend he'd live forever and they had decades to make up for lost time.

Especially now that she'd forgiven him.

Ruby hadn't woken one morning and experienced an epiphany—it wasn't like that. Her heart had been softening toward him since he'd stomped his cigarette out after Mia had said grandpas shouldn't smell like ashtrays.

"Mia's lucky to have you for a mother."

"I think she might argue that point with you."

The knocker banged against the front door, the sound echoing through the house. Hank left the room, and she set her cup on the counter before following him.

"I need to speak with Ruby."

"Deputy Randall." She moved past Hank and stepped outside. "What brings you by?"

The officer stared at Hank, eavesdropping behind the screen door.

Hank muttered beneath his breath, then walked off. Ruby sat in a chair. "Did you catch the person who's been vandalizing the ranch?"

"No." Randall leaned against the porch rail, his gaze shifting from the door to the porch steps to the rosebushes and then back to the door.

"Is this about the little scene I witnessed in the sheriff's office?"

His face paled, catching her off guard.

"You're afraid I'll tattle on you." Call her stupid for provoking him, but his attitude pissed her off. "Oh, wait. I forgot," she said. "Women aren't welcome in town . . . except the ones you want to screw."

He clenched his jaw. "It's not what you think."

Ruby struggled not to laugh. "I know what I saw."

"Leona and I are friends. We grew up together."

"So that excuses you two for cheating on her husband?"

"We're not having an affair." He shoved a hand through his neatly styled hair, leaving a clump sticking up at the back of his head. He looked like a lost little boy.

"Then what happened in your boss's office?" she asked.

"A mistake. A onetime mistake."

Ruby had a history of onetime mistakes. Who was she to judge?

"I'd appreciate you not bad-mouthing Leona. She doesn't deserve it."

Randall was worried about his job. "I won't." Maybe if she granted him this favor, he'd work harder to find the bad guys.

"Is there a problem?" Joe walked up to the porch.

"No problem," Randall said. "I was just telling Ruby that the local Little League is having a fund-raiser tonight at the ballpark in Guymon." He nodded to Joe. "We need an extra outfielder for our team if you're interested."

"What time does the game start?" Ruby asked.

"Six. But come early. There'll be hot dogs and activities for the kids. Your daughter might enjoy it." Randall got into his patrol car and left.

"Why do I get the feeling a softball game isn't the real reason he stopped by?"

She pointed to the chair next to her. "Take a load off."

Joe accepted her invitation, and she caught a whiff of male sweat and faded cologne when he sat down. He studied her, his warm stare reeling her in. This was the first time they'd been alone together since they'd kissed in the barn after the carnival. "The deputy has a dirty secret."

"Oh?"

"The sheriff's wife."

"No kidding."

"I caught them in the act when I stopped by the jail to report Hank's stolen oil lease. Randall's afraid I'll spout off about it while I'm working at the saloon."

Joe rubbed his knuckles against Ruby's cheek, and she shivered when his finger brushed her mouth. "I know you can take care of yourself, but if you didn't work at the Possum Belly, you could spend more time with Mia and Hank." His finger moved back and forth over her lower lip. "And me."

"You haven't been acting like you want me around."

"I'm sorry." His brown eyes darkened, but he didn't look away. "I got scared."

"We can take things slow." Slow was good. "We should just enjoy being with each other." And not think. Thinking too much led her down the path of self-doubt.

Joe's mouth closed over hers, but he ended the kiss too soon. "Will you let me give you a ride to and from the bar?"

She could take care of herself, but after he'd lost his son, she could understand Joe's need to protect her. If they were going to be together, she couldn't call all the shots like she'd done in her previous relationships. "Okay, you can play chauffeur."

"Good." He rewarded her with a real kiss.

"Mom!" Mia waltzed into the yard. "Hey, you guys were kissing."

Ruby smiled at Joe.

"Come see the trick I taught Poke. Hurry." Mia ran back to the corral.

"Wait." Ruby clutched Joe's arm when he made a move to stand. "Are you going to accept Randall's invite to play softball tonight?" She didn't want to push him to be around families with little boys, but she knew Mia would appreciate the chance to socialize with other kids.

"Sure. It'll be fun."

Hand in hand they walked to the backyard. With a final squeeze, Joe released her fingers and veered toward the barn. Ruby joined Hank and Friend at the corral.

"What did the deputy want?" Hank asked.

"He invited us to the ballpark in Guymon for a Little League fund-raiser."

"He had to ask you that in private?"

She ignored his frown. "There will be other kids at the park. Mia might like the chance to hang out with someone her own age."

"Joe can take you gals. I'll stay here."

Ruby had figured Hank would want to remain at home rather than sit on uncomfortable metal bleachers in the hot sun. "We don't have to go if you'd rather we stay." She recalled meeting Hank for the first time and her determination not to care about him. Now look at her—she was worried about leaving him alone at the ranch.

"I'll be fine. You all go without me." He nodded to Mia. "She taught Poke this move all by herself."

"Mia never told me she was teaching him tricks."

"She wanted to surprise you."

That her daughter wanted to impress Ruby warmed her heart. It didn't always seem like it, but she and Mia were taking tiny steps forward together.

"Ready, Mom?"

"Ready!"

Mia guided Poke across the corral. Then she dropped the reins and stood in front of the horse. Poke's attention remained on Mia, the animal's gaze never wandering. After a few seconds Mia raised her arms above her head and Poke stood on his hind legs. Then Mia turned in a slow circle and Poke did the same before lowering his front hooves onto the ground.

Ruby clapped. "I can't believe you taught him that trick in such a short time."

Mia jogged over to Ruby. "Grandpa thinks Poke was once a circus pony."

"Circus pony or not, you've got the magic touch with horses."

Mia's smile lit up her face. Ruby made a mental note to praise her daughter more often.

After Mia walked off, Ruby said, "Sure I can't change your mind about the baseball game tonight?"

He shook his head.

"I'll see what I can scrounge up for your supper."

"I can make my own food."

"I know." She took a step toward the back porch, but Hank's voice stopped her.

"Ruby."

"What?"

"I asked Charles to search for Cora."

The enormity of his statement took a moment to sink in. He'd lived for three decades not knowing where Cora had gone, all the while holding on to the hope that one day she'd return to him. "You didn't have to ask Charles to look for her."

"I didn't do it for me. I did it for you."

Ruby went into the house carrying his revelation with her. Hank believed she deserved to know what had happened to her birth mother. Maybe this was his way of saying he was sorry.

How many times would he have to apologize before she allowed her heart to love him?

Chapter 29

"April and I are gonna hang out on the swings." Mia took off with the redheaded fourteen-year-old she'd met when they'd first arrived at the ballpark. Ruby watched the pair for a few minutes, glad Deputy Randall had invited them to the game. It was reassuring to hear Mia's laughter—maybe her daughter hadn't lost all of her innocence when she'd slept with Kevin.

Ruby escaped to the shade of an oak tree and watched the men warm up on the field. Joe played catch with the deputy and a man wearing a T-shirt with a picture of a plunger on the front and ACE PLUMBING: CALL THE BEST, FLUSH THE REST written on the back.

Several women close to Ruby's age had introduced themselves and chatted with her. They'd teased her about living near Unforgiven and encouraged her to find a place in Guymon, where there were more activities for kids and better shopping. The idea had merit. If she and Mia made their home in Guymon, they'd have a chance to make friends and become part of the community yet still be close by to keep an eye on Hank.

"Hello, Ruby." Leona Carlyle joined her by the tree.

The woman was the same height as Ruby but runway-model slender. Her perfectly styled bob sat on her head like a shiny brunette helmet. Strappy sandals showed off her pedicure—bloodred nails with a white flower on each big toe. Her beige linen slacks and blue sleeveless blouse had been pressed to perfection, and the silver bangles on her wrist jingled when she swatted at a fly buzzing near her head. Not your usual picnic attire.

"Paul said he talked to you." Leona had whispered even though they stood twenty yards away from the nearest pair of ears.

"He mentioned that you two grew up together," Ruby said.

"We were in the same grade in school."

"It's really none of my business what you and Randall do, but you might want to be a little more discreet about it."

Leona's gaze shifted to the sheriff, who joined Randall, Joe, and Mr. Plumber's throwing circle. She waved at the group, but only her husband acknowledged her with a smile. "I've always had a crush on Paul."

"People have affairs for all kinds of reasons." Ruby didn't care why the pair was screwing around.

"I wish we were having an affair." Leona watched Randall walk to the dugout, where he traded his ball cap for a batting helmet.

"I don't get it. Your husband is a hell of a lot better-looking than the deputy." Ruby shrugged. "Looks aside, Randall's an ass."

"I wanted to date Paul in high school, but he ran with a wild crowd and my parents would have locked me in my bedroom until I turned eighteen if they'd suspected I was interested in him." A dreamy, faraway look filled Leona's eyes. "I went away to college. Dated other guys. After I graduated, I moved back home, hoping Paul and I would get together." She forced a smile. "He wasn't interested, and instead he introduced me to Mike. We hit it off well enough and got married." Leona had settled for the sheriff.

Ruby considered her situation with Joe. He was a complicated man. She was a complicated woman. If they met in the middle, maybe neither of them would have to settle.

"What can I do to convince you to keep what you saw the other day to yourself?"

Ruby had no intention of shouting Leona's infidelity to the masses, but she'd be stupid not to take the woman up on her offer. "Find out why your husband is turning a blind eye to Roy Sandoval's shenanigans. Hank's neighbor is behind the vandalism at the Devil's Wind."

"Roy's a nice man. He wouldn't harass Hank."

"There's bad blood between the men. I'm guessing you've heard the stories about my mother having an affair with Roy."

"I'll speak to Mike." Leona motioned to the bleachers. "I'm tired of standing. Let's sit down."

The game lasted a little less than two hours. Mia joined Ruby and Leona when Joe's team was up at bat. Joe acted as if he was having fun, joking with the other men in the dugout and high-fiving the first-base coach when he hit a single to left field. But she imagined everything about tonight—kids chasing one another, the smell of grilled hot dogs, women sitting in groups gossiping—reminded him of the life he'd once lived.

At the end of the game, Leona went off with the sheriff while Randall and Mr. Plumber carried a five-gallon orange Igloo cooler through the crowd, soliciting donations for the Little League program. When they stopped in front of Ruby, she opened her purse and dumped two days' worth of tips into the cooler. The deputy's eyes widened, but all he said was "Thanks" before he moved on.

She met Joe by the dugout. "You were awesome." Not just because he'd caught two fly balls but because he'd been brave enough to come tonight and battle memories of playing catch with Aaron.

Ruby signaled Mia, and she ran over from the playground. "Do we have to go? They're gonna set off fireworks."

"We've been here almost four hours," Ruby said.

Mia looked longingly at the kids congregating near a picnic table. "I guess we'd better check on Grandpa."

Although she appreciated her daughter's devotion to Hank, Ruby knew when the day came to say goodbye to the old man, Mia would need more than her mother and the horses to lean on—she was going to need friends.

"Mom?"

"I'm awake." Ruby tossed back the top sheet, and Mia slid beneath the cover. "Don't tell me Friend is hogging your pillow again."

"He's sleeping on the rug in Grandpa's bedroom." She yawned. "Who was the pretty lady you sat with at the baseball game?"

"That was the sheriff's wife, Leona."

"Oh. Did Joe have a good time?"

"He did. How about you and April? Was it fun to hang around someone your age for a change?"

"April's really nice. She asked if I was going to school in Guymon this fall."

"What did you tell her?"

"That I might."

"Would you consider living in Guymon instead of at the ranch?" Ruby asked.

"Why would we live there when Grandpa and Joe are here?"

"I'm glad you like Joe, but if we end up together, I want it to be different this time." She held Mia's hand. It didn't seem so long ago when her daughter's whole fist fit in Ruby's palm. "I need to be sure about my feelings for Joe." Her feelings weren't the issue—her fear was. She didn't want to panic at the first sign of trouble and send Joe packing. "I want to get it right this time, Mia, because I don't want you to get hurt again."

"I won't get hurt. Grandpa will always be there for me."

If only that were true.

"Are you reading Grandma Baxter's diary?"

"Yes." Hank had twisted Ruby's arm.

"What does it say?"

"I learned how I came by my name."

"How?"

Ruby lifted the gemstone resting against her neck. "Your grandparents gave this necklace to me on my thirteenth birthday. I thought it was from them."

"But it wasn't?"

"It belonged to Cora. She left it in my hospital bassinet before she ran away. When your grandparents adopted me, the social worker gave them the necklace. It was Grandpa Baxter who said I should be named Ruby so that I'd know my birth mother had loved me."

"If Cora loved you, she wouldn't have left you behind."

Mia's words jarred Ruby. One day her daughter would have a child and understand that a mother could do horrible things yet still love her offspring. Ruby was a perfect example—she'd made bad decisions that her daughter had unfortunately paid the price for. "No one's perfect, honey."

"Does Grandpa know Cora left you the necklace?"

"He recognized it when we first arrived at the ranch."

"What happened to Cora?"

"No one knows. Hank asked his lawyer to search for her."

"What are you gonna do if she's still alive?"

"I'll cross that bridge if and when we come to it." Ruby was more worried how Hank would take the news if Cora was alive and hadn't bothered to contact him all those years.

"If Cora married some other man and had kids with him, you'd have half brothers and sisters and maybe I'd have cousins."

"We'll have to wait and see." Ruby was still getting used to the idea of her, Mia, and Hank becoming a family—and maybe Joe. She didn't want to invite anyone else into the circle.

"Do you have to work tomorrow?"

"Stony doesn't return from Dallas until Wednesday."

Mia hopped off the bed. "If we stay at the ranch, I'm gonna need a computer to do homework when school starts. And Grandpa's gonna have to get the Internet."

"I know. 'Night, honey."

It was a long time before Ruby fell into a restless sleep. Then she dreamed of a happy-ever-after with Joe and woke feeling hopeful for the first time in a long while.

Chapter 30

"Where are Hank and Mia off to?" Joe hovered in the kitchen doorway Sunday afternoon.

"A movie in Guymon." Ruby had been invited along, but she'd declined, wanting to spend a few hours alone with Joe. Lately it felt like they were under a microscope, Mia and Hank monitoring their every move and gauging their progress.

Ruby shut the fridge door. "Can you take a break from chores?" she asked.

"I'd planned to replace the gearbox on the windmill." His gaze darted to the porch.

She wasn't opposed to an afternoon quickie, but if she wanted more from Joe than she'd experienced with other men, she couldn't let her fear win. She was ready to take a leap of faith and get to know Joe on a deeper level.

"Can the windmill wait?" She gestured to the supplies on the table. "I packed a picnic lunch."

"You must think I'm an idiot," he said.

She walked up to him and brushed her mouth against his. "I don't think you're an idiot. I think you're good-looking. Kind. And sexy. But it's too soon. Rather than mess up the sheets, I thought we could spread a blanket beneath the cottonwood."

"I'd like that." He carried the picnic supplies out to the backyard. The afternoon temperature hovered near ninety degrees, but the tree's thick branches provided plenty of shade. He spread the quilt across the ground, then propped his back against the trunk. Ruby sat next to him and held out a sandwich and a bottle of water.

"Someone wants to join us." Joe got to his feet and opened the back door for Friend. The mutt trotted over to the blanket, then whined until Ruby tossed him a piece of lunch meat.

"This is good." Joe had finished half his sandwich in two bites.

"I added dill seasoning to the mayo."

He grasped her necklace between his fingers. "Is this a gift from one of your past boyfriends?"

"My parents gave it to me."

"Is it real?" Joe asked.

"Yes."

He rubbed the gemstone, his calloused knuckles bumping her throat. "I bought Melanie a diamond pendant after Aaron was born, but she lost it."

"Did the clasp break?"

He released her necklace. "She never said. One day I asked why she didn't wear it anymore and she claimed she couldn't remember how she'd lost it."

"I only take my necklace off to clean it." The ruby had been a reminder of happier times with her parents, and she refused to allow the memories to become tainted just because the necklace had belonged to Cora.

"Were you close to your mother?" he asked.

"Not real close. I ran with a wild crowd and tested her patience."

He grinned. "You look like the rebel type."

She landed a playful punch against his arm. "Go ahead and mock me. I bet you were the perfect son."

"Not a chance. I got pulled over for drunk driving in high school. The cop didn't write me up because he knew my father. I left the clunker on the side of the road and got a ride home in the backseat of a patrol car."

"Did your father have political connections in your town?"

Joe laughed. "Heavenly connections. He was a preacher."

She would never have guessed Joe had been raised in a religious family.

"You ran with a wild crowd and I drank to rebel," he said.

"Every kid tests their parents." Mia knew all of Ruby's hot buttons.

"My folks were good people," Joe said. "They didn't deserve the negative attention my partying brought them."

"But you straightened out."

"Only because of Melanie."

"How do you mean?"

"She was the daughter of one of my father's minister friends. They set us up on a date, and we hit it off. I quit drinking and focused on my studies. We married a year after we graduated from high school. I was a freshman in college at the time, so we moved into an apartment and Melanie became active in the local church, directing the children's choir. Once I earned a degree and landed my first job, we bought a small house and then Melanie got pregnant with Aaron."

"I wanted to go to college once." Her junior year of high school she'd taken the SATs and had gotten an acceptable score. "But then I got pregnant with Mia and . . ."

"Your parents were killed."

"After that I was just trying to keep it together. Work every day so I could pay the bills and buy formula and diapers for Mia."

"If you'd been able to go to college, what would you have studied?" he asked.

"I hadn't thought that far ahead. I figured after I took a few classes I'd find my niche."

"What's stopping you from going back to school now?"

"Seriously?"

"You could enroll in online classes."

"College costs money," she said.

"Apply for financial aid. I received grants and scholarships because of my father's occupation. You're a single mother and"—he raised his hands in the air—"no offense meant, but I'm guessing you don't make a lot of money."

"What gave it away? Arriving in town on a Greyhound bus or"—she tugged the hem of her plain tank top—"my stylish wardrobe?"

Joe's gaze skimmed over her, his eyes warming. "The peach dress and cowboy boots you wore when you first arrived in town looked good on you."

"You liked that outfit, huh?"

He smiled.

Ruby changed the subject. "Do you keep in touch with Melanie?"

"We communicated off and on to finalize our divorce, but I

haven't seen her since Aaron's funeral." He guzzled his water. "If our son hadn't died, I'd like to believe we'd still be together."

Ruby couldn't say that about any of her past boyfriends—not even Sean.

"But now . . ." He shook his head. "Melanie and I aren't the same people. We'd feel like strangers if we ever met up again."

Life changed people—for better and for worse. The changing part was an ongoing process. When Ruby thought of the storms she'd weathered in her short life, she'd emerged a different Ruby from each one.

"I had it all." He snapped his fingers. "And it was gone in the blink of an eye."

"Joe?"

"What?"

"I wish Aaron hadn't died. And I wish you could still be with Melanie. Still have your family." And she meant it.

He threaded his fingers through hers and rested her hand on his thigh. "What went through your mind when you found out you were adopted?"

"After it sank in, I was finally able to make sense out of some things in the past." She tossed the remainder of her sandwich to Friend. "All these years I'd believed me and my mother had been at odds because of my rowdy behavior, but that wasn't the reason at all."

"What do you mean?"

"When I was twelve, I found my father's stash of *Hustler* magazines. I snuck them into my bedroom to look at the photos. I was fascinated by all the boobs and remembered thinking I never wanted mine to be that big."

Joe quirked a brow at Ruby's ample bosom.

"They're not quite *that* big." She laughed. "I bet you wondered how big your . . ." She flicked her wrist toward his crotch.

"My what, Ruby?"

She blushed. "Never mind. When my mother found me looking at the magazines, she muttered something about my bad genes. At the time I thought she was talking about the ripped blue jeans I always wore. Now I know she was referring to my biological mother."

"What about your birth mother?"

"Cora worked in a brothel." Because Hank had left Ruby's adoption open, Cheryl Baxter had dug into Cora's past and had probably been horrified by what she'd discovered. Ruby didn't blame her mother for worrying that her daughter might follow in Cora's footsteps because her worry had been grounded in love. But it was too bad her mother's fear had prevented them from enjoying a close relationship.

"We're quite a pair, aren't we . . . ? The son of a minister father and the daughter of a prostitute mother."

No kidding. "I almost didn't answer Hank's letter."

Joe's eyes shone with sympathy. "Why not?"

"I was angry and I wanted to hurt him."

"What were you afraid of?"

Of course Joe would guess that Ruby had used anger to mask her fear. "I was worried that Hank wouldn't like me." Memories of Glen Baxter ignoring her, then Dylan blowing her and Mia off, followed by a history of broken relationships, had made Ruby hypersuspicious. By the time she'd read *Sincerely Yours* at the bottom of the lawyer's letter, she'd decided to reject Hank before she gave him the opportunity to break her heart.

Joe held her chin between his fingers, forcing her to look him in the eye. "For both our sakes, I'm glad you're here."

"How was the movie?" Ruby asked when Hank and Mia returned to the ranch an hour after Joe left to fix the windmill.

"Good, but Grandpa slept through it." Mia patted her leg. "Come on, Friend. Let's check on Poke." The old dog got to his feet and followed Mia outside.

Hank took a mug from the cupboard and helped himself to the half inch of brew remaining in the coffeepot from earlier in the morning. "I didn't sleep through the whole movie." He carried his mug to the table.

"How much, then?"

"Two-thirds."

Ruby sat across from him. "I wanted to discuss the possibility of you signing up for Internet service."

"I don't need it."

"I know you don't, but Mia will need it for school this fall."

He sat up straighter. "Are you and Mia staying here?"

"Haven't decided yet. But even if we live in Guymon, Mia will want to be here with you and the horses every chance she gets. It'll be easier for her to keep up with homework if I buy a cheap laptop that she can bring with her to the ranch."

"I'll call the phone company tomorrow and see what my options are." He slurped his coffee. "You and Joe have a nice day?"

"Nothing happened between us, if that's what you're asking."

His eyes twinkled. "Mia and I will take in a double feature next time."

"Wait a minute." Ruby pointed her finger at him. "It was your idea to go to the movies, not Mia's."

"Guilty as charged."

"So you're trying to find a way to convince me to stay at the ranch, too?"

"Whether you stay here or not is your decision. I just don't want you to end up alone like me."

Ruby didn't want that, either, but she hated feeling pressured. If things fell apart with Joe, it would be awkward between them if he continued working for Hank. "Joe and I are taking things slow."

"Don't take them too slow. I won't be around forever."

"You don't need to remind me."

Chapter 31

"Are you and Joe Dawson an item now?" Stony had waited until the last customer left the bar to strike up a conversation with Ruby. For a Friday night the saloon hadn't been crowded, and the shit-kicker was only half full.

"Why do you care what I do with Joe?"

"I don't. I saw his truck parked outside last night."

True to her word, Ruby had allowed Joe to drive her to and from the bar each day she worked. "I like Joe. He's a nice man."

Stony grimaced.

"What?"

"A nice man isn't your type."

She slid a tray of empty shot glasses into the sink filled with soapy dishwater and tried to ignore Stony.

He whispered over her shoulder, "How long before Mr. Nice Guy becomes Mr. Boring?"

"Joe's not boring." Ruby grabbed the spray bottle and a clean cloth, then attacked the beer stains on the tabletops. She scrubbed hard until a sharp pain shot through her elbow. Things between her and Joe had been perfect the past few days. Each time he smiled at her or held her hand, she'd grown more convinced that she was ready to give their relationship an honest chance.

"I bet Joe doesn't have any tattoos." Stony's gaze darkened. "I'm tattooed in places you've never seen ink on a man before."

She snorted. "Don't get your hopes up, pal." Stony was an insensitive, selfish, ignorant jerk. There wasn't one thing she liked about the man, except that he hadn't been afraid to give her a job.

"It won't last with Joe."

"Oh, yeah?" Her trigger finger itched to spray him with disinfectant, then wipe the smirk off his face.

"You've got your mother's blood running through your veins, Ruby. Like her, you'll never settle for one man."

Damn Stony for opening his big mouth and reminding Ruby of her biological connection to Cora. It hadn't escaped her that maybe more than a necklace connected mother and daughter. What if the reason she couldn't commit to a man was a combination of fear *and* biology?

If Ruby had inherited the tramp gene, it wouldn't matter if she overcame her fear of commitment because she'd never be more than a woman who slept with too many men. If she opened her heart to Joe, genetics would eventually win out and she'd punt him down the road. Ruby didn't want to hurt Joe—not when he was the first man she'd ever envisioned going the distance with.

Numbness settled in her bones as she studied her reflection in the mirror behind the bar. Her vacant stare sent a chill through her. Then something moved in the background. *Joe.* He was here to take her home. She emptied her tips into her purse.

"Have a nice evening, Ruby."

Ignoring Stony, she followed Joe outside to his pickup.

He opened the passenger-side door for her. "What's the matter?"

"Everything." Tears filled her eyes.

"Rough night at work?" He caressed her cheek with his knuckles.

If he knew what she was thinking, he wouldn't be so considerate. They drove in silence, Ruby staring out the window, searching the dark for answers that weren't there.

"Did Stony say something to upset you?" Joe glanced across the seat at her, but she didn't have the courage to look him in the eye.

She bit her lip, focusing on the pain and not the trash clogging her head. "I made a mistake."

"What kind of mistake?"

Maybe she should give herself time to calm down. Stony had been his typical asshole self tonight, undermining her confidence because it made him feel powerful. Then again, time wouldn't change the truth. No matter how fearless Ruby believed herself to be, she was still Cora's daughter.

"I made a mistake thinking I could be with you."

He gripped the steering wheel with both hands, drew in a deep breath, then exhaled heavily. "Is it because I screwed up and Mia took off on Pretty Boy that afternoon?"

"No. Not at all."

His choke hold on the wheel loosened. "Then what did I do wrong?"

Nothing. You did nothing wrong. "It's not you, Joe. It's me."

"I can help if you explain what's going on."

No one could help her. Even if she could find the words, the lump in her throat blocked them from escaping.

"Ruby?"

"I don't want to talk about it." She went back to staring at the darkness outside her window.

The remainder of the drive to the ranch took forever. Joe stopped in front of the house but kept the engine running. Ruby owed him an explanation—then again, what did it matter? Eventually he'd realize she'd done him a favor. She got out and slammed her door, then sat on the porch steps and cried angry tears. She damned the ugly, desolate ranch for playing tricks on her, for making her believe she was stronger than she was.

When no more water leaked from her eyes, she wiped her nose with the hem of her blouse and went into the house. Before she'd even shut the front door, her daughter's voice rang out.

"Mom?" Mia stood on the landing.

"What?"

"Have you been crying?"

"It's nothing." She set her purse on the staircase.

"Did you have a fight with Joe?" Mia tapped her foot against the loose board on the landing. The squeaky sound grated on Ruby's nerves.

"We didn't have a fight."

"Your mother home?" Hank joined Mia in the hallway. His murky gaze zeroed in on Ruby's swollen eyes and blotchy face. "What happened?"

"Your choice in women stinks, Hank." She should walk away before she said something she'd regret.

"I asked Mom if she had a fight with Joe."

She and Mia had come too far for Ruby to start lying now. "It's not going to work out between us."

Mia stamped her foot. "You ruin everything!" She fled to her room.

"You want to talk about it?" Hank asked.

Suddenly the men on the ranch had turned into therapists. "You can't fix this, Hank. You picked Cora and now I'm stuck with being her daughter and everything that entails."

Hank dropped his gaze, then shuffled back to his bedroom, the quiet click of his door sounding like a bomb detonating inside the house. Ruby went to her bedroom, gathered her pj's, then went up to the bathroom. She stood beneath the showerhead, the hot water erasing the tears that streamed from her eyes.

She hated herself. Hated that she'd let Mia down. *Again.* Hated the censure in Hank's eyes—hated even more how it mattered to her that she'd disappointed him. But most of all she hated herself for hurting Joe.

The morning after Ruby dumped Joe, she wanted nothing more than to escape Mia's accusing glare. She borrowed Hank's pickup and drove into town to speak with the sheriff about the oil lease. When she entered the jail, Randall was sitting at his desk filling out paperwork.

"Hello, Ruby."

She skipped the pleasantries. "Is the sheriff in?"

"He and Leona went to Ponca City for the day."

She waited for him to follow up with a snide remark and send her on her way, but his next words surprised her.

"Thank you for the generous donation at the ball park. We collected enough money to buy new equipment for the minor league division."

"You really like Little League baseball, don't you?"

"Kids who can't afford to play deserve a chance to experience being on a team."

"What made you decide to go into law enforcement?"

He blew out a loud breath, the air rustling the papers on the desk. "I wanted to help people." His eyes skittered to the door, then back to the pile of paperwork.

"Well, that's good, because I need your help with Hank's oil lease."

"What's the matter with it?"

"The copy Steward Kline made for Hank shows the lease expiring this September, and it should be in 2050."

"Sounds like a simple mistake."

"Maybe Steward changed the date before he made the copy."

"Are you accusing him of falsifying the document?"

"Is that so unreasonable, considering all the trouble at the Devil's Wind?" Ruby placed her hands on the edge of the deputy's desk and leaned forward. "Someone wants Hank's ranch, and they're trying to scare him into selling."

"Kline doesn't want the property."

"Maybe not, but he might be helping out the person who does."

"And who would that be, Ruby?"

"I don't know. It's your job to find out."

"I'll talk to Kline. More likely than not, it's a typo." Randall waited until she opened the door, then said, "I'm curious."

"About what?" Ruby asked.

"Why you're still here. I thought by now you'd be tired of this place."

"Who says I'm not tired of it?"

"The oil workers leave their families back in the cities because there's nothing out here for women."

"Hank's a pain in the ass, but he grows on you after a while." Ruby left the jail, then stood in the hot sun, eyeing the four-way stop at the end of the street. A faint rumble reached her ears right before a Greyhound rode a wave of dust into town. The bus stopped across the street, and the driver opened the door and looked at Ruby. "You boarding?"

What would happen if she left town? Would Mia and Hank miss her? And Joe . . . Would he miss her, or would all three of them be relieved? A gust of wind shoved Ruby from behind, and she stumbled into the street.

If you get on that bus, you'll only ever be Cora's daughter.

But if she didn't get on the bus, she might still have a fighting chance to be her own person.

Ruby shook her head at the driver. He closed the door and drove off. When the dust cloud settled, she caught Big Dan watching her from the window of the mercantile. Neither of them broke eye contact as she crossed the street.

"You decided to stay," he said when she entered the store.

"You don't sound surprised." She followed him as he zigzagged between the clothing racks. He climbed the stool behind the checkout counter. Today the tufts of white growing along the side of his head looked like jagged bolts of lightning. "You need a haircut."

He ignored her and stuck his fingers inside a tobacco pouch, then slipped a pinch between his gum and cheek.

"At least pluck the fuzz out of your ears. It looks like you're hiding kittens in there."

He struggled to keep a straight face, then gave up. "Cora used to tease me, too."

Ruby hated being compared to Cora—they had too much in common as it was. "Did Cora love Hank?" If she'd cared about him—in whatever way she'd been able to—at least Hank would have something to hold on to when he learned her fate.

"She never said."

"I get that Cora was bored at the ranch, but she could have driven into Guymon to shop or joined a club to meet women her age. Why did she spend her time with you?"

"She didn't have to pretend she was anything other than a hooker with me." The corner of his mouth curved upward. "I know what it's like to be different. To be looked down upon by society. We're both outcasts."

"But Hank didn't see Cora that way."

"Hank's intentions were good, and Cora was always grateful that he cared enough to offer her a normal life."

Was there such a thing as a normal life?

"After Cora had been at the ranch a while"—Big Dan spit tobacco juice into a Styrofoam cup—"she knew she could never be what Hank wanted her to be."

"And what was that?"

"Happy. Hank just wanted Cora to be happy. But she couldn't leave her past behind. It was a part of who she was and she felt lost without it."

"Did she tell you that she was unhappy?"

He nodded. "But she didn't tell me she was going to leave. I didn't know she'd taken off until Hank came into the store and said he was putting you up for adoption."

"Were you surprised Hank paid you a visit?"

"Not really. I think he hoped Cora had told me where she was going. He'd already contacted the brothel, but none of the women had seen or heard from her."

"What about the women who attended Hank and Cora's wedding? Wouldn't one of them have kept in touch with her after she left Nevada?"

"Cora didn't marry Hank." Big Dan's pudgy fingers scratched his cheek. "She knew even before she came that she wouldn't stay."

Her mother hadn't even tried to give Hank a chance. A lump swelled in Ruby's throat, threatening to block her airway. She felt sad for Hank and sad for herself, because she was nothing if not her mother's daughter. Ruby had given birth to a daughter out of wedlock. She'd never been married. And to be brutally honest: Ruby ended her relationships without giving them a real chance, just like Cora had done with Hank.

Big Dan handed Ruby the envelope of Cora's photos. "She'd want you to have these."

"What mother would want her daughter to see her in skimpy lingerie?"

"It's who she was, Ruby. Maybe not by her choice in the beginning, but by her choice in the end."

Ruby stuffed the envelope into her purse. She'd hide the photos in Cora's trunk in the attic.

"Did she ever contact you after she left town?" Had Cora cared even a little about what had happened to Hank and her daughter?

"About three years after she disappeared, Cora got off the bus in town and came into the store."

Ruby's heart beat faster.

"She was on her way to Amarillo and wanted to know if you were okay. I told her that you'd been adopted."

"Did she seem sad?" At Big Dan's blank look, Ruby said, "Forget I asked. "What had she been doing all those years?"

"She didn't say."

"Why was she going to Amarillo?"

He shrugged.

"You didn't ask?"

"She was back on the bus in less than two minutes."

Disappointment filled Ruby, but the knowledge that at least Cora had returned to check on her daughter and later made an attempt to communicate with her through Glen and Cheryl Baxter redeemed her a tiny bit in Ruby's eyes. "Did you tell Hank that Cora had stopped in town?"

"She asked me not to."

Cora had been heartless. "Hank's lawyer hired a private investigator to look for her."

Big Dan's head swung back and forth like a pendulum. "It's too late."

Ruby hoped not. "Maybe you're wrong." She weaved between the clothing racks.

"Ruby?"

"What?"

"It's time you faced your fears."

"I'm not afraid of finding out that Cora's dead."

"That's not what scares you."

Curse the midget and his clairvoyance. He knew she was running from herself, just like Cora. "Mind your own business."

Ruby drove fifteen miles below the speed limit back to the Devil's Wind because her watery eyes washed out the road in front of her.

Chapter 32

It was no surprise that Mia was exercising the horses when Ruby returned from her visit with Big Dan. The corral had become her daughter's safe place. Hank sat in a lawn chair in the shade, Friend sleeping on the ground at his feet. Ruby stayed in the pickup, watching the pair engage in an animated conversation involving hand gestures and lots of smiling.

She held her breath, anticipating the wallop to her stomach—the sensation she always experienced when she witnessed the closeness between Hank and Mia. But the pain never materialized and her heart melted. Ruby had stopped at the Devil's Wind to find answers for herself—she hadn't expected the desolate, dusty ranch to help her daughter grow stronger.

Because of Hank and the four-legged misfits in the barn, Mia would survive her mother's latest screw-up with Joe. Her relationship with her daughter was an ongoing project and unfortunately they'd taken a step back yesterday, but Ruby no longer feared that

Mia would do anything drastic again—like sleep with a boy—if her mother disappointed her.

And they both knew Ruby would mess up again.

Mia tipped her head and laughed, her long blond hair cascading down her back. Her daughter's looks were changing—faster than Ruby would like. It wouldn't be long before she blossomed into a full-grown woman. Mia would need a strong, guiding hand to help her steer clear of the abusers and losers in the world. What would happen when ornery old Hank wasn't there to threaten the bastards with his shotgun?

Joe would have stepped in and looked out for Mia, but you made certain that wouldn't happen.

Ruby went into the house, set her purse on the bed, then stood behind the screen door and watched Hank teach Mia how to play poker. Mia had a huge heart with lots of love to give, and Ruby was counting on her daughter to save a little of that love and forgiveness for her mother.

When Hank folded, Mia shouted, "I won, Grandpa!" She flung her arms around his neck and hugged him.

Feeling left out, Ruby went into the kitchen. A few minutes later Hank joined her. "You're like an old hound dog," she said. "You can sniff out a fresh pot of coffee a mile away."

He hung his hat on the hook by the door, then pulled out a chair at the table. The sound of the ticking wall clock and Hank's slurping broke the silence.

Ruby sat across from him, and they engaged in a squinty-eyed duel over the rims of their mugs. "Might as well speak your piece."

"I don't mind saying I'm disappointed that you gave up on yourself so easily," he said.

The old Ruby wanted to shout, *You don't have a right to be disappointed. You gave me away.* But she held her tongue until the urge passed. The new Ruby—the woman she needed to become to save her relationship with her daughter and maybe save herself—accepted Hank's admonishment.

"But I still love you," he said.

Her eyes widened.

"I've always loved you." He held her gaze. "And you know what?"

Still reeling from his proclamation, she whispered, "What?"

"I know you love me."

Hold on, now. Hank was pushing her too fast.

"You want to know how I'm sure about that?"

No.

"You got off the bus."

The ache in Ruby's stomach spread through her limbs, and the mug in her hand turned to lead. "I needed to learn my medical history for me and Mia." But it was more than that. From the moment she'd read the lawyer's letter, Ruby had yearned to connect with Hank, and the need had never wavered even when he'd opened the front door with a shotgun in his hand.

He set his cup aside, then leaned across the table and patted Ruby's cheek with his calloused hand. "Nothing you say or do will keep me from loving you, daughter."

There was still plenty of hurt and anger inside Ruby, but she recognized that the only way to move forward with Mia was to forgive Hank—fully and unconditionally. She knelt in front of his chair and collapsed against his bony chest.

Cigarette smoke, dust, and old age hugged her, and she held on tight, afraid if she let go, she'd lose him. "I forgive you . . . Dad." The word *Dad* had burst from her mouth like a boulder breaking through a dam. The anger and hurt rushed from her body, leaving her gutted.

"I'm grateful for your forgiveness, daughter."

Each wrinkle, brown spot, and scaly freckle reminded her of Hank's frail health. Would they have enough time to make up for the thirty-one years they'd been apart? "Promise me you won't die."

His eyes twinkled. "I'll hang on until Mia graduates from high school."

"Until she gets married." If Ruby had her way, Mia wouldn't walk down the aisle until she turned forty. "What if we never find out what happened to Cora?" Ruby wasn't sure she cared to learn the woman's fate. If her life mirrored her mother's, then maybe it was better if she didn't know how it would all end.

"Never mind Cora," he said. "What are you going to do about Joe?"

"Nothing." She'd blown it with him. "Women like me don't get second chances."

"You're talking like Cora."

Ruby returned to her chair. "What do you mean?"

"I've had three decades to figure out why she left me." He swirled the coffee in his mug. "I looked the other way when she slept with Sandoval, because she couldn't help herself. But that didn't keep me from loving her."

"Then why did she run off?"

"Cora didn't believe she deserved to be happy." Hank swung his gaze to Ruby. "You're a stronger woman than your mother was. Don't let your insecurities and fears rob you of the happiness you're entitled to." He took his cup to the sink. "I better go out there before Mia spoils those damned nags rotten."

Ruby sat alone in the kitchen, thinking back on the years following her parents' deaths. Life had been tough when she'd had to raise Mia alone. She'd shut down inside and focused solely on surviving. She went to the window and watched Mia and Hank in the corral. If there was ever a time in her life to grow a backbone, it was now. She was tired of running. It was time to stand her ground and reach for the happiness that she'd denied herself for so long.

Ruby stood in the hallway outside Mia's bedroom, holding a plate of cold pizza slices. Ever since the satellite Internet service provider had installed a dish on the roof earlier in the day, Mia and Hank had been holed up inside the bedroom. Ruby had gone to the bottom of the stairs twice and called them down for supper, but they'd ignored her.

"Can I come in?" When no one acknowledged her request, Ruby opened the door and poked her head inside the room. Hank sat on the bed beside Mia, holding a brand-new laptop.

"Click on the link," Mia said.

"What link?" Hank asked.

"That one." Mia tapped the keyboard. "I added it to your favorites list."

"I don't want to see pictures of Pinky's band," Hank said.

"I do."

"Why does she have pink hair?"

"Because her name's Pinky."

"Stupid name if you ask me."

"Check out this photo. I think that's a dance club in Paris. Have you ever been to Paris?"

"No."

"Would you like to go someday?"

"No. Now get me back to that game I was playing a minute ago."

Mia sighed dramatically. "Mom won't like it if she finds out you're playing Internet poker."

"She won't find out unless you tell her."

"I won't find out what?" Ruby struggled not to laugh at the startled expressions on both their faces.

"Nothing." Hank closed the laptop.

"I was standing in the hall for five minutes and neither one of you answered me."

"I've been showing Grandpa all the stuff he can do on his new computer."

"I brought you supper." She held out the plate.

Hank took a slice of pizza off the plate as he walked by. "I'll eat in the kitchen." He closed the door behind him, leaving Ruby alone with her daughter.

"I'm not hungry," Mia said.

If they didn't talk, the tension between them would grow worse. "I need to apologize."

Mia groaned and flung herself back on the mattress.

Ruby put the plate on the dresser, then sat in the rocker. She'd rehearsed her speech before coming upstairs—funny how she couldn't remember a word of it now. "I don't know what else to say other than I'm sorry."

"You hurt Joe."

"I didn't mean to, but I realized that I have some things to work out." *With myself.*

Mia rolled her head sideways and stared at Ruby. "You hurt everyone."

Shame filled her when she thought of all the men who had come and gone from their lives—several of them decent guys who hadn't deserved the way Ruby had treated them.

"I think you did it to hurt me, too. I like Joe and I was hoping you guys would get together." Mia wiped her eyes, and Ruby died a little with each tear that slid down her daughter's cheek. "I wanted all of us to be a family."

"I can promise that you, me, and Hank will always be family."

"What do you mean?"

Now that Ruby had forgiven Hank and let go of the hurt and anger, she intended to take care of him for as long as he stuck around. "We're going to make the Devil's Wind our new home." *Home*—she'd never thought she'd equate the word with Hank like Mia had, but they were now one and the same in Ruby's heart.

"What about Joe? Is he gonna stay, too?" Mia wanted stability in her life. A man she could look up to as a father. A mother who put her first. Hank was the frosting on the cake—a grandfather who made her feel extra special.

"I don't know what Joe's plans are, but he'll always be welcome here."

"Make him want to stay, Mom."

Ruby wished life were that easy—that if you just tried a little harder, everything would turn out okay. "Honey, I'm sorry I let you down." *Again.*

"I'm tired." Mia stuck her iPod buds into her ears.

Ruby left her daughter alone and went downstairs, where she spotted the pruning shears on the table next to the umbrella stand. She took them outside and knelt on the ground in front of the rosebushes, then went to work clipping the dead twigs—each snip representing bits and pieces of her past that she needed to shed in order to bloom again. It was rough acknowledging that she'd made more bad choices than good and had hurt the ones she cared about most. She dropped the dried stems on the ground, where the blowing dust would eventually bury them.

"Don't cut 'em back too much."

Ruby hadn't heard Hank come outside.

"Cora said red roses reminded her of home."

"Where was Cora's home?"

"Arkansas."

"Nevada's a long way from Arkansas. How did she end up that far away?"

Hank sat in the chair. "Her mama died when she was real young."

"Any siblings?"

"An older brother."

"What was her last name?"

"Johnson."

Ruby rose from her knees and sank down on the porch step. "Do you think she made up the name?"

"Cora never lied to me."

"What about her affair with Sandoval?"

"I never asked Cora if she was sleeping with Roy."

His answer made Ruby both angry and sad, so she changed the subject. "What was Cora's childhood like?"

"Her daddy gambled." Hank's fuzzy eyebrows lowered, deepening the wrinkles across his forehead. His mouth pressed into a thin line and his nostrils flared. "The bastard let his friends have turns with Cora to pay off his gambling debts."

Cora had turned to a life of prostitution because that's all she'd known, thanks to her father. "I'm surprised she wanted anything to do with you after you won the ranch in a poker game."

"I promised Cora I wouldn't gamble anymore."

"Did you keep that promise?"

Hank nodded. "Haven't set foot in a casino since I beat Roy at cards."

And he'd kept his promise to Cora even after she'd left him. "How did she end up in Nevada?"

"Ran away from home at fifteen and met a gal on the streets who'd worked at the Love Ranch Cathouse. She told Cora that they treated the girls well."

That Cora had survived her teen years was a testament to her strength. "Why was she so special?"

"Because she was kind to a piss-poor cowpuncher with little education." He rubbed his eyes. "To tell you the truth, I never thought I'd be able to sweet-talk her into coming here."

"You . . . a sweet-talker?"

He chuckled. "I was better-looking back in the day."

"Did you ask her to marry you?"

"I did, but she said I could do better."

Yet he still loved her. "You could have gone after Cora." Maybe if Hank had found her, he could have persuaded her to return to the Devil's Wind and the three of them could have been a family.

"I didn't go after your mother because I knew she wouldn't come home until she was ready."

So Hank had waited at the Devil's Wind year after year, hoping Cora would stop running.

Ruby understood all too well that fear played crazy games with a person's reasoning. Wanting to shield herself from hurt, she panicked and ran at the first sign of trouble instead of trusting in herself and her partner to work things out.

Ruby climbed the porch steps and sat in the chair next to him.

"I'm sorry Cora disappointed you." She was apologizing a lot lately. She held his hand and asked, "Any news from your lawyer?"

"Charles said the investigator found a promising lead." He pulled his hand free and patted his empty shirt pocket. "Dad blamit."

"What?"

"My Winstons are in my room." He offered a sheepish smile. "Mia says I'll quit sooner if I have to walk upstairs to get my cigarettes every time I want a smoke."

"Is it working?"

"Maybe," he grumbled.

"Thank you for trying to please Mia." Lord knows Ruby hadn't done a good job of it lately.

"Didn't promise to quit, but I'm cutting back." He got up from his chair. "Man's gotta have a vice in life or it ain't worth living."

"Speaking of vices, I Googled online gambling laws in Oklahoma, and I'm not sure it's legal."

"By the time they catch me, I'll be six feet under." He puffed out his chest. "My poker name is the Dusty Devil." He chuckled. "I won fifty bucks earlier."

"What about your promise to Cora?"

"I promised not to gamble in a casino."

It dawned on Ruby that Hank taking up gambling again might signify that he was done waiting for Cora to return. Maybe he was moving on, too.

"You don't have to work at the bar," he said. "I've got enough money to pay the bills and feed us."

"I appreciate that, but I need to keep busy." She'd never been a stay-at-home mom, and her job had been her social life. She'd go nuts wandering around the ranch with nothing to do all day.

"The house could use a makeover."

That was an understatement. "What kind of makeover?"

"Update the kitchen. Maybe turn the back porch into a real bedroom and add a bathroom. You could take my room. Then I wouldn't have to go up those damned stairs each time I wanted a cigarette."

Ruby laughed. "If you're serious, I'll look into getting bids from local contractors."

"I'll let you handle it, then." He went into the house and left her alone with her thoughts.

Ruby was no Suzy Homemaker, but working on renovations would allow her to spend time with Hank while Mia was in school. And she'd be right by his side if he fell ill. She got up and knelt in front of the bushes again. Every few snips, she glanced at the barn. Sweet longing almost propelled her toward the structure.

She owed Joe an apology—at the very least.

Like Hank preferred not to know what had happened to Cora, Ruby would rather not know if Joe wanted to give her a second chance.

Chapter 33

"I'm ready, Grandpa." Mia's voice arrived in the kitchen before she did.

"Did you feed the horses?" Hank asked.

She nodded. "Joe said Lonesome needs a pedicure and you're supposed to call a fairy."

Hank chuckled, no longer embarrassed that his smile showed the world his missing teeth. "Farrier."

"Whatever."

"Where are you two going?" Ruby set the laundry basket on the kitchen table.

"Guymon. Grandpa said I could buy some movies to play on his computer." Mia patted her leg. "Come say goodbye to me, Friend." The dog followed her outside.

Ruby knew what they were doing—leaving her alone with Joe, forcing her to talk to him even though she wasn't ready. "You want me to tag along?" she asked, hoping Hank would say yes.

"Nope." He handed her his empty coffee mug, then kissed her cheek.

"I don't know what to say to Joe."

"You'll think of something." He walked out the front door.

Ruby listened to the rumble of Hank's pickup fade as the oxygen in the room evaporated, making her heart pump faster. She wanted so badly to get this right.

Fear won the first round. She took a cool shower, then a cold one, standing under the spray until her skin turned blue and shivers forced her out of the tub. Ruby's beauty routine was minimal at best, but today she slathered lotion on her body. Then she shaved. Brushed and flossed her teeth. And gargled with Listerine twice, hoping the numbness in her mouth would loosen her jaws and make talking easier. She wore a pink bra beneath a black lace top and a pair of cutoff jeans shorts. She studied her reflection in the mirror—sexy but not slutty.

As she made her way to the barn, she walked past Joe's pickup, and it wasn't until she heard a clanging noise behind her that she noticed his legs sticking out from beneath the front end. She backpedaled and waited for him to acknowledge her. Seconds ticked by, and when he didn't speak, she thought he intended to ignore her. "I'm sorry."

Silence.

Now she was ticked. "You're not going to give me a chance to explain?"

The clanking stopped. Joe slid out from under the engine and stood. His sober expression gave nothing away. She couldn't tell if he was mad, hurt, or indifferent about how she'd treated him.

"I panicked."

He wiped his hands on an oil rag, the lines around his eyes

softening as he stared at her. "Okay." Then he knelt on the ground and rummaged through the toolbox next to the front wheel.

Okay? What the hell was happening? Why wasn't he upset—or at the very least telling her she'd hurt his feelings? She didn't know how to fight like this. "I've never been good at trusting men . . ."

He glanced up at her.

She tapped her chest with her fist. "With my heart."

"I figured that." He sifted through the tools.

"Would you stop!"

"Stop what?"

"Acting like what I'm telling you is no big deal." She kicked a pebble in the dirt and sent it flying over the roof of the truck. "Damn it, Joe. You scare me."

He got to his feet. "I know being with me worries you. I'm worried, too."

"You are?"

He slipped a finger beneath her pink bra strap and pushed it back under her shirt. "I buried the pain of losing Aaron so deep inside me that I couldn't feel it anymore. But watching you and Mia work through your problems reminded me of the joy my son brought to my life. I want to feel that joy again, but I don't want the pain that comes with it."

"My history with men doesn't make me a sure bet." She snorted. "And it's not enough that serious relationships scare me, but now I have to accept the fact that I'm genetically predisposed to being a whore."

Joe's eyes widened, and then he busted up.

"It's not funny." When he wouldn't stop laughing, she yanked the front of his T-shirt. "If my biological mother couldn't settle down with one man, then the future doesn't bode well for me."

His smile faded. "You're not your mother, Ruby. You're you."

"That's what I'm trying to make you understand. *Me* isn't such a hot deal, and you deserve a woman who's not afraid to love you."

"Then don't be afraid."

"Damn it, Joe. I'm trying to do what's best for you."

"You're what's best for me." He tucked a strand of hair behind her ear. "Give us a chance, Ruby. Let's see if together we can move on with our lives and find something better with each other."

She wanted Joe. Wanted to prove to Mia that she was capable of being in a committed relationship. "I don't want to fail you." Or Mia and Hank.

"You won't fail this time."

"How can you be sure?"

"Because this time it's with me." He pulled her close, and she buried her face in his neck. He smelled of cheap laundry detergent, and—God help her—he smelled like *forever.*

"When you smile at me," he said, "I can almost believe Aaron wouldn't want me to keep punishing myself."

Ruby's heart hurt for Joe. She thought of Cora and all the men she'd slept with and how none of them had made her happy—not even Hank, who truly loved her. Ruby didn't want that life for herself.

Joe pressed a kiss to her mouth. "Let me be there for you and Mia."

She closed her eyes, drew in a deep breath, and held it in her lungs. She was strong—stronger than she'd been just weeks ago when she'd stepped off the bus in Unforgiven. If and when—because there would be ifs and whens—she began to doubt herself, Hank and Mia would keep her on the straight and narrow.

"Okay." She exhaled and opened her eyes. "Let's do this." Then she rose on tiptoe and kissed him, gifting him with her heart and her trust. She took his hand and led him to the house, where they entered the back porch and tumbled onto the mattress.

No words were spoken. The only thing left to do now was just love each other.

"Who's that?" Mia pointed to the BMW parked in front of the house as Ruby drove into the yard late Thursday morning.

"I don't know." She stopped the truck next to the car. She and Mia had taken a quick trip to Lonny's Icehouse five miles down the road to buy Hank his favorite ice cream—boring vanilla. She glanced at the barn. Joe's pickup was missing.

"I'm gonna put the horses in the corral."

"I'll come out and help you after I take the ice cream inside."

"That's okay. I can do it by myself." Mia skipped off toward the barn.

"Hank?" Ruby called out when she entered the house.

"In here."

She stowed the ice cream in the freezer, then went into the parlor. Hank sat on the piano bench, staring at his boots while a distinguished-looking man wearing a tan suit stood in front of the window. The gentleman's gray hair was neatly trimmed, and his expensive cologne overpowered the furniture's musty odor.

Hank looked at her with bloodshot eyes, and Ruby's stomach dropped. "What happened?"

"This is Charles Walker." Hank's finger shook when he pointed to the visitor. "Charles, my daughter, Ruby."

The lawyer offered his hand along with a strained smile. "Pleasure to meet you, Ruby."

Her heart beat faster. There were only two reasons Mr. Walker would pay Hank a visit in person—he had news about the oil lease or the investigator had located Cora. Ruby sat next to Hank on the bench and grasped his hand.

Charles cleared his throat. "The PI I hired to look into Cora's whereabouts—"

"Is she alive?" Ruby interrupted. She hadn't realized how badly she needed Cora not to be dead—for Hank. And maybe a little bit for herself, too.

"Cora's alive."

Ruby breathed deeply through her nose until her light-headedness disappeared. "Where is she?"

"Amarillo."

Where she'd told Big Dan she was headed when she'd stopped in town all those years ago. "How long has she been there?" Ruby asked.

"Approximately twenty years."

All this time Cora had lived a little more than a hundred miles down the road from Hank. "This is good news, right?" Hank wouldn't make eye contact with her.

"Cora was admitted to a convalescent home nine months ago," Charles said.

"What else did you learn about her?"

"I'm not a relative, so the home wouldn't give out any information on her condition." Charles removed a piece of paper from his suit pocket and handed it to Hank. "The address and phone number of the nursing home. I informed the manager that you might call to inquire about Cora."

Charles checked his watch. "I'm meeting with the Petro Oil executives in two weeks. I'll be in touch about your lease."

"I'll see you out." Ruby followed the lawyer onto the front porch, closing the door behind her. "The nursing staff wouldn't tell you anything about Cora's health or state of mind?"

Charles shook his head. "They mentioned that she hasn't had any visitors since she's been there."

"Thank you for your help." Ruby waited until the BMW was out of sight before returning to the parlor. Hank hadn't budged from the piano bench. "If you want to see Cora, I'll go with you. We can leave right now."

"I'll pack a bag." He was halfway up the stairs before the words registered in Ruby's head. She retreated to the porch and threw a few changes of clothes into a duffel bag, then went out to the corral, where Mia had just turned Poke loose. She spotted Joe's pickup barreling toward the barn. After he parked, he joined them at the corral.

"You're spoiling Poke," he said.

"I know." Mia laughed. "But he's sooo cute!"

Joe's gaze swung to Ruby, and his brown eyes grew darker. It had been like that between them since they'd made love—their touches were hotter, their looks deeper, their words softer. "How was your morning?" he asked.

"Hank's lawyer was just here. They found Cora."

Mia walked closer. "He found my grandma?"

"Cora's in a nursing home in Amarillo, Texas."

"I can drive Hank down there to see her," Joe offered.

"I want to go, too," Mia said.

Ruby would love for Mia to meet her grandmother, but there was no predicting Hank's reaction when he laid eyes on the love of his life for the first time in thirty-one years. What if he lost it? Or what if Cora refused to speak to him? Or worse, what if she didn't remember Hank anymore? Ruby wasn't even sure how she'd react when she came face-to-face with her biological mother.

"Maybe next time, honey."

"Take my truck," Joe said.

"Thanks." Hank would have a real heart attack if his old jalopy broke down before they arrived in Amarillo. "I'll call when we get there."

"Are you gonna bring her home?" Mia asked.

Home. The sick feeling Ruby usually got in her gut when Mia called the Devil's Wind home didn't materialize. She'd finally acknowledged what Mia had seen all along—that the ranch was a safe haven for both of them. "I'll let you know our plans after we see her." Hank would insist on bringing Cora back to the ranch. Ruby didn't like the idea of having to take care of the woman, but she'd do it for Hank.

"We'll be fine," Joe said.

When Ruby rested her head against his chest, he wrapped his arms around her and she thought how fortunate she was to have him to lean on.

"I'm glad you guys made up."

"Me too." She released Joe, then kissed Mia's sweaty head. "Stay out of trouble."

"I'm gonna say goodbye to Grandpa."

Left alone with Joe, Ruby said, "Will you sleep on the porch while we're gone? I don't want Mia alone in the house at night."

He rubbed the pad of his thumb across her forehead. "Stop frowning. Everything will be okay." He left her to get his truck, and Ruby walked to the front yard.

As soon as Hank stepped outside with his overnight bag, Ruby said, "I'll be right back." Then she went into the house and retrieved Hank's heart pills from the kitchen cabinet. There was no way to predict how he'd react to seeing Cora, and she wanted to be prepared just in case.

"Buckle up," Ruby said when she got behind the wheel. She waved to Mia and Joe as they drove off.

"Gun it," Hank said when they reached the highway. "I'll pay for the speeding ticket if you get pulled over."

She pressed the accelerator until the needle on the speedometer hovered at eighty. Hank slouched in his seat and pulled his hat over his face, leaving Ruby alone with her thoughts and a hundred miles of asphalt.

Chapter 34

Ruby decreased her speed on the outskirts of Amarillo. The two-hour drive had taken an hour and twenty minutes. She'd been lucky the highway patrol hadn't pulled her over. Hank had had little to say during the trip. He'd spent most of the time staring at the notepaper clutched between his fingers.

She passed him her cell phone. "Turn on the GPS and type in the address of the convalescent home."

His finger hovered over the screen, his mouth puckering like a raisin.

"Never mind," she said. A half mile later she pulled into a gas station and parked in front of the convenience store. With a few taps of her finger, she opened the GPS and typed in the address.

"You want anything to drink?" Hank asked.

"A diet cola would be nice, thanks." Ruby watched him through the windshield, his shoulders hunched, shoes barely clearing the ground. She worried that this visit would take a huge toll, both physically and emotionally, on his heart. She could only hope that Cora had a kind word for him after all the heartache she'd caused.

"The place isn't far from here," Ruby said when he returned with their drinks. She left the gas station and merged onto the main road. After three traffic lights and two right turns, they arrived at the Angel of Mercy Care Center.

The one-story brick facility looked every bit as worn and tired as Hank. The landscape was overrun with weeds, and only a few stubborn blooms clung to the daisy bushes. Narrow prison-style windows ran the length of the patient wings. Only a handful of vehicles sat in the lot—probably the nurses and aides who worked in the home.

Ruby parked by the front doors, where an angel statue, leaning precariously to one side, guarded the entrance. Dirt filled the cracks in the cherub's face, and a chunk of plaster was missing from her left wing. A lifetime of guarding departing souls had beaten her down and she begged to be relieved of her duties.

The strong odor of urine welcomed them inside the facility. A crowd of wheelchairs sat parked before a big-screen TV. The residents stared in trancelike states, their gazes attached to various objects in the room—a fish tank, an oil painting of a Victorian woman, a matted teddy bear left on a chair, a wastepaper basket filled with plastic drink cups.

"Do you see her?" she asked.

Hank shook his head. "But my eyes aren't what they used to be."

A nurse in a blue blouse, white slacks, and a gray sweater walked into the room and noticed them. "Hello. I hope you haven't been waiting long. Our maintenance man is on vacation, and the alarm on the door won't be fixed until he returns." She offered Hank her hand. "I'm Janelle. I assume you'd like to tour the facility."

Hank stiffened, and Ruby jumped to his defense. "We're here to visit Cora Johnson."

"The name doesn't sound familiar."

They accompanied Janelle to the nurse's station on the other side of the room. While she flipped through the patient register, Ruby peeked into the dining hall. An elderly resident in a hospital gown and bib sat alone at a table, a tray of untouched food in front of him. It was three in the afternoon. If the man hadn't eaten by now, he didn't want to.

Cold fingers clutched Ruby's arm, and she jumped inside her skin. A woman with desperate eyes stared at her.

"Take me home." Her rank breath hit Ruby in the face, and she stepped back.

"What's your name?"

"I don't belong here."

"Margaret!" A nurse marched toward them. "You should be in your room, resting."

"I don't want to be here," Margaret whined.

"This is your home now." The nurse escorted the woman away.

Ruby returned to the station and spoke to Janelle. "Does Margaret ask to go home all the time?"

"She's new here. She'll settle down soon."

"She seems to have all of her faculties. How did she end up in here?" Ruby asked.

"Her son moved to Florida, and he and his wife decided not to take her with them. They sold her house and brought her here."

No matter how bad off Hank got, Ruby would never put him in a home. A few weeks ago she'd been determined to give him a piece of her mind and then head to Kansas. Now, as she stared at the haggard face that had won her forgiveness and a piece of her heart, she couldn't imagine her and Mia not being with him for however many days he had left on earth.

Janelle glanced up from the register. "I can't find Cora's name in our records. Is it possible she's in a different facility?"

"I don't think so," Ruby said. Unless the private investigator had gotten the name of the convalescent home wrong.

"How are you related to Cora?"

"She's my birth mother," Ruby said.

Janelle picked up a walkie-talkie. "Heather, will you please come to the front desk?"

A few minutes later a second nurse joined them. "These folks are looking for Cora Johnson. I don't see her listed in the book."

"They moved Cora to the hospice wing three days ago."

Hospice?

Hank swayed, and Ruby clutched his arm. "Can we see her?"

"I'll take you to her room," Heather said. They walked through a second set of doors and down a hallway. "I wasn't aware that Cora had any relatives."

"How did she end up here?" Ruby asked.

"Her landlord found her passed out in front of her apartment. He called 911."

They moved aside when two men wearing scrubs pushed a gurney around the corner and headed in their direction. Hank stiffened as the sheet-covered body passed by.

"That's not Cora," Heather said. "Her room is this way." They continued down the corridor. "Cora suffered a stroke. The hospital did all they could for her, but because no next of kin were ever located, she was released into the state's care and transferred here."

"When did her health take a turn for the worse?" Ruby asked.

"She stopped eating five days ago. We're giving her IV fluids and making her as comfortable as possible." Heather stopped outside room seven. "I'm afraid her pneumonia isn't improving, but she's a fighter." The nurse offered a sympathetic smile, then left them in the hallway.

Ruby closed her eyes and thought back to the afternoon she'd opened the envelope from Hank's lawyer and learned she'd been adopted. No way could she have predicted that a few months later she'd be visiting her birth mother on her deathbed.

Hank looked scared. And too damn old.

What if, after seeing Cora, he stopped caring if he lived? They'd been robbed of a lifetime together, and the thought of Hank choosing to go with Cora and leave her and Mia behind was too painful to consider. Cora had already destroyed Ruby's relationship with Glen Baxter. Couldn't she leave Ruby's other father alone?

"I'll stay here if you want privacy," Ruby said.

"We'll go together." Hank grabbed her hand, and Ruby clutched it tight. He might not have said the words, but he needed her, and no matter her feelings for Cora, Ruby would help Hank through whatever awaited him inside the room.

"Ready?" With a gentle nudge, she urged Hank through the doorway.

A single bed sat behind a partially drawn curtain that concealed the upper half of Cora's body. A beige blanket covered her from the waist down.

Hank scuffled across the floor, his gait uneven. Ruby hoped it was his bad hip giving him trouble and not the pacemaker ticking out of whack. He removed his cowboy hat and placed it over his heart. Ruby waited by the doorway, allowing him a private moment with the woman who'd held his heart prisoner for a lifetime.

A single tear slid down Hank's wrinkled cheek and dripped off his chin. Ruby could almost hear the voice in his head begging Cora to accept his love. Nothing would make him happier than believing she carried his heart with her to heaven.

He'd offered Cora his love and a better life, but she'd turned her back on him. Pity was all she'd get from Ruby.

She joined Hank at the foot of the bed. The moment seemed surreal, as if she watched the scene unfold from somewhere outside her body. Cora didn't look like a woman who'd spent her life breaking men's hearts. A cloud of pearl-white curls threatened to swallow an innocent doll face. Only a few wrinkles and age spots marred her porcelain skin. Even with one foot in the grave, Cora's beauty shone through.

A clear tube fed oxygen into her nose while her buxom chest rose and fell in shallow, quick movements. A frail arm rested above the covers, where IV fluid fed into a blue vein on the back of her hand. Had that hand caressed Faith's head before she'd dropped the ruby necklace into the bassinet and fled the hospital?

Hank moved to the side of the bed and grasped Cora's fingers. Ruby pushed a chair across the floor, made him sit, then leaned against the wall and watched the scene unfold.

"It's Hank, Cora."

Cora's eyeballs moved beneath the closed lids—maybe she recognized his voice.

"You gave me a scare when you ran off after giving birth to Faith."

Ruby felt the urge to punch the wall. Hank had gone to bed every night for decades not knowing if the woman he loved was safe or had met an ugly fate. It wasn't right. This whole situation was messed up.

"I never quit hoping that you'd find your way home." He rubbed his eyes. "But we're together now. That's all that matters."

Hank drew in a deep breath. "You should see Faith. You'd be real proud of the woman she's become. Her parents named her Ruby. Every day she wears the necklace I gave you."

Why hadn't Hank told her that *he'd* purchased the jewelry? Ruby felt better about wearing it now that she knew one of Cora's admirers hadn't given her the gift.

"You've got a granddaughter named Mia. She's smart as a whip. Wants me to quit smoking. I know you told me to quit, too. I've cut way back." Hank played with Cora's fingers as if he could will them to squeeze back.

"My lawyer found Faith, and she's staying with me now. You get better so you can come home. Faith'll look after us."

He slouched in the chair as if settling in for an afternoon chat. "Heard you tried to see Faith when she was sixteen." He shook his head. "I know I disappointed you because I didn't keep her with me, but I couldn't raise her. Not by myself. Not without you."

Ruby had heard enough. She slipped from the room and returned to the nurse's station, where Heather was dropping blue pills into tiny disposable soufflé cups.

"Do you know if the name of the apartment complex where Cora lived is in her file?"

"Let me check." Heather pulled out a black binder with pocket folders. She read through the patient notes. "Belmont Estates. It's not far from here. Go south on Winchester—that's the street out front. Turn left at the first light, and it's down the block."

"I'm going over there to speak with the manager. If Hank asks where I am, will you tell him I'll be back soon?"

"Sure."

Ruby stepped outside and drew in deep breaths—one after the other until she flushed the stench of death from her nostrils. Then she got into the pickup and drove off.

When she arrived at Belmont Estates, a neon sign in the office window blinked Vacancy. The units were single rooms, not apartments. The trailer Ruby had leased in Missouri had been nothing to brag about, but it had been downright homey compared to this dump.

The rental office was the size of a closet. The man behind the counter set aside his newspaper and offered a yellow-toothed grin. The first four buttons of his purple silk shirt were open, showing off a thick gold chain and a clump of dark chest hair that looked like the stuff you pulled out of your bathtub drain. He hadn't shaved in at least two days. Food crumbs stuck to the beard stubble at the corners of his mouth. His greasy hair was thinning on top, but rather than sport the popular comb-over style, he'd used a brown spray-in concealer on his scalp—two shades darker than his natural hair color.

His sleazy gaze zeroed in on Ruby's bosom. "I rent by the hour or by the day."

"I don't want a room. I was hoping you might remember a former tenant. Cora Johnson."

"You a cop or something?"

"Family."

"The name sounds familiar. Maybe." He leaned back in his chair and winked.

Jerk. Ruby pulled a twenty-dollar bill from her wallet and tossed it on the counter. He ignored the money.

"I can go get a cop if you want."

The smile slid off his face, and he stuffed the twenty into his pocket. "I called 911 after I found her."

"How long had she lived here?"

"She was here when I took over as manager three years ago."

Three years? "Any idea where she'd been before that?"

"Lady, do I look like I'm friends with my renters?"

"What happened to her belongings?"

"Put them in storage." He narrowed his eyes. "What do you want with Cora?"

"She's my birth mother."

"We've got a roomful of personal possessions from former residents." He came out from behind the counter with a set of keys. "It'll cost you fifty bucks to have a look."

"On top of the twenty I gave you?"

"I'm losing rent money off the room I store everyone's crap in."

"This is all I have." She held out another twenty-dollar bill, and he snatched it from her fingertips. They went outside, and he opened the door to room one, next to the office, and flipped on the light switch.

Mounds of clothes covered the king-size bed. Suitcases lined the walls. Two cardboard boxes overflowed with mismatched shoes. A plastic tote filled with kitchenware had been shoved beneath the bathroom sink. "I'm guessing you don't remember which things were Cora's," Ruby said.

"The yellow suitcase was in her room, but the rest of this junk . . ." He shook his head. "Let me know when you're done, so I can lock up." He left the door open.

Ruby passed over the piles of clothing, boxes of shoes, and kitchen gadgets and went straight for the luggage. If suitcases could talk, she'd love to ask about all the places this one had been. Scuff marks and scratches marred the leather. No tag. She set the yellow bag on the bathroom vanity, then opened it.

Empty. Unless . . . She unzipped the side pocket. Bingo! A faded Polaroid snapshot of a bald-headed baby sleeping in a hospital bassinet. Only the word *March* was discernible from the smudge of blue ink along the white border. She turned the photo over. *Faith.*

Ruby's first baby picture.

Cora must have borrowed a camera from a nurse or maybe a new father hanging out on the maternity floor. Ruby put the Polaroid in her purse, then carried the suitcase to the door. She had no idea why she was taking the bag—she just knew she couldn't leave it behind. She stopped at the office, but the manager was gone. He'd probably left the property to buy booze or more hair dye with the forty bucks he'd swindled from her.

When she returned to the nursing home, she found Hank right where she'd left him—snoozing in the chair by Cora's side. He'd aged twenty years since he'd entered the hospice wing, his complexion as gray as the ash from his beloved cigarettes. He'd hung on all these years because he hadn't known Cora's fate, and now that he'd found her, the woman was draining the life out of him right before Ruby's eyes.

As much as she hated Cora for hurting Hank, she wished the woman would gain consciousness and answer for her actions. But answers didn't seem to matter to Hank. Cora had put him through hell, but all he cared about was getting one more chance to tell her that he loved her.

Careful not to wake Hank, Ruby moved to the opposite side of Cora's bed and reached for her hand—soft as silk. Cold as ice.

You must have missed me a little if you kept my baby picture all these years.

Ruby needed to speak her piece, even if it was only in her head.

I didn't know you tried to see me when I was sixteen. I wish we could have met, but my mother was afraid you'd be a bad influence on me.

Hank shifted in his chair, and Ruby held her breath, willing him not to wake up.

You know, it's pretty shitty of you to die without telling Hank why you left him. Why you left me.

Cora's fingers moved in her hand.

Hank's got a bad heart, but I'm going to take care of him. A tear escaped Ruby's eye, and she brushed it away.

I wish his lawyer had never found you.

It was the honest truth.

You broke his heart, Cora, but he never stopped loving you.

The tears kept coming. *I know you can't take back all the pain you caused Hank, but you can make amends for it by convincing God or whoever's in charge up there not to call him home too soon. My daughter and I need him.*

Cora's white lashes fluttered.

I haven't been a perfect mother, either. Like you, I've made mistakes. Big mistakes. But because of Hank, Mia's giving me a chance to make it up to her.

Ruby pressed her lips together to prevent the sob in her chest from breaking free. *It's too late for you to make it up to me, but I'll forgive you anyway.*

Cora's fingers moved again.

And when the time comes that you and Hank are together, you'd better treat him right and not run off on him again. Ruby squeezed the frail hand one final time, then stepped away from the bed. When she glanced up, Hank was staring at her. "I'm hungry," she said. "Let's grab a bite to eat."

“I’ll stay here.” Hank wasn’t going to let Cora die alone.

“I’ll bring you something back.” When she got into the truck, she called Mia’s cell. No answer, so she left a detailed message and a promise to phone again later.

Then Ruby sat and stared at the guardian angel’s broken wing and bawled her head off.

Chapter 35

It took Cora three days to die.

After thirty-one years, the love of Hank's life was finally coming home. The cardboard box rested in his lap, his hand absently caressing the lid. He seemed at peace with Cora's passing, reassuring Ruby that his spirit was a lot stronger than his frail body. He'd sat with her until the end, holding her hand as she'd drawn her last breath. Then he'd kissed her cheek and left the room.

They'd remained in Amarillo two additional days while Cora's body had been cremated. This morning they woke early, ate breakfast at Denny's with the Tuesday regulars, then sat in the parking lot of the Angel of Mercy Care Center until the crematory delivered the ashes. Ruby tried to keep the conversation going when they hit the road, but Hank wasn't in the mood to talk, so they made the drive home in silence.

"Where do you want to spread her ashes?" Ruby turned onto the ranch road.

"Beneath the rosebushes. You can put my ashes there, too, before you get rid of the place."

"What makes you think I'll sell the property? Your granddaughter won't want to leave the horses." Ruby wasn't keen on spending the rest of her life caring for old nags, but she admired her daughter for devoting herself to a good cause. Mia must have inherited that quality from Hank, because Ruby had never gone out of her way to help animals in need.

"Mia's a good girl," he said. "She's got a big heart."

"Joe thinks you should run more cattle."

"Then you two will have to dig a second well."

"Would you please stop talking as if you won't be here tomorrow?"

"Might not."

"Just because Cora's gone doesn't mean you have to follow in her footsteps. You've lived without her this long. You can hold out a few more birthdays before you see her again."

Hank's lips twitched.

She squinted out the windshield. "Do you see that dark cloud?"

"Smoke."

"The barn's on fire." She pressed on the gas pedal.

Hank set Cora's ashes aside and leaned forward, straining the seat belt.

When they drew closer, Ruby said, "The horses are in the corral and Friend's barking in the driveway." The dog paced in front of the barn doors. A shiver raced down her spine. "I don't see Mia or Joe." She parked in front of the house, then sprinted toward the barn.

Flames shot through the roof at the back of the structure, and smoke poured from the open door and windows. She hit a wall of heat fifteen feet from the barn and stopped. "Mia! Joe!"

Joe staggered out of the barn, carrying Mia in his arms, both coughing and covered in soot.

Heart banging against her rib cage, Ruby held her daughter's hand as Joe carried her into the backyard. He set Mia on the porch steps, and Ruby stared into her watering eyes. "Are you hurt?"

"No," Mia wheezed.

"Joe?" Ruby tugged his shirtsleeve.

"I'm okay." He bent over at the knees and coughed.

Ruby went into the house and grabbed bottles of water for Mia and Joe, then returned outside.

"Everyone okay?" Hank came around the corner of the house. As soon as he saw Mia, he went over and sat next to her. Ruby pressed her palm against his chest, as if the pressure would prevent his pacemaker from short-circuiting. "Don't get riled up, Dad. Everyone's okay."

"I couldn't get down from the hayloft because the ladder was on fire," Mia said before guzzling her water.

"I called the fire department, and the sheriff's on his way, too." Joe stared in a trancelike state at the burning structure. "I shouldn't have left Mia alone."

"What do you mean, alone?" Ruby asked, but Joe ignored her and walked over to the tree, where he stood by himself and watched the barn burn.

"I saw him do it, Grandpa." Mia rested her head on Hank's shoulder.

"Who?" Ruby asked. "Who did you see?"

"The man who set the fire."

Dear God. If Joe hadn't rescued Mia . . . Ruby couldn't finish the thought. Twice now someone had tried to harm her daughter.

Joe had risked his life when he'd carried Mia out of the barn. "I'm glad you're both okay."

The whine of sirens grew louder as the sheriff's patrol car escorted a fire truck and a water tanker onto the property. A section of the roof collapsed as the emergency vehicles pulled up to the property. A fireman hooked up the hose to the water tanker, and then two others carried the line to the back of the barn and attacked the flames there.

"Looks like no one was hurt." Sheriff Carlyle glanced between Joe and Mia. "What happened to you two?"

"My daughter was in the barn," Ruby said. "Joe saved her."

The lawman narrowed his gaze on Mia. "What were you doing in the barn when it caught fire?"

The suspicious tone in his voice rubbed Ruby the wrong way. "You better not be accusing my daughter of setting—"

"Don't get your tinsel in a tangle, Ruby. Just asking a question."

"Did all the livestock get out?" A fireman walked into the yard.

"We only have the four horses." Joe nodded to Friend, sitting at Mia's feet. "And the dog."

"I was asking if they knew how the blaze started," the sheriff said.

"Arson." The fireman pointed to the rear of the structure. "The smell of gasoline is pretty strong in that corner. We should have this out in a few minutes." He returned to his crew.

Ruby planted her fists on her hips and glared at the sheriff. "Don't tell me that arson is just another prank against Hank's ranch."

The sheriff frowned. "I understand this is serious."

Dumb-ass. The other incidents were serious, too.

"I saw who started the fire," Mia said.

The sheriff removed a pen and notepad from his shirt pocket.

"I was in the hayloft, listening to my iPod. It got too hot, so I was going to leave; that's when a man in a black ski mask walked into the barn with two gas cans. I couldn't see what he was doing, but I heard him open and close the stall doors before he ran out."

"Why didn't you leave the barn?" Ruby asked.

"I was scared he might be waiting outside. Then it got all smoky and the ladder caught fire."

"Can you describe the man?" the sheriff asked.

"He wore a dark hoodie that covered his head."

"How tall was he?"

Mia glanced at Joe, then Ruby. "Shorter than Joe but taller than my mom."

The sheriff walked over to Joe. "Where were you when Mia was in the barn?"

"Checking the windmill I'd repaired the other day." Joe looked at Ruby, his gaze beseeching her. "I was gone less than an hour."

The firemen shut off the water, then stowed the hoses and waited for their boss to report in to the sheriff. "Fire's out, but everyone should steer clear of the debris for a few days until the timber cools."

"Thank you," Ruby said.

After the two trucks drove off, the sheriff put away his notepad. "If you remember anything else, Mia, have your mother give me a call." He got into his vehicle and left.

"I better have some hay delivered." Hank went into the house.

"I'll drive into Guymon to buy feed for the horses."

"What about your clothes?" Ruby called after Joe. All his personal possessions had been in the storage room where he'd slept.

He waved off her concern. "I'll pick up a pair of jeans and a couple of T-shirts in town." Then he hopped into his truck and sped off.

They were all upset about the fire, but there was something else bothering Joe. She'd have to wait until he returned to talk with him. Ruby hugged Mia. "I'm glad you're safe, honey." And grateful that the jerk who'd set the fire hadn't seen her daughter in the hayloft. If he had, who knows what he might have done.

"Is Grandpa sad, Mom?"

"About the barn?"

"No, Cora dying."

"Yes, he's sad."

"Did he cry?"

"Your grandpa's a strong man. He'll be okay."

Mia's arms squeezed tighter, and Ruby buried her face in her daughter's smoky hair. "Are you upset that you couldn't talk to your birth mom?"

"A little." Ruby wished she'd been able to ask why she'd been left behind, but discovering that Cora had kept her baby photo—proof that she'd loved *Faith* as best she could—was enough for Ruby to forgive her.

"While you take a shower, I've got an errand to run."

"Where are you going?"

"To pay Hank's neighbor a visit." No one believed Sandoval was behind the pranks against the Devil's Wind, but Ruby wasn't convinced.

Ten minutes later she pulled up to the Bar T. Sandoval's home looked more like a fancy bed-and-breakfast than a ranch house. She parked next to the fountain in the circular drive. The stupid water statue looked out of place in the bleak landscape.

She climbed the porch steps and rang the bell. Expecting a maid to answer, she was surprised when Sandoval opened the door. If he was shocked to see her, he didn't show it. Even at home the man was impeccably dressed—Western shirt, pressed slacks, brown cowboy boots, and a spit-shined belt buckle.

"What do you want?" he asked.

"Did you send one of your men to burn down Hank's barn?"

"His barn caught fire?"

"Like you don't know."

Sandoval stepped outside, forcing Ruby to retreat or get knocked over. "I had nothing to do with any fire."

"Maybe you didn't pour the gasoline or light the match, but one of your ranch hands did."

He pointed his finger. "My father should never have given Hank that parcel of land and I'd like nothing better than to take it back, but I'm not a swindler like Hank. I don't steal from others."

"Maybe you don't cheat at cards, but you're pissed at him for winning the girl."

"What are you talking about?"

"Cora. You're angry that she had Hank's baby, then took off and left you both behind."

His shoulders slumped and the anger seeped out of him, leaving a tired old man standing before her. "Cora and I had an affair. A very short affair."

"How short?"

He lifted one hand and spread his fingers apart, then folded two digits. "That's how many times we slept together."

"So you didn't love her?"

"No. And I never wished her or Hank any ill will." The truth shone in his eyes.

Damn it. "Do you have any idea who's sabotaging the Devil's Wind?"

"I do not. Now get off my property."

Before he shut the door in her face, she blurted, "Hank found Cora."

"Where?"

"A nursing home in Amarillo."

"How is she?"

"Cora had suffered a stroke a while back, but pneumonia took her. Hank brought her ashes home."

"I'm sorry to hear that," he whispered, then closed the door in Ruby's face.

Chapter 36

Wednesday morning Ruby woke with a headache. She'd gotten little sleep last night, her mind in turmoil. She had some tough decisions to make, and convincing Hank and Mia to go along with her plan might be her biggest challenge yet.

The sound of the front door opening and closing drifted down the hallway. Hank had finally woken up. Ruby went outside and found him picking through the rubble. "You're supposed to wait until the debris cools off."

"I'm being careful." He tossed a wrench into a pile of objects worth salvaging.

"Sandoval isn't the one making threats against the ranch."

"Didn't think he was. If he'd wanted to, he could have forced me off the land years ago."

"Then why didn't he?"

Hank kicked a chunk of scorched wood. "He loved Cora, too."

Oh, Dad. Is that what you've told yourself all these years to make Cora's betrayal easier to live with?

"Roy sends his sympathies."

He stopped searching the burned remains and stared into the distance. She followed his gaze to the rosebushes. Last night after everyone had gone to bed, Ruby had heard the stairs creak. She'd tiptoed through the house to the front window and had watched Hank spread Cora's ashes beneath the bushes. Then he'd sat on the porch steps in the dark for almost an hour before returning to bed.

Cora had finally come home, and now Ruby was going to ask Hank to move.

"We can't stay here." Ruby's first responsibility was to keep Mia safe, but she couldn't leave Hank at the ranch. And then there was Joe. She didn't want to leave him behind, either. "I know the Devil's Wind means a lot to you, but Mia and I need you."

His watery eyes blinked against the sun. "You asking me to go with you gals?"

"We're a family now."

His gaze swung back to the front of the house.

"We'll take the rosebushes"—and Cora—"with us."

"You want me to sell the place?"

"You don't have to live on the property in order to lease it to the oil company, do you?"

"No."

"For now let's sell off the cattle and board the horses closer to Guymon."

Hank didn't say anything.

"We could rent a house in Guymon; then after school you and Mia could check on the horses wherever they are, and Joe could drive back and forth to the ranch to keep an eye on the property. Just until the sheriff makes an arrest."

"Mia won't want to leave," Hank said.

"That's why I need you to tell her." Mia would follow her grandfather anywhere.

"You're a good mother and a good daughter."

The Devil's Wind was the only real home Hank had ever known—it was the linchpin that held him, Ruby, and Mia together as a family. The dusty wasteland had helped Mia and Ruby forgive each other. Helped Ruby forgive Hank . . . even Cora. And in between all the forgiving, the ranch was where Ruby and Joe had found each other.

"We'll come back here as soon as it's safe," Ruby said.

"I'll talk to Mia."

She was grateful for Hank's support, but leaving would be stressful for him and she worried about his health. "Let's hold off telling Mia until I speak with the sheriff one more time." If there was the slightest chance the lawman was close to apprehending the arsonist, then they'd stand their ground.

A cloud of dust formed along the road. "Joe's back." He'd been quiet since the fire, and any attempt to engage him in conversation had been met with a grunt or a nod. She'd invited him to share her bed since the cot he'd slept on in the barn had been destroyed in the fire, but he'd purchased a sleeping bag the day he'd gone into town to get horse feed and at night he bunked down in his pickup bed. Ruby wasn't sure what was going through his mind, but she gave him his space, believing he'd open up when he was ready.

"What have you been up to?" she asked when Joe parked in the driveway.

"I bought extra feed for the horses."

Ruby peered into the truck bed. He'd also purchased a forty-pound bag of dog food. There was enough feed to last the animals for a month.

"I'll go with you when you talk to the sheriff." Hank took two steps, then stopped. "You make a fresh pot of coffee?"

"Four scoops—strong enough to blow a hole through your gut."

"That's my girl."

Ruby waited for Joe to make eye contact with her, but his gaze skipped across her face, causing alarm bells to ring in her head.

He set the last bag of feed on the ground, then shut the tailgate. "I'm leaving."

When the meaning of his words sank in, her heart froze inside her chest.

"I thought I could do this." The pain in Joe's voice alarmed her as much as the vacant look in his eyes.

"Do what?"

"Be with you. Be a part of"—he waved his hand at the house—"a family."

Nooo! A shrill voice screamed inside her head.

"I'm sorry, Ruby."

Anger shoved aside her hurt. She didn't want an apology—she wanted a fight. "Don't go." *Damn you, Joe. Don't leave me.* She'd finally found the courage to give him her trust and he was flinging it back in her face.

His head dropped forward, and he stared at the ground. Ruby threw herself at him, wrapping her arms around his waist. "I need you." She buried her face in his neck. "Hank and Mia need you." She swallowed a cry when his arms came around her and he crushed her against him.

"You don't understand," he mumbled in her ear. "Mia could have died in that fire and it would have been my fault."

Wanting to shake him, Ruby clutched fistfuls of his shirt. "My daughter's safe. Because of you."

His body turned to stone, and he stepped away from her. "I shouldn't have left Mia alone, not even for a few minutes."

She smacked her palm against his chest, wanting to hurt him. "Don't lie. You're not leaving because you think you failed to protect Mia. You're walking out on me."

"I'm no good to anyone, Ruby, especially you."

"Shit." She spun away, pressing her fingers against her skull, willing her brain to find the words to change Joe's mind. She had no experience arguing this side of it's-time-to-move-on. "Don't go."

When she and Mia had left Pineville, Ruby had never imagined that their fresh start would be the Devil's Wind and not Elkhart, Kansas. The ranch had forced her to let her guard down and open herself up in a way she hadn't done before with any of her relationships, including with Mia. She was confident and strong now. And she knew what she wanted—forever with Joe. But like the blowing dust in the Panhandle, he was slipping through her fingers.

"You make me want more out of life than to just exist. But I can't be the man you deserve."

"Please don't go."

He shook his head. "Be happy, Ruby."

Be happy? When he was giving up on her . . . them? She damned the tears welling in her eyes and poked her finger in his gut. "You're a coward, Joe Dawson!"

He clasped her face between his hands and pressed his mouth to hers, his kiss hot, hard, and urgent. Then he drove off, leaving her gasping for breath and knowing what it felt like to be kicked to the curb.

It didn't feel so hot.

"Mom?" Mia walked toward Ruby. "You want to help me groom . . . ?" She stopped. "You're crying." She glanced at the road. "Where's Joe going?"

"He's leaving."

"Did you guys have a fight?"

"No." She wished Joe would have argued with her. Maybe then she'd have stood a chance of changing his mind.

Hank stepped outside, and Mia called out to him. "Mom's crying."

Ruby's whole body was numb, her face included, and she didn't even feel the tears running down her cheeks.

"What happened?" Hank joined them, his bushy eyebrows fused together.

"Joe left." Ruby wiped her runny nose across the back of her hand.

"He's coming home, right?" Mia asked.

"I don't think so." But Joe had said that Ruby made him want more out of life than to just exist. She tucked the tiny scrap of hope inside her heart.

"It wasn't very nice of him to leave." Mia put her arm around her mother's waist.

"We'll be okay, honey." Ruby hugged her daughter. "Hank and I are going into town. You'll have to come with us."

"When?" Mia asked.

"Right now."

"I better use the bathroom first." Mia called to Friend, and the two went into the house.

Hank looked as miserable as Ruby felt, and when he opened his arms, she gladly accepted his hug. "I'm sorry," he said.

She sniffed against his shirt. "Life is funny."

"How so?"

"I came here determined to give you a piece of my mind and then spit at your feet and move on."

"I wouldn't have blamed you for doing that."

"We both fell for people who ran away from us." Her laugh turned into a sob.

"We're a pair, all right," he said.

No matter that she'd lost her fresh start with Joe, Ruby would always be grateful Hank had called her home.

When they arrived in Unforgiven, Ruby parked the pickup at the diner. "Here's a few dollars." She handed Mia the money. "Get yourself a snack. Hank and I will fetch you when we're ready to leave town." Ruby waited for her daughter to enter the Airstream, and then she and Hank crossed the street.

"Don't let on that we're thinking of moving," she said. "I doubt the sheriff and deputy will spend much time investigating if they know we intend to leave the property."

Inside the jail, Sheriff Carlyle and the deputy were engaged in a heated debate. Ruby closed the door hard and the argument abruptly ended.

"I was updating Paul about the fire out at your place, Hank," the sheriff said.

"Heard the barn was a total loss." Randall read the file on his desk as if he couldn't care less about Hank's troubles.

"I'm sending Paul out to talk to the ranchers in the area," the sheriff said.

Questioning ranchers must be their standard protocol. "You can cross Sandoval off your list," Ruby said. "Not that he was ever on your radar."

"You seemed pretty confident he was involved," the sheriff said.

"I spoke with him after the fire. Based on what he said, I don't believe he had anything to do with sabotaging the Devil's Wind." She waited for an I-told-you-so, but the sheriff let her off the hook. "Whoever torched the barn has to be someone local."

"We're checking every angle," the sheriff said.

Randall set aside his paperwork. "What do you plan to do now, Hank?"

"Build a new barn."

"Why not sell? Rumor has it your oil lease is up at the end of September."

"My lawyer's looking into that," Hank said.

"I know Ruby believes Kline changed the date." Randall narrowed his eyes.

"Maybe he's in cahoots with the man who wants to buy my ranch." Hank went to the door. "I'll be in the mercantile, Ruby."

"Who wants to buy the Devil's Wind?" the sheriff asked Randall.

"One of those wealthy corporate people looking for a place in the country."

The sheriff's gaze swung to Ruby. "Those responsible for the vandalism and the fire will eventually slip up, and we'll catch them."

"If you don't crack this case soon, I'll make a big stink about it to the Guymon police."

"They won't help you investigate a crime that's not in their jurisdiction," Randall said.

Ruby shrugged. "I'll take my chances."

Chapter 37

Ruby left the sheriff's office, doubting her threat to contact the Guymon police had done much good. She hurried along the sidewalk and caught up with Hank before he reached the mercantile.

"Would you rather I wait with Mia in the diner while you speak to Big Dan?" she asked. Cora was a touchy subject between the two men, and Hank might have a few words for the fortune-teller that he'd just as soon Ruby not hear.

"Doesn't matter to me." He opened the door and she followed him inside.

"Heard about the fire." Big Dan stepped into view as if he'd been expecting them. "Glad no one got hurt."

"We stopped by the sheriff's office to"—Ruby shook her head—"never mind." He knew why they were in town.

Big Dan's Roman nose twitched. "You found Cora."

"In Amarillo," Hank said.

"And . . ." The merchant's bug eyes swung between Ruby and Hank.

He doesn't know.

"She died six days ago." That was all Hank intended to say on the subject. He looked at Ruby. "I'll be in the diner." Then he left the store.

Big Dan's eyes watered. "Tell me everything."

This time the little man depended on Ruby for information about Cora, rather than the other way around.

"Cora was living in a rented motel room when she suffered a stroke. She never fully recovered, so she was placed in a nursing home, where she contracted pneumonia. When Hank and I got there, she'd already been moved to the hospice wing."

"She deserved better." He retreated behind the counter, where he sat stooped over on the stool.

"Cora was offered better, but she snubbed her nose at it."

Big Dan nodded, his stare distant and empty.

"Hank spread her ashes beneath the rosebushes at the ranch."

"She'd be proud of you for taking care of Hank."

"I'm not doing it for Cora." That was the God's honest truth. Ruby would watch over Hank for herself. Their relationship had gotten off to a rocky start, but the old man had claimed a piece of her heart. When the time came for their final goodbye, she'd be at his side. "I better go."

"Ruby?"

"What?"

"I'm here if you need to talk."

The ache that had been stuck in her throat since Joe left slid down and settled in her chest. "Thanks." Although she appreciated the offer, Ruby would not be using her mother's confidant as her own.

She cut across the street to the diner. The place was crowded with oil workers and ranch hands. She approached the lunch counter, where Hank sipped water and Mia flirted with a young roughneck.

"Too bad about the fire, Ruby," Jimmy said.

"Thanks." She sat on the stool next to her daughter, then leaned behind her and tapped the young man on his shoulder. "How old are you?"

He flung a ten-dollar bill onto the counter and left the diner.

"We were just talking, Mom."

"Talk to boys your own age."

"He said he had a fourteen-year-old sister, right, Grandpa?"

Hank nodded.

"C'mon, Mia." Ruby touched Hank's shoulder. "We'll wait by the truck." She followed Mia out the door and almost ran into Stony. "Go on." Ruby handed the keys to Mia. "I'll catch up."

"I assume you'll be giving me your two weeks' notice."

Before the fire Ruby had tossed around the idea of working at the bar until Mia began school. Then she'd planned to stay home with Hank and work on the house renovations. "Who says I'm quitting?"

Stony frowned. "Didn't think you'd stick around after the fire."

"You should know I don't scare easily." The threats might force them to relocate until it was safe to return, but no one was going to steal her and Mia's new home from them.

"I heard about Cora." He opened the door and Hank stepped outside. "My condolences," Stony said, then entered the Airstream.

"It's hot out here," Mia complained when Ruby and Hank reached the pickup.

"I'll drive." Hank took the keys from Mia and slid behind the wheel.

"If you intend to keep driving, you need to get your eyes checked," Ruby said.

"I can see the road fine. Just don't see good at night anymore."

Ruby added an eye doctor appointment to the mental to-do list with Hank's name at the top of it. If he intended to chauffeur Mia places, she'd insist he have his cataracts removed. Until then it was reassuring that he drove well below the speed limit.

Three miles outside of town they passed the first oil pumps. The nodding donkeys brought back memories of the afternoon Joe had given her and Mia a ride to the ranch. She'd almost had it all with Joe and there was no use pretending Joe hadn't hurt her by giving up on them so easily.

Ruby shot forward in her seat, abruptly jerked from her reverie. "What was that?"

"Damn fool hit us."

She checked the side mirror and spotted a dark sedan riding their bumper. She leaned across the seat and pressed the button for the flashers. "Ease onto the shoulder and let him pass."

Hank slowed down and moved over in the lane. The car refused to go around them. "What a jerk. Tap your brakes," she said.

Before Hank moved his foot to the brake, the sedan hit their bumper again.

"What's going on?" Mia removed her iPod earbuds and glanced out the rear window.

"We've got trouble." Ruby leaned over the seat and pressed her hand against Mia's shoulder. "Stay down." Ruby stared out the back. "I can't get a good look at the driver's face."

The car moved into the oncoming lane. "Be careful. He's sneaking up next to you." Ruby pulled her cell phone from her purse and called 911—still close enough to town to get a signal.

She relayed their location and the situation to the operator, who assured her that help was on the way. "Nice and easy," Ruby said after the sedan was forced to fall behind them when an approaching vehicle passed by. Ruby prayed Hank's pacemaker would withstand the stress and the three of them wouldn't end up in a cow pasture.

"Slow down some more," Ruby said. Hank let the speed drop to thirty miles per hour. "He's backing off." Then suddenly the sedan swerved toward the shoulder. "He's heading back the other way. You've got to follow him." Ruby didn't want the bastard getting away.

By the time Hank turned around, the sedan was a speck on the horizon. "Can this thing go any faster?" Ruby asked.

Hank pressed the gas pedal to the floor and the truck sputtered and coughed its way up to fifty-five miles per hour.

Mia stared out the rear window. "Here come the cops."

The blue-and-red flashing lights were gaining on them.

When the patrol car pulled alongside them, Ruby leaned across Hank and shouted, "It's a black sedan with dark tint on the windows!" The officer sped off.

"I didn't catch any numbers on the license plate." Ruby glanced at her daughter. "Did you?"

Mia shook her head. "Nope."

Hank leaned forward, his nose bumping the steering wheel.

"The cop pulled him over." Ruby waited until Hank parked behind the patrol car. Then she got out of the pickup. "Stay here."

The officer signaled Ruby. "Ma'am, I need you to get back in your vehicle."

"Call Sheriff Mike Carlyle or Deputy Paul Randall in Unforgiven. They're investigating an arson fire at Hank McArthur's ranch. That might be the guy they're after."

The patrolman leaned down and spoke to the driver. A second later the sedan's car door opened and the driver stepped out.

Ruby gaped when she recognized Randall. "You're the one who's been sabotaging Hank's ranch?"

The highway patrolman walked over to Ruby. "I don't know anything about an arson complaint. Deputy Randall claims he attempted to pull you over for speeding, but you refused to cooperate. Is that true?"

"He's lying." She pointed to Hank. "My father was driving fifteen miles below the limit when Deputy Randall rammed the back end of our truck. Go see for yourself. The bumper's probably dented."

The officer ignored her suggestion. "Deputy Randall says he tapped the bumper when your vehicle drifted into the oncoming lane."

Holy hell. Randall was going to talk his way out of this and there wasn't a damned thing she could do. "We never crossed the center line."

"The deputy insists he stopped pursuing you because he was afraid of causing an accident."

Ruby wanted to slap the smug look off of Randall's face.

"So you're going to believe his version of the story when he's not even in uniform?" Randall had changed clothes before coming after them.

"An off-duty officer has the right to enforce the law." The patrolman slipped on his sunglasses. "Deputy Randall has offered to let you go with a warning this time."

"How generous."

The highway patrolman returned to Randall's car and spoke to him. Once the deputy took off, the patrolman said, "Ma'am, I suggest you continue on your way and watch your driving. Consider yourself lucky that you didn't get a ticket." He sped away.

"What happened?" Mia asked when Ruby got in on the passenger side.

"Unfrickin' believable." She looked at Hank, who still clutched the steering wheel. "Randall told the patrolman that you were driving recklessly and he tapped your bumper to get you to pull off the road. When you didn't, he let you go to avoid an accident."

"What a jerk," Mia said.

Jerk was too nice of a word to describe the deputy.

"Now what?" Hank asked.

"We head back to town to speak to the sheriff."

And this time the lawman wasn't going to brush off her concerns.

Chapter 38

When they arrived in town, the dark sedan, the sheriff's patrol car, and a pickup with the Bar T logo sat parked in front of the Possum Belly Saloon.

"Wait in the diner for us, Mia."

"I want to go with you."

"Listen to your mother, young lady," Hank said.

Once Mia was safely inside the Airstream, she and Hank got out of the truck. "What are you looking for?" she asked when he ducked his head behind the seat.

"A little persuasion." He stepped back and shut the door.

She nodded to the shotgun. "How many of those do you have?"

"Keep one in the house, one in the truck, and had one in the barn."

"Is it loaded?"

"Wouldn't do much good if it wasn't."

"Maybe you should leave the bullets—" He marched past Ruby, and she hurried after him.

They found Randall speaking to Sheriff Carlyle, no doubt trying to cover his tracks before his boss heard Ruby's version of the events.

No one in the noisy room paid any attention to them. But Hank solved that problem. He fired the shotgun at the ceiling.

Plaster rained down on their heads, and men dove for the floor. If Ruby weren't so pissed off, she might have laughed at the beef necks taking cover under the tables.

Sheriff Carlyle yanked the shotgun from Hank's hands. "Give me that before you kill someone."

"Don't believe a word your deputy told you." Ruby glared at the lawmen.

Randall puffed out his chest. "He was driving like a maniac."

Hank waved a crooked finger at Randall. "You tried to run us off the road."

"Let's take this discussion over to the jail." When the sheriff made a move toward the door, Ruby blocked his path.

"Did you ask your deputy why he isn't in uniform?"

The sheriff stared at Ruby as if she were a petulant child. "After our earlier visit, Paul said he wasn't feeling well and decided to go home to rest."

The corners of Randall's mouth twitched.

The bastard's cockiness irked her, and she lashed out. "What happens when the parents of those Little League boys find out their hero set a rancher's barn on fire? They'll never let you near another baseball field again."

Randall glanced over his shoulder at Stony, as if he expected the bartender to step in and defend him.

"It all makes sense now why your investigation into the trouble at Hank's ranch has gone nowhere. Deputy Randall's the one who shot at Mia the day she went horseback riding near Fury's Ridge."

The sheriff glanced between Ruby and his deputy. "What's she talking about, Paul?"

Randall turned to Stony and said, "I'm not taking the fall for this."

The bartender picked up a shot glass and dried it with a towel, looking bored with the drama playing out in his saloon. "I have no idea what the deputy is talking about."

"The hell you don't." Randall's chest heaved. "Stony's the one who wants the Devil's Wind. He paid me to harass Hank to get him to sell."

Stony locked gazes with Ruby, and her skin crawled at his cold stare. "Randall's lying."

"I've got a canceled check for twenty thousand dollars to prove I'm telling the truth," the deputy said.

"Shut up, you stupid ass." Stony flung the towel at Randall's head.

Eyebrows squished together, the sheriff asked, "Why would you do this, Paul?"

Randall perspired profusely, large wet stains spreading under his armpits. "They were going to cancel the Little League unless they came up with a way to fund it. I asked Stony for a donation, but he said I had to earn it by doing him a favor."

"He's lying." Stony banged the shot glass on the bar.

"He wants the Devil's Wind for himself." Randall threw the bartender under the bus.

"You don't know when to shut the fuck up, do you?" Stony said.

"You son of a bitch." Sandoval stepped from the shadows behind the sheriff. He glared at his half brother. "All this time you made it appear as if my ranch hands were vandalizing Hank's property."

"What the hell do you care?" Stony came around the bar and

got in Sandoval's face. "That land was supposed to go to me, but you lost it in a poker game."

"This isn't about the land." Sandoval balled his hands into fists. "You're angry because you're the bastard son."

"I deserved half the Bar T when our father died." Stony swatted the air with his hand. "I got nothing."

"You got nothing," Sandoval said, "because your mother tried to blackmail our father."

"Bullshit. You—"

"Enough!" the sheriff shouted. "Stony, you're coming with me."

"I didn't touch Hank's ranch."

"Doesn't matter. Get over to the jail or I'll slap handcuffs on you." The sheriff looked at Randall. "Same goes for you, Paul."

Stony shoved Randall aside. The deputy careened into a table, knocking beer mugs to the floor. Then Stony stopped in front of the sheriff. "Why don't you ask *Paul* how he knows your wife has a butterfly tattoo on her right ass cheek."

The air in the bar went out as everyone held their breath. The sheriff kept his temper in check. "Go." Then he took Randall by the shirtsleeve and dragged him out the door.

A few seconds later the rest of the men vacated the premises. "My condolences on Cora's passing," Sandoval said.

Hank nodded.

"Are you staying or selling?"

"We're staying," Ruby said.

"Let me know when you're ready to put up a new barn. I'll send my men to help."

Ruby took Hank by the arm, and they followed Sandoval outside. "I'll fetch Mia," she said, "while you give the sheriff your statement."

Hank hesitated. "Ruby?"

"What?"

"You sure you want to stay? There's nothing out here but wind and dust."

"There are good people, too." She'd met several at the Little League game. "Besides, I'm getting used to dirt in my teeth."

"We've got a lot to talk about, then," he said.

"We do?"

"I won't live forever, and I've got plans I want you to carry out for me."

"Can we hold off talking about you dying until tomorrow?"

He chuckled. "I suppose my funeral plans can wait."

Ruby kissed his cheek. "See you in a bit." She walked to the diner, her thoughts switching to Joe. She wanted to tell him what had happened today. Assure him that Mia was out of danger and he didn't have to worry about keeping any of them safe. She wanted to ask Joe to come back to her—to give them a second, third, or as many chances as they needed to get it right.

Joe parked his pickup in front of a three-bedroom, two-bath brick ranch—the home he and Melanie had purchased after Aaron was born. The shrubs he'd planted in front of the house were twice their original size. A flower wreath hung on the door, and a welcome mat sat on the stoop.

It didn't look like a house where a little boy had died.

He couldn't put his finger on it, but something was different. He scanned the homes along the street and realized the hedges were missing. Every house up and down the block had removed the four-foot hedges next to their driveways—the evergreens that had hidden

Aaron from view before he'd flown into the street on his bike. Anger squeezed the air out of Joe's lungs. Why did it have to be his child who died before the parents realized the danger the hedges posed?

His gaze moved down the sidewalk to the sign at the corner—Slow, Children Playing. That was new. And so were the speed bumps in the street.

The days following Aaron's death had been a blur. Neighbors had come by to pay their respects, but Joe had been so numb he couldn't remember their faces, let alone what they'd said to him. Melanie had taken a sleeping pill each night. But Joe had sat in Aaron's room, staring at his empty bed. And then one morning he'd woken up and realized Melanie was gone. Her clothes were gone. Her makeup in the bathroom was gone. Her medications were gone. The only thing she'd left behind was him.

Joe pulled away from the curb and drove to the end of the block, then turned the corner and pulled into the neighborhood park. It was the middle of the afternoon, but the playground was empty. He got out of his car and walked over to the monkey bars. Aaron's face flashed before his eyes. Laughing, smiling, shouting to his friends as he swung by one arm.

He hadn't recalled there being any trees on the playground when Aaron had played here, but one had been planted across from the swings. A bench sat in its shade. He went over to sit down, but stopped short when he noticed the engraved placard on the backrest.

In Memory of Aaron Dawson

Life had gone on. Kids still played, laughed, and grew up on the same street that had taken Aaron's life. But they hadn't forgotten him. Joe wanted to believe his son's spirit remained here, riding his bike through the neighborhood, swinging on the monkey bars.

Joe sat and bowed his head. *Aaron, buddy, I'm sorry.*

If he could go back and do that day all over again . . .

I'll always love you, son. He gave in to the memories, to the good times he'd had with Aaron and Melanie, and let go of the bad memories, the darker days, the sleepless nights, the drinking.

A car door slammed shut and he opened his eyes. Three young boys raced to the swings, and their mother walked over to the bench and sat at the opposite end from him.

"Hello," she said.

Joe nodded.

"Are you new in the neighborhood? You don't look familiar."

"My wife and I lived here several years ago."

"Oh? My neighbors Margie and Gary Johnson have been here forever."

Joe remembered the Johnsons. Melanie and Margie had played Bunco together.

"What's your name? I'll tell them I ran into you."

"Joe Dawson."

"Cindy Nelson. My husband and I moved here last year." She clapped her hands to get the boys' attention, then shook her head and the kids stopped arguing. "Boys are a handful." She smiled. "Do you have any children?"

"I had a son." Joe stood. "I better get going."

"It was nice meeting you."

He cut through the playground, taking one last look at the monkey bars. He would never return to this park or this neighborhood. Before he pulled out into the street, he glanced in the rearview mirror and caught the young mother reading the plaque on the bench.

He'd never forget the day Aaron died, but it was time to move on. With his son's memory safely tucked inside his heart, Joe turned the pickup north and headed back to the Panhandle.

Chapter 39

"Mia's worried about you." Hank sat next to Ruby on the front porch.

"I'm fine."

"Could have fooled me." His fingers dove inside his empty shirt pocket, and then his hand fell back to his lap. "You've been watching the road every night since he left."

She didn't want to talk about Joe. It hurt too much. "Sears called earlier. They're delivering the new appliances tomorrow."

Two weeks had passed since the barn fire, and with Hank's encouragement Ruby had begun renovations on the farmhouse. The kitchen had been first on her list. They'd hired a woodworker from Guymon to refinish the cabinets. He'd stripped off the stain and painted them white. The linoleum floor had been pulled up and neutral cream tile put in its place. The baseboards had been repaired and painted to match the cabinets.

Hank had grumbled when Ruby bought a Keurig machine to

replace the coffeemaker. She insisted they'd waste less grounds if they made a cup at a time, even though the real reason she'd purchased the expensive gadget was because she'd always wanted one for herself. But Hank complained that his coffee was never strong enough, so Ruby gave in and put the ancient appliance back on the counter next to the Keurig.

Usually after a loved one passed away, a person kept a piece of jewelry, a trophy, or a painting to remember them by. Ruby already knew the Mr. Coffee machine would remain on the counter long after Hank's footsteps no longer echoed in the house.

"Hank?"

"Yeah?"

"After we finish the renovations, I was thinking about enrolling in a couple of classes at the community college in Guymon." She would register for night classes so that Mia would be home with Hank in case he fell ill.

"What are you interested in studying?"

"I don't know." She thought she'd answered Hank's letter not only to learn about her medical history but because she wanted to discover if she was meant to be anything more than a waitress or a desk clerk the rest of her life. Thanks to Joe, Ruby finally understood that she'd always possessed the power to determine her own future—she just hadn't had the courage to exercise it until now.

"I won't start classes until after the winter break."

"Why not?"

"I need to apply for financial aid and—"

"I'll pay for your school."

"I'm capable of paying my way."

"I missed out on all the things fathers do for their kids." He winked. "I'd like to send my thirty-one-year-old daughter to college."

When he put it like that, she couldn't refuse.

"I'll make a deal with you," he said. "If you flunk out, you have to pay me back."

"That's fair." She reached across the space between their chairs and grasped his hand.

"Are you in love with Joe?" he asked.

Not a day went by that Joe wasn't inside Ruby's head, messing with her thoughts. Inside her heart, messing with her feelings. "I want to be."

"What's that supposed to mean?"

"I've never been in love before, but I think I could have been with Joe, if we'd had more time together."

"After Cora left, I didn't want to go on living."

Ruby's eyes stung.

"Don't look at me like that. I'm still here, aren't I?" He dropped his gaze to their hands. "Every morning I'd get out of bed thinking this was the day I'd look out the window and see her walking up the road. Days turned into weeks. Then months and finally years."

"When did you stop looking out the window?"

"The day after we brought Cora home."

Dear God. Ruby didn't want to watch the road for Joe every day for the rest of her life.

"Go after him."

She wasn't a chaser. She was a kicker-outer—a woman who told men to beat it, not one who begged them to take her back. "I don't think he's ready to be part of a family again."

"Convince him to stay here while he figures it out," Hank said.

"And if he says no?"

"Life goes on. You've got your daughter and me. We love you."

"You're going to make me cry." She wiped her eyes. Each day

with Hank was a gift. There was no guarantee he'd come down the stairs tomorrow morning, much less a month or a year from now.

"Don't make the same mistake I did," he said.

"You regret not going after Cora."

"If I had, I might have been able to change her mind and talk her into coming home."

"What if you had found her but she'd refused to return to the Devil's Wind?"

"Then I would have had to let her go. After a while I might have found the courage to open my heart to someone else."

All her adult life Ruby had been afraid of being left behind. Because of that fear she'd never allowed herself to trust a man and at the first sign of trouble she'd cut him loose rather than risk him leaving her.

Joe had left her, but she was still here. Still breathing. Still okay. And she still had Mia and Hank. Ruby was far from perfect, but she was a good person with a good heart. She deserved to be happy, and if Joe made her happy . . .

"Okay. I'll go after him."

"You want me to ask Charles to contact his private investigator?"

"Give me until the end of September." If she couldn't find Joe by then, she'd ask for Hank's help. "Joe mentioned his sister and her husband live on a farm in Nebraska." That was as good a place as any to start.

"We'll come with you. I'll pay one of Roy's hands to take care of the animals."

"I have to do this on my own. And Mia can't miss school." Each morning Hank drove Mia out to the highway to catch the school bus into Guymon. And each afternoon he was there waiting for her when she got dropped off.

Her gaze shifted to Hank's jalopy parked in the front yard. "I'll need your truck." But she didn't like the idea of Mia and Hank stranded at the ranch without a vehicle.

"Take it. There's an old ATV in the shed I can use to drive Mia to the school bus."

"Or she could walk the mile to the road." The exercise would do her good.

"Why are you looking at me like that?" he asked.

"I'm concerned about your health."

"Don't worry. Mia will call the Bar T if I bite the dust."

"That's not even funny."

"When are you leaving?"

"First thing in the morning."

Hank went into the house and Ruby went back to staring at the road.

"Oh, come on!" Ruby coasted to the shoulder of the highway and turned off the engine. Go figure. She'd finally screwed up the courage to chase after Joe, but she'd made it only forty miles before the truck broke down. Forget checking the engine—she had no idea what to look for. She turned on the flashers, then retrieved her cell phone from her purse. No signal.

Crap. She'd figured it would take time to find Joe, but she hadn't counted on hiking to Nebraska. She'd wanted to look pretty if she caught up with him by the end of the day, so she'd worn the peach dress and cowboy boots that he'd said looked good on her. She wasn't sure how far she'd make it in boots, but she for sure wouldn't get anywhere sitting on the side of the road. She took her purse, locked the truck, and started walking.

A horn honked and she jumped inside her skin. A white utility van pulled up alongside her. The passenger window lowered. The driver wore a blue work shirt with Ted embroidered above the pocket. "That your truck back there?"

The guy is an idiot. "Ah, yeah."

"Want me to call a wrecker for you?"

No, actually, I'd like you to call a pizza-delivery service and have them send out a medium pepperoni and mushroom. "That would be great."

"I'm turning off a mile up the road. I can take you that far."

A lot could happen in a mile—she'd seen the show *CSI: Crime Scene Investigation.* "Thanks. I'll wait with my vehicle."

"Suit yourself." He sped off.

Once Ruby was confident Ted wouldn't turn around, she retraced her steps, then removed her luggage from the backseat and used it to sit on. An hour later she worried that Ted had forgotten her. She stowed the suitcase in the truck and shut the door. She'd hiked only fifty yards when she noticed help approaching in the opposite lane. She waved her arms.

The pickup slowed—a black Dodge. The driver crossed the center line and parked facing Hank's vehicle. She held her breath . . . waiting . . . hoping . . .

Joe.

He got out of the pickup and strode toward her. "Don't you know hitchhiking is dangerous?" His brown gaze skimmed over her. "Damn it, Ruby, you could have been hit by a car or abducted and left to rot in a ditch."

She stared wide-eyed, afraid to blink for fear he'd disappear. His gaze softened as it swept over her. "I tried to leave, Ruby. I tried so damn hard, but you kept calling me back."

His confession split her heart wide open.

"For years I buried the pain of Aaron's death, hoping it would go away if I ignored it. I knew if I allowed myself to feel, I'd fall apart, and I was afraid I wouldn't make it back from that dark place a second time."

Tears burned her eyes, and she sniffed.

"But you made me do things with you and Mia, and before I realized it, I was living again. Feeling again. Then I panicked after the fire and the scare with Mia. All I could think about was how I'd failed Aaron, and I didn't want to be responsible for losing someone else I cared deeply for. So I left."

"Where did you go?"

"Back to the house where Melanie and I raised Aaron."

He'd returned to the place his son had died.

"I realized that punishing myself will never bring Aaron back." He shoved a hand through his hair. "My son wouldn't want me to stop living."

"No, he wouldn't." She gripped his arm, wanting to never let him go.

"I'm ready to start living again. I want to learn to laugh and smile without feeling guilty." He caressed Ruby's cheek. "And I want to do it all with you by my side and Aaron in my heart."

The tears she'd held at bay leaked from her eyes. "I was coming to get you. To bring you home." She gathered her courage and put her heart on the line. "I think I'm falling in love with you, Joe."

"I want to say those words back to you, but not until I know I mean them." He pressed her hand to his heart. "No matter how long it takes or how hard I have to fight to get there—I will say those words to you, Ruby. And when I do, you'll know it's for forever."

Ruby vowed that each day she'd show Joe he was worth loving.

And with Hank and Mia's help, she'd convince him that he was worthy of a place in their family and in their hearts.

"I don't want to lose you, Ruby."

"You won't." She pressed her lips to his, the kiss filled with the promise of forgiveness.

Then Ruby rested her cheek against Joe's chest and listened to his heart pound strong and steady. As the sun rose higher in the sky, Ruby's life righted itself and the world around her took on a rosy glow.

Even the dirt carried off by the wind shimmered like gold dust.

Acknowledgments

I write stories about family drama because family is important to me. Without my family's support and encouragement, this book would not have survived the journey to publication. I might make up stuff in my head every day, but all of you are my reality, and I'm blessed to have you in my life.

To my husband, Kevin—whose golf game has improved immensely, thanks to my writing deadlines. I appreciate all the Saturdays you sacrificed on the golf course so that I could have a quiet house to write in while tackling revisions for this book.

To my adult children, Thomas and Marin—I'm so proud you both chose careers that serve people in need. It's an honor to write under your names.

To my father, James Milton Smith—we both tell stories: you with a paintbrush, me with a keyboard.

To my sister, Amy Smith-Lalonde—I've never met a person who works as hard as you do. You're an inspiration to all those around you.

To my brother, Brett Smith, who often suggests that I write a book about him—I believe your life story is best left in the hands of Hollywood screenwriters.

To my canine writing partners, Bandit and Rascal, who've slept at my feet beneath my desk for the past fourteen years. We've written a lot of stories together, and I'm counting on you fur balls to hang around for a few more books.

As with all of my stories, writing the first draft is the easy part. The real work begins during the revision and editing process. Thank you to my editor, Danielle Perez, for taking a chance on me and helping to transform this story from a chunk of coal into a shiny diamond.

And because the last thing an author wants to do is frustrate her readers with grammar mistakes and inconsistencies, many thanks to copy editor Penina Lopez, not only for keeping the hyphen queen in check but for keeping an eagle eye on my characters' ages and the passage of time.

My thanks to the artistic talents of Laura Corless for the lovely interior pages design, Tom Hallman for the cover art and Katie Anderson for the cover design. I love how you captured the warmth and vibrancy of the story's theme of forgiveness.

To my publicist, Danielle Dill—thank you for helping Ruby, Hank, Mia and Joe find their way into the hearts of first-time readers.

To my agent, Paige Wheeler of Creative Media Agency—thank you for supporting this new path in my writing career and for your invaluable feedback and encouragement on the numerous versions of this book proposal before it sold.

To Karin Dearborn—thank you for helping me brainstorm the original idea for this book. Go figure Ruby would steal the show.

To author Erin Quinn, who writes a killer synopsis—thank you for taking the time to help me fine-tune my synopsis for this book.

To author Barbara White Daille—thank you for your support and the numerous business lunches discussing the publishing industry. The pizzas weren't bad, either.

To the many talented authors at www.tallpoppy.org—thank you for your generous support and guidance in helping me navigate this new world of women's fiction.

To my faithful readers—thank you for purchasing my books, taking the time to post reviews online and recommending my stories to friends and family. Without your loyal support, I wouldn't be able to do what I love.

And last, but never least, to my Ohio author assistant, Denise Hall—thank you for your immense patience with this technically challenged author and for always being one step ahead of me and my next book. Without you, Marin Thomas would be forever wandering aimlessly around the Internet. Most of all, thank you for your friendship and keeping me sane in a whirlwind business that changes faster than the speed of light.

CONVERSATION GUIDE

the promise of forgiveness

MARIN THOMAS

This Conversation Guide is intended to enrich the individual reading experience, as well as encourage us to explore these topics together—because books, and life, are meant for sharing.

Questions for Discussion

1. Do you believe the author intended for the Oklahoma Panhandle to be a character in the novel? Does it play the role of villain or savior? Maybe both?

2. There's a lot of dust in this novel. What does it symbolize for Hank? At the beginning of the book, Ruby views the blowing dirt as a symbol of nothingness, bleakness, hopelessness. How does she view the dust particles at the end of the story?

3. Forgiveness is a major theme in this story. Have you ever withheld forgiveness from someone close to you? Does your reason still make sense after reading this novel, or are you more open to the possibility of forgiving your offender?

4. Raising teenagers is difficult. Do you believe Ruby handled Mia losing her virginity at such a young age appropriately? Was it right to move away from their small town? Or do you think Ruby was more concerned with how people would judge her and her motherhood skills? Why is it so difficult for parents to tell their children they're sorry?

5. If Cora had lived, do you think Ruby's relationship with Hank would have weakened or grown stronger? Why?

6. Life isn't always fair and a parent never gets over the death of his or her child, but do you think it's possible to move on with your life and find some semblance of happiness and peace without feeling guilty?

7. Being left behind is a major theme in this book. Do you think Ruby gives herself enough credit for breaking the cycle with her own daughter?

8. When in the book do you believe Ruby really forgave Cora? When she learned Cora left her the ruby necklace before she fled the hospital? When she found her baby picture in the suitcase at the motel where Cora had lived out her final years? Or when she said her final goodbye at the nursing home?

9. Ruby's adoptive mother, Cheryl, was afraid to tell Ruby her birth mother wanted to connect with her. What would you do in Cheryl's situation if your child were rebelling and challenging your authority and another parent wanted to enter your child's life? At what age do you feel it's appropriate to tell a child they're adopted?

10. Why do you think Hank and Mia hit it off right away? How much did it have to do with their shared love of animals?

11. What are some of the traits that Hank and Ruby share?

12. What is the significance of gambling in the book? When did it help Hank and when did it hurt him?

13. Ruby has built Hank up to be a huge obstacle to overcome or to fight against, but he turns out to be a frail man with a pacemaker in his chest. Do you believe it would have been more difficult or easier for Ruby to forgive Hank if he'd been healthy? Why do you think Ruby is so reluctant to forgive Hank?

14. Do you keep a diary? If so, are there any secrets that will turn your loved ones' lives upside down?

Why Unforgiven–Why Ruby?

I'm a big fan of small towns. Small towns provide built-in conflict for stories. People know one another—maybe a little too well. In small towns, secrets are guarded closely, because once they're revealed, the repercussions travel through the community like shock waves after an earthquake. On the one hand, it's comforting to know you have help nearby, but on the other, it's disconcerting when you discover your neighbors know more about you than you realized.

When I brainstormed this novel, I needed a location that would challenge the book's theme of forgiveness. I then filled the town with men, because Ruby has a deep mistrust of men, and I didn't want her to feel too comfortable, because only when we're uncomfortable do we accept the need to change.

Unforgiven is a safe haven for men. A place where roughnecks and cowboys check their morals and values at the door. A place where they can say what they want without fear of backlash or condemnation. The men have secrets and regrets. Their lives have been built on mistakes and bad decisions—but no one holds them accountable in Unforgiven. At home these men toe the line for their wives and families, their actions and words guided by a moral conscience. For some men, the women in their lives are the only link between them and civilized society.

Ruby is nothing like the wives and girlfriends who are at home waiting for their roughnecks and cowboys. Ruby is as hard as the gemstone she's named after. She, too, has secrets and has made her share of mistakes and bad judgment calls. The town is a reflection of Ruby—unforgiving and suspicious.

Why did I pick Ruby to be the story's protagonist? Because Ruby is a fighter. There's something very real and honest about middle-class America. The middle class doesn't make enough money to buy their way out of the messes they create in their lives like the wealthy, who have the means and connections to make things "go away." Few people in the middle class experience having opportunities handed to them like the wealthy, yet they're often held to higher standards and made accountable for the consequences of their choices and actions while the wealthy get away with their mistakes and indiscretions.

The middle class is the heartbeat of America. They love deeply and hate deeply. And because these attributes can lead them down the wrong path, the need for forgiveness plays a greater role in their lives than perhaps in the lives of the more fortunate in society.

Forgiveness is not about the offender—the person who committed the offense. It's not about deciding if the offender deserves forgiveness. It's only about what's inside the heart of the person who's been hurt. If you've carried a grudge against someone for a long time and you finally let it go, you'll feel a weight lift off your shoulders. And only when you forgive can you begin to heal, because you no longer carry the burden of being the injured one.

Ruby arrives in Unforgiven determined to hold a grudge against her biological father, but what she doesn't understand until later is that she needed to give forgiveness more than she needed to receive it.

As I've grown older, I've learned a few valuable lessons in life. You can't change people. And sometimes those who profess to love you will hurt you. But the most important thing I've learned is that offering forgiveness frees the soul and gives us a path forward in life that is richer and sweeter than the one we walked before.

About the Author

Marin Thomas is an award-nominated author of more than twenty-five novels, including the Cash Brothers series. She grew up in Janesville, Wisconsin, and attended college at the University of Arizona in Tucson, where she played basketball for the Lady Wildcats and earned a BA in Radio and Television. Following graduation, she married her college sweetheart in a five-minute ceremony at the historic Little Chapel of the West in Las Vegas, Nevada. While her two children were young, Marin coached youth basketball. Now that her son has graduated from college and her daughter is in graduate school, Marin writes full-time. She and her husband currently live in Houston, Texas. *The Promise of Forgiveness* is her first women's fiction novel.

CONNECT ONLINE

marinthomas.com
facebook.com/authormarinthomas
twitter.com/marinthomas